CURSED: BELOVED

BOOK 3 (M/M MODERN RETELLING OF BEAUTY & THE BEAST)

※

X ARATARE

RAYTHE REIGN PUBLISHING

Copyright © 2017 by Raythe Reign Publishing

All rights reserved.

No part of this book may be reproduced in any form or by any electronic or mechanical means, including information storage and retrieval systems, without written permission from the author, except for the use of brief quotations in a book review.

SUMMARY OF CURSED: BELOVED

Nick Fairfax believes that his romance with Lord Bane Dunsaney is over. Bane has chosen revenge against Nick's family over his love for Nick. And Bane's secret - that he is the guardian of a tiger spirit - has also caused a wedge between them with Nick still in the dark about Bane's true nature. Can they overcome these seemingly insurmountable problems and find their happily ever after?
  This book completes the m/m modern retelling of *Beauty & the Beast*!

SIGN UP FOR FREE STORY

Download this sexy alternate retelling of how Nick and Bane meet.

In this 20,000 word story, Nick is an aspiring photographer looking for a patron, and Bane is a reclusive, lonely billionaire. Both meet at an exclusive club, Smoke, only to find that their relationship is much more than a one-night affair. It seems almost fated!

Cursed: Smoke is a fun extra that does not have anything to do with the main Cursed timeline. Use coupon code SMOKE to get it free:

https://shop.raythereign.com/shop/cursed-smoke-short-story/

CHAPTER ONE - SCARRED

Over one hundred years ago in India during the British Raj ...

A COLD CLOTH was pressed to Bane's forehead. He was so hot. His skin was *burning*, especially the right side of his face.

My face. Something happened to my face.

The memories of a withered hand being dipped in boiling mud and that hand coming towards him had Bane's eyelids flying open.

The world was a blur. He saw the silhouette of someone leaning over him. His breathing came in frightened gasps. He remembered a wizened female face with ancient, sad eyes who hated him and he thought that *this* vague silhouette was *her*. He remembered no pity in those eyes for him in the past. She had punished him before for a transgression he couldn't quite remember yet. Was she back to end his life now? He cringed from the silhouette, but then the figure spoke to him.

"Bane?" a soft female voice asked.

Mother!

"Bane? Can you hear me?" his mother asked.

The tension drained from his body and he sank back against the pillows. His vision was still blurry, but he now could recognize the woman that had given birth to him as opposed to the woman who had harmed him..

"M-mother." Bane's mouth was so dry that he could hardly speak.

"Missus sahib, I think he needs more water," Nadal's voice rose up to the right of him.

"You're right, Nadal! Where is the pitcher --"

"Do not worry! I will get it." There was a shuffling sound as Nadal moved away and then came back. "I have it. Here."

"Thank you, Nadal, now put it down there. He's got to be sitting up to drink and I can't lift him myself." His mother brushed her hand over Bane's forehead to get his attention. "Darling, we are going to lift you up so you can drink."

Bane gave a jerky nod. He felt her and Nadal's hands on his back as they lifted him up and stuffed pillows behind him. He found that he was able to move surprisingly easily. If only his vision and ability to speak were restored as quickly and completely!

"That's good, Bane," his mother praised him. "That's very good."

He felt like a child that had been rewarded for taking his first steps. In a way, he felt strangely *new* as if he, indeed, were a child again just starting out. He had a sense that there was a reason for this feeling, but the thought drifted away before he could catch it. He was having trouble thinking. He sensed something momentous - or *terrible* - had happened to him, but his mind didn't want to remember it just yet.

"Bane, here's some water," his mother cooed softly.

A cool glass was pressed against his lower lip. At first, she tipped only a teaspoon's worth of water into his mouth, but then Bane took the glass from her and drained it in one go. Though his mother and Nadal were still blurry, his vision was clear enough now that he knew where to thrust the glass to ask for more. The glass was refilled swiftly and Bane drank the water down greedily again. After a third glass, the tightness in his throat was relieved and he could speak much more easily. He picked out the silhouette that looked most like his mother and reached towards it.

"Mother?"

"Oh, thank God. Yes, Bane, it's me!" she cried, her voice choked with tears as she took his hand.

"Why are you crying?" he asked.

"You've ... you've been *ill*, my darling," she answered.

He had guessed that. But *why* was he ill? Had his father come back and *attacked* him again? That didn't *feel* right to him and he had no memory of a fight. But, then again, he had no real memory of anything at the moment. So what terrible thing had happened that landed him in bed? His mind answered it for him. The image of a burning hand appeared before him and he rocketed back against the headboard. It smashed against the wall. The glass left his hand and crashed on the floor as he raised both of his arms up to ward off that terrible burning hand.

He screamed, "No! Don't touch me!"

His mother and Nadal took on twin horrified expressions. They were the only ones in the room. There was no burning hand. No withered woman wielding it who was stronger than seemed possible. He lowered his arms slightly. But his breathing still came in shuddering gasps and he was shaking so badly that the bed rocked with it.

"Bane, you're all right now! You're safe! You're back home!" his mother cried. "Oh, Nadal, what do we do?"

Nadal shook his head, clearly speechless, as to Bane's behavior. His hands were pressed before his chest as if in prayer. Perhaps praying was the only thing to do.

"You're *home*, Bane," his mother repeated. She patted the air in front of him, almost as if not daring to touch him. "You're *home*."

Home.

That word had his arms lowering fully down to his lap. The other two leaned towards him. It was as if everyone in that room were holding their breath to see what he would do next.

Home, he repeated the word to himself as if it was a talisman, but it didn't have the same power to soothe him as it originally had.

Because somehow this place didn't feel like home any longer. It felt more like a *prison*. The soft bedding did not feel right against his skin. He wanted to be up higher from the ground than he was. That would mean he was out of reach of other predators. He wanted the sun on him so he could bask in its warmth. But, instead, he was in this box. All he wanted to do was flee.

"What -- what has happened to me? I *know* something is *wrong*, but I cannot -- I cannot remember all of it!" Bane's balled fists slammed down on the bed.

His mother tentatively took one of his hands and stroked the back of it. "You've just woken up, Bane. Give yourself time."

He looked into her eyes. He could see far more clearly now. There was something in her eyes that had him realizing that she *knew* what had happened to him, but she didn't want to tell. This just confirmed his belief that the acrid taste of fear in his mouth was justified. She wouldn't hold back the truth if it was anything good.

"Mother, tell me what you know! Tell me the truth!" he demanded and started to rise up from the bed as if he could *walk* to the answer of his missing memory. At least moving would ease the horrible trapped feeling he had.

But his mother gently tried to push him back down flat on the bed. Nadal moved to the other side of the bed and tried to do the same, but he resisted both of them. Despite being ill, he was *strong*.

Stronger than before, a voice whispered in his mind. He shuddered at the sound of it. What kind of illness could make him stronger?

Nadal cried, "Sahib, you are not well!"

His mother pleaded "Bane, you must remain still until the doctor --"

"I don't need a doctor! I need answers!" he barked and his mother shied away from him. That brought him up short, because that was the motion she made when his father yelled at her. She cringed away from his father in an attempt to avoid a blow that would always accompany those sharp words. Bane would *never* hurt her. He softened his tone, "I -- I just need answers, Mother."

She shot Nadal a concerned look as she told him hesitantly, "I know you do, but we're not ... not altogether sure what happened to you."

"But you know *something*, do you not?" he pressed her.

At that moment, his eyes began to water. Bane blinked and rubbed them furiously. When the watering and itching eased, he looked up at her and all the blurriness was *gone*. The room was amazingly sharp and clear. Sharper and clearer than he had *ever* seen it.

He gazed about his own bedroom as if it was *new*. Indeed, it felt like seeing it for the first time with these improved eyes. The mahogany four-poster bed came into stark relief against the lighter floors. The white walls were almost blinding as sunlight sifted through the gauzy curtains that hung over the balcony doors.

Those doors were cracked open and he could smell cooking meat from the kitchen. He took in another breath and he could smell the dung of the horses in the stables. The moment he focused on the smell of the horses, he could hear the soft breathing of the stable boy as he cleaned the stalls. He then could *smell* the boy's sweat and *hear* the rasp-rasp of the rake.

This is impossible! The stables are over five hundred feet away!

"Bane?" his mother's voice jerked him back to the room.

He focused on her. She was so *vivid* in her white muslin dress with blue ribbons. Her dark hair was fastened up on top of her head, but a few stray tendrils had fallen down around her face. The heat of the day had plastered them to her neck in places. He watched as a stray trickle of sweat slowly rolled down the side of her throat and wetted the top of her collar. The white material darkened slightly as the sweat was absorbed. He heard her swallow and the quick bird-like thump of her heart. There was a slight coppery smell rising from her and he realized it was her time of the month. He grimaced and tried to withdraw his senses within himself.

It is not natural or right for me to know any of this!

She sat down on the edge of his bed. One of her delicate hands fluttered on top of his right shoulder. Her fingers were clear of paint that usually covered them no matter how assiduously she scrubbed them. He smelled no scent of oils or astringents on her person either.

Bane frowned. That meant she had not painted in some time. That caused him further alarm. She *needed* to paint every day. But she clearly *hadn't*. And the only reason she wouldn't have painted would have been to take time to care for him.

"Can you, at least, tell me how long have I been ill?" Bane asked.

"Five days," she answered. She was trying very hard to keep her voice neutral and calm.

He stiffened. "Five days?!"

What could have kept him unconscious for five days and left him with such heightened senses? His mind offered him the image of a dead tiger and that awful ancient woman staring at him accusingly.

"She burned me," Bane whispered, not knowing why he said that or what he even meant.

His mother exchanged a worried look with Nadal. Bane's gaze swung to the servant. The man had started to clean up the broken glass. He was walking with a decided limp. He'd acquired that limp when he had bravely tried to defend Bane and his ex-lover Alastair from Bane's father after his father had found Bane and Alastair in the bath together. His father had thrown Nadal against the wall in a fury.

Alastair ... I saw him ... I cursed him ... cursed ...

The old woman's face was in his mind's eye again. He rubbed his forehead furiously, trying to erase the image or have it make more sense.

"Do not worry about that now, Nadal," his mother said about the cleanup.

"I must, missus sahib. You or Bane might cut yourself on the glass if it is left here," Nadal said with quiet firmness.

Nadal had become his mother's most trusted confidant since the attack. He had a very large place in Bane's heart, too. And that was when he realized that *Nadal* shouldn't be here. *Tarun* should be. As soon as he thought of Tarun, there was another flurry of images. One of them was a dead tiger. Another was a group of villagers with knives at Tarun's throat. Finally, there was the impossibly ancient priestess who had made the mud bubble and then ...

"Where is Tarun?!" Bane's voice was high and tight. "Is he -- please tell he isn't --"

"He is well." His mother stroked his forehead with a cool hand.

"Then where is he? Why is he not here with me?"

"He just had to go to the train station to …" She broke off and again looked at Nadal who was bending over to pick up glass. Even with the blood rushing to his face, the Indian servant went gray at her words.

At that moment, Bane heard the clip-clop of horses' hooves and the creak of a carriage as it pulled up outside by the front doors. There was a click-click sound as the stairs extended and he heard the solid thump of boots descending them.

"I don't need your help to get from the carriage! I am not a woman!" his father's quarrelsome voice rose up.

"Forgive me, sahib," came Tarun's almost whispery apology.

"So where is he? Where's my son?" Richard demanded. "Upstairs in bed? Why am I not surprised! Such a weakling!"

All three of them were frozen in Bane's bedroom as the solid clomp-clomp of his father's footsteps came into the foyer, up the stairs and down the hallway towards them. Bane swore that with every step his heart threatened to beat out of his chest. The door to his bedroom was thrown open and Lord Richard Dunsaney stood in the threshold.

His father was bigger - and *angrier* - than ever. In that moment, his hulking figure made him seem more like a monster than a man. His face was flushed red with drink and there were plentiful broken veins around his nose. Oily sweat coated his skin and there were sweat stains beneath his armpits. His dark gray eyes zeroed in on Bane's face and he stilled. One of Bane's hands half lifted to his face, confused by whatever it was there that seemed to shock his father to the bone. But he lowered it almost immediately. His father's face broke into an ugly smile and he gave out a bark of laughter that cause Bane to jerk.

"Well! If only this had happened *before* Alastair had come here then none of the trouble would have occurred!" his father chuckled.

Bane winced at the name of his traitorous lover on his father's lips. He had believed his father had killed Alastair, as the man had disappeared directly after they had been discovered by Richard in a naked embrace. His father had told him he'd paid the Honorable Alastair Hillingham to simply leave. But Bane hadn't believed him.

Yet his father had been telling the *truth* all along as he'd discovered. The throb of that memory of what had happened after that discovery pressed against the front of his mind, but Bane still held it away from his consciousness. Now though Bane was sure that whatever else these strange words of his father's meant, they were likely true as well.

"Richard, don't say anything more! He's just woken!" his mother's voice was shrill with warning.

"What is he talking about, Mother?" Bane asked. His gaze was fixed on the hated figure of his father.

His father's eyes danced with malevolent amusement. "You don't know? You haven't seen yet?"

"Richard! Stop it!" His mother's hand tightened on Bane's shoulder protectively.

"What haven't I seen?" Bane asked.

"Let me show you."

His father swaggered further into the room. Nadal dashed out of his way as quickly as his wounded limb would take him. Richard let out another cruel laugh at the man's fear. His father then picked up a handheld mirror from Bane's dressing table and threw it at him. Bane wasn't meant to catch it, but he did. His hand moved faster than it should have. His father blinked in surprise. Bane felt a stab of satisfaction. But it did not last long. Because it was then that Bane looked at his face in the mirror.

He stilled.

"You see?" his father said with evident relish. "Now you have a face that only a *mother* could love."

Bane's breathing accelerated as he saw the handprint burned onto the right side of his face. The skin was raw and red and raised. He looked ... like a *monster*. Like a *beast*. He pulled his hair around so that it covered the horrible mark.

He heard a splintering sound. It took him a moment for him to realize where the sound had come from. He had crushed the metal and glass mirror as if it were a piece of paper. He hardly noticed his father's consternation or his mother's alarm.

He then remembered everything.

After discovering Alastair's betrayal, he'd felt the need to kill something *beautiful* and *precious*. And he'd done just that. He'd taken down a white Bengal tiger. This tiger was not a normal beast, but the *spirit* of all tigers. And for his transgression, he had been *cursed* by a priestess.

But he knew his punishment wasn't just the disfiguring scar on his face.

No, something else had changed in him, too.

He had a feeling that he would soon find out exactly what that was.

CHAPTER TWO - STALKED

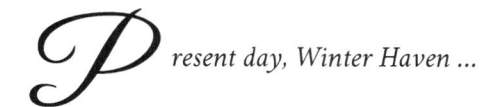

Present day, Winter Haven ...

NICK HUNKERED down over the top of his motorcycle as he raced back to Winter Haven and away from the beloved mansion, Moon Shadow. The trees that bordered the two-lane highway whipped by on either side of him. Nick felt the air nipping at his leather jacket and finding its way through the holes in the knees of his jeans. Even though it was summer, a slight chill held him in its grip. He practically laid his body across the top of the motorcycle and increased his speed so that he would get back to the city as quickly as possible.

Normally, he would have drawn out a ride like this. The moon was bone white and the stars glittered like so many diamonds in a deep black sky. But he found no beauty or joy in it this time. He was just trying to get from point A to point B as fast as he could without thinking too much.

Without thinking of Bane ...

Tears pricked his eyes behind the visor of his helmet. He quickly blinked them away though his vision blurred for a few moments. He tried to force his thoughts away from the billionaire, but they kept circling back to him like he was on an endless loop.

Tonight was supposed to have been a triumph. The first showing of his photography to the public had been a success. Over half a dozen of his photographs had sold for a good cause and good money. People had genuinely seemed to like his art. Even his father and brothers had grudgingly admitted that he might have some talent.

They should have all been back at the party, celebrating with champagne. Nick's face should have hurt from smiling too hard. His best friend Jade Lessitor should have been taking her high heels off and dancing barefoot with Omar Singh, Bane's servant and Nick's friend. His father Charles Fairfax should have been red-faced with whisky and pride. His two older brothers, Jake and Steven, should have even been tolerating the evening. Even Devon Wainwright, Bane's ex-boyfriend, should have been there with his cat-like smiles.

But that hadn't happened.

Instead, Bane had been *awful*, but also, frighteningly out of control. He and Bane had met just a few months ago under terrible circumstances. Nick's father and brothers, through their venture capital firm Fairfax International, had attempted a hostile takeover of one of Bane's companies. The end result was quite different than what his family had planned. Bane stopped the takeover and ended up owning Fairfax International instead.

Bane was morally repulsed by what he saw as Nick's father and brothers' pure avariciousness. In Bane's eyes, all the Fairfaxes did was destroy and make the world a worse place than how they found it. He had been set to destroy them when Nick had, unexpectedly, walked into his father's office. Nick's intent had been to tell his father that he was choosing his art over his family's financial and emotional support. Upon seeing Nick, Bane appeared to come up with a *new* plan to punish the Fairfaxes.

Bane offered them a *deal*. Part one of this deal had Nick's father and brothers working for Bane for a year. At the end of that year, they had to show that they had absorbed Bane's business practices and left their old ways behind them. Though Nick had nothing to do with his family's company, Bane required Nick to also serve him for a year in any capacity he asked for at his mansion, Moon Shadow. In return, Fairfax International could be theirs again. In order to save his family, Nick had agreed to his part of the deal, though he had been *adamant* that he drew the line at sleeping with the beautiful, if tempestuous, billionaire.

But as his time at Moon Shadow went by, he'd found himself falling for Bane and the feeling appeared to be mutual. Bane even released Nick from his part of the deal so that they could pursue a romance. But things had not all been rosy at the mansion. Nick was badly sunburned and then almost raped by Bane's business associate. But the greatest surprise had been when Nick found a white Bengal tiger spooning with him instead of Bane. The tiger had even accidentally injured Nick and fled into the night.

The next day, Omar had explained that Bane had a sacred charge to take care of the tiger, something Nick had known nothing about. But Nick wasn't *completely* surprised as he had been dreaming of tigers since the first night he'd come to Moon Shadow. Yet he needed explanations from the billionaire. Bane reappeared, only it wasn't with apologies or explanations, but instead to flee from him. The billionaire left Moon Shadow for a month without any explanation or even a goodbye.

During this month, Bane did not call Nick. He did not write. He simply *vanished*, supposedly to introduce the tiger into a zoo in Europe. But Nick chose to stay at Moon Shadow and help transform the decrepit mansion back to its former glory. He documented the process with his camera. He also hoped that Bane would return to him and maybe the nascent romance they'd shared could be rekindled.

Bane had finally returned and their romance had burned brighter than ever. Bane had actually confided in Nick why he did not believe in love. The truth was that Bane *had* believed in it, deeply and profoundly, in the past but he'd been betrayed on every level by a man named Alastair Hillingham. Alastair was Bane's father's dashing best friend. He'd seduced a teenaged Bane and introduced him to male love, but then abandoned him for money. Bane's father, Lord Richard Dunsaney, had brutally beaten Bane for being gay, even though Alastair had revealed that he and Richard had pursued male lovers all through school and Richard had only married Bane's mother for money.

Convinced that Alastair loved him and would never leave him to the tender mercies of his father for base coin, Bane believed Richard had killed Alastair. It was only at a party where Bane ran into the older man did he realize the truth: Alastair had left him for money even though he knew Richard's violent tendencies. This realization had spurred Bane to go on a hunting trip in a secret valley in India where he'd received the burn that was shaped like a handprint was over the right side of his face.

As Nick and Bane's relationship deepened, it seemed that Bane's demons lessened. Nick had even been so bold as to confess his love for Bane and the billionaire returned it - though he was still seemingly afraid to say the words. But Nick was sure those words were to come. Only there were other obstacles for them to overcome far larger than "I love you". Bane had other secrets that he would not share with Nick.

The billionaire seemed to have moments when his eyes would *glow* and he would be out of control. These most often happened when they were about to be intimate. Bane confessed at those times that he feared he might *hurt* Nick. Nick hadn't believed Bane capable of harming him, but he could see that Bane's fear was real to him and vowed to go slow with their physical intimacy.

Nick could have dealt with lack of verbal "I love yous" and Bane's secrets, but he could not accept Bane's insistence on keeping Nick's father and brothers under the terms of the deal. Jade warned Nick from the very beginning that his and Bane's relationship could not survive with the billionaire still having control of the Fairfax family's fate. Nick claimed that Bane couldn't be the man he seemed if he actually tossed Nick's family out on the streets, but Nick, at the same time, veered away from actually *asking* Bane to let his family go.

Until that night, just outside of the party where his art was being presented to world.

And that was what had brought everything crashing down. Bane had been ill for the two days before the party, but he had insisted on going to Nick's opening. It was there, after overhearing part of a conversation Nick had with his father - one where Charles Fairfax had urged his son to continue dating Bane for the year of the deal - that Bane and Nick had a final argument.

Bane revealed that he had no intention of letting the other Fairfaxes out of the deal and giving them the business back. He revealed to Nick that his family was failing to pick up his business practices and he fully expected to put them out on the street at the end of the year. Not realizing the absolute hypocrisy of his stance, Bane also revealed that he believed Nick would be *glad* when he did this. Nick's family was horrible to him and the faster they were out of Nick's life the better.

While Nick had little fondness for his family's business practices, they were still *his family*. He would never want to see them out on the street, let alone be *glad* about it. He realized then what Jade had said from the beginning: if the whole deal wasn't unwound, he wasn't really free of it. He couldn't be with a man who would destroy his family.

But as their argument had progressed, Bane had become stranger and stranger. He had seemed almost *animalistic*. He had snarled and growled and, at one point, Nick was convinced that the man was going to actually *harm* people. He attempted to calm Bane down, but while he was partially successful, Devon had wandered out into the fray and Bane had run off yet again.

Nick had Omar take Jade back to her apartment and asked the Indian man to take him back to Moon Shadow. But he wasn't going back there to wait for Bane. He was going there to get his things and then he was leaving the beloved mansion and his beloved Bane. Perhaps forever.

Nick had taken only the things he'd come to Moon Shadow with, leaving everything Bane had gifted to him, including a credit card, in the room. He'd then gotten on his motorcycle and headed back to Winter Haven, which was what he was doing now. He was going to live with Jade, figure out a way to pay back Bane for funding off his last year of school, and *hope*, somehow, that Bane determined that punishing his father and brothers meant less than losing *him*.

People don't change, Nick thought sourly as he took one of the road's many curves. *Bane told me that he hated my family and intended to make them pay for how they'd run Fairfax International. Yet I ignored what he said and even what he did! I pretended that somehow love would overcome! I was a coward. I didn't ask him to let my family go in the beginning of our relationship because I knew what his answer would be: no. And here we are. The answer is, in fact, no. But my heart is already his.*

He put a little more pressure on the gas and followed the snaking highway through the dense forest that surrounded Winter Haven. With all the wealth that was located in that town, Nick would have thought that the land would have been claimed by McMansions or luxury condos for the rich-but-not-quite-rich-enough to live in Winter Haven proper. But that was not the case. One man was responsible for keeping Winter Haven's forests intact and pristine: Alric Koenig.

Nick had only once glimpsed him across a room at a crowded party that his father had dragged him to. The Fairfaxes, though wealthy and incredibly successful, were not in the same league as Alric Koenig, no one really was. But Nick's impression had been that the man's press was not as good as it could have been. Even if Nick had not been impressed with the man personally, Alric's decision to buy up all the surrounding land around Winter Haven and keep it undeveloped forest won Nick's heart completely.

As he rode the winding highway through the trees, the moon began to rise higher into the black sky. The full moon was tomorrow. Nick's breath caught at its beauty. It cast a hard, white light onto the road, silvering the asphalt. He and Bane had talked about the moon while looking at it through a telescope in Moon Shadow's small observatory. Bane had been surprisingly knowledgeable about it, telling Nick the names the moon went by each month and it's almost magical power over people.

Nick's throat tightened. That night the moon had seemed mysterious and inviting. Tonight it appeared cold and uncaring. But his thoughts were interrupted as his headlamp flickered.

What the?

Then the motor shuddered.

Oh, come on! No way!

It sputtered.

Don't break down, baby! I just need you to make this one last ride!

The engine shut off completely.

You've got to be kidding me!

His bike was dead. He was coasting. With a curse, Nick steered his motorcycle over onto the narrow shoulder. Once stopped, he turned the key in the ignition. The first time it clicked, but after that, the motor made no noise at all. Nick let out a fluid string of curse words. To have his bike break down after having to leave Bane was adding insult to injury. He felt like screaming or crying or both. But he didn't.

Instead, he reached into his back jean's pocket to grab his cell phone and call a towing company. It was too far to walk back to Moon Shadow - and the very thought of returning there was like a stab to the heart - or forward to Winter Haven. Jade only had her moped so she couldn't come get him. So he went to dial for a tow, but then he saw the "No Service" at the top of his phone and swore.

Now all I need is for a car to come by and run me down! That would just top the night off!

But there were no cars. In fact, the silence around him seemed almost *threatening*. Without the motorcycle's engine roaring, no lights, and no cars in sight, Nick felt like he was alone in a primeval forest. His earlier love for Alric Koenig took a sharp dive. If this place had been developed there would have been a gas station nearby! But there wasn't.

"Well, this utterly sucks," Nick growled.

He turned and looked back at where he had come and then

forward towards where he had to go. It was incredibly dark. Nick realized he had seen only a handful of cars since he took off from Moon Shadow. He might not see any more. This area was mostly rural, large estates or farms, but nothing else. Lots of land, but few people to occupy it. And fewer still were interested in driving out there or back into the city. That meant there was only one choice: walk until he got cell service.

Nick's shoulders slumped. He took a few deep breaths to steady himself and then dismounted from the bike. He began to walk the motorcycle towards Winter Haven. The bike was far heavier than he had anticipated and he found that it took him almost double the usual time to walk a mile than it would have without the bike. Nick unzipped his leather jacket and hung it over the handlebars. His white t-shirt was already sticking to his skin. He swiped a hand over his sweaty forehead and continued to push the dead hunk of metal.

And not one car has passed me by either way! If there wasn't an asphalt road here, I could believe I really was lost in the forest.

At that moment, the hair on the back of Nick's neck stood up on end though he had no idea why. He froze and scanned his surroundings. The two-lane highway was still empty. He found himself staring at the space between two trees trunks nearest to him. The darkness in the forest was surprisingly absolute. Nick strained his eyes as he *swore* he saw movement between those trees.

Someone was there.

Some*thing* was there.

Watching him.

Nick shook his head and tried to laugh at himself.

There is nothing dangerous in the woods around here! No wolves or bears or even bobcats. The most dangerous animals are deer and they are only dangerous to cars not people!

But despite this knowledge, Nick's heart beat rapidly and the copper taste of fear coated his tongue. He found himself hunching his shoulders and pushing the motorcycle faster along the highway. He wanted to get to Winter Haven. He wanted the safety of heavy locked doors between him and whatever it was that flickered out of the corner of his eye. He checked his cell. Still no service.

He caught sight of another flicker of movement of something white between the trees. He could not chalk it up to his imagination this time. He had truly seen something!

Nick turned his walk into a run. But he wasn't able to shake the white thing that raced just beyond the first line of trees. It kept up with him. And it was *big*. It wasn't a fox. It wasn't a cat. It wasn't a dog.

It's so much bigger than that ... It's ... It's .... Oh, my God ...

The creature crossed into a pool of moonlight ahead of him. Nick stumbled to a halt even as his motorcycle tried to drag him forward towards the thing that had been stalking him.

Except it *wasn't* a thing.

It was a white Bengal tiger.

And, somehow, through the terror, that felt like *fate*.

The majestic, terrifying beast headed straight towards him.

CHAPTER THREE - CHASE

When Bane was in the tiger form, he was the passenger, not the driver. Most times, he would lose consciousness altogether and have no memory of what the beast did. When the beast escaped from its basement cage, he would wake up the next morning, naked and in a field, with blood on his hands and face, but no memory as to what he had done. He'd always hoped - hoped beyond hope - those times when his body was stained crimson that it was animal blood and not human blood. He'd then stumble back to Moon Shadow where Omar would be anxiously waiting for him. The Indian man would help him bathe and put him to bed where he would stay, nearly insensate, for several days.

But this time Bane was completely awake and aware of what was going on.

The moment he'd realized that Nick had left him, the beast had shredded through his thin control and shifted them into the tiger form. Bane was fully present as the beast had raced down the stairs, past a shocked Omar, and barrelled out the front doors into the night. The beast had paused then, for a brief moment, head raised in the air to sniff it. Nick's scent, though faint, was on the wind. The tiger began to run again. Yet it didn't head out to the road where Nick was riding, but instead it headed into the woods that bordered the two-lane highway. It would be able to go faster that way, cutting off miles from the trek to Winter Haven.

Bane had no idea how long ago Nick had left. The speed limit was forty-five miles per hour in parts and up to fifty miles per hour in others. The road was bound to be empty and Nick might be inclined to speed. Nick had told him many times about the lure of speeding under the light of the moon on his motorcycle.

He'd have wanted to get away from Moon Shadow as quickly as possible, too, Bane realized. He felt sick at the thought of Nick fleeing from him, but it was a good thing at that moment, because it might take the young man out of the beast's reach. *It won't go into downtown Winter Haven. It won't make its way to Jade's apartment. That is too exposed. So long as Nick gets to the city's limits before the beast finds him, he'll be safe.*

But the beast was determined to find Nick and bring him home no matter what it had to do. Bane wished to find Nick, too, but not like this. *Never like this.* He clung to the thought that Nick was simply too far ahead for the beast to catch up. The beast would reach the edge of the city and have to turn back. No matter how much it wanted to find Nick, it knew the danger in being seen. It would have to retreat.

Bane addressed the beast then, *You should give this up. You can't convince Nick to come back. All you'll do is scare him. And you might hurt him.* Bane said "might", but he feared that the "might" was really "would". *Turn back. Leave Nick alone. I will speak to him -*

No, a single word from the beast and it chilled Bane into silence for a moment. It had never been this angry with him. *You have done enough. I will retrieve our mate. He will understand.*

He won't understand! He'll just be afraid of you! Bane argued then added, *He's out of your reach.*

You are wrong, the beast said. *As you are wrong about many things.*

And then the beast went silent. It would not respond to him any further no matter what he said. As the beast ran and ignored him, Bane's thoughts went to what had happened earlier in the night.

He'd earned Nick leaving him. The things he'd say at the charity event to his lover were unforgivable. Bane had been struggling to keep the beast under control - any time near the full moon his moods were atrocious and his short-fused temper even more so - but his words had been especially cruel. He'd told Nick that both of them would be *glad* after Charles, Steven and Jake Fairfax failed in their part of the deal and Bane put them out on the street.

The Fairfaxes were supposed to learn and apply his methods of business. What they were doing instead was trying to use *their* methods on *his* companies. They looked for ways to lay people off, cut salaries, and reward senior management, which mostly meant themselves. While these acts might have made Bane's companies more profitable in the short term, they would be disastrous in the long. The employees *were* the companies. Depress them, overwork them, or make them feel like disposable cogs in a great grinding wheel and one wouldn't get the best out of them. Yet despite being told no, over and over again, and being directed towards better practices, the Fairfaxes kept falling back on their old ways. At least, that's what Charles had been doing. The brothers less so, but *still*. They had no idea that they were *failing*.

Bane's disgust with them, and his own out of control emotions from the nearing shift, had caused him to crow to Nick about his family's fate. He gleefully reminded the young man that not only would his family not have their company anymore, but they would be *destitute*. He'd make sure they had no place to go. No one would take them in. Nick's family would have a *taste* of what they'd done to others over a lifetime of destroying companies. Maybe then they would understand that they had failed. This kind of punishment appealed to a cold, hard part of Bane. Justice without mercy.

But it wasn't a *good* part of him. It was a part that he sensed Charles Fairfax might actually be impressed by, but Nick would *never* be. Yet he'd vomited it all up for Nick anyways and *expected* Nick to be grateful that he was going to destroy his family. Even when Nick told him that he wanted the deal unwound and his family freed, Bane had *persisted* in his refusal, in clinging onto the punishment he had in store for the other Fairfaxes. He'd tried and failed to get Nick to see how *right* it was. He'd even gone so low as to use Nick's outsider status with the family to justify hurting them.

They behave like he's some kind of foundling instead of one of them. Charles traded Nick to me to save his own skin! They don't deserve to be rewarded with their company back. Nick has to be protected from them!

These might be valid reasons to hate the other Fairfaxes, but they weren't the *real* reason he had refused to unravel the deal fully. The *real reason* was far from noble and it had nothing to do with Nick's family.

I wanted Nick to have no place else to go. I wanted to keep him imprisoned. I couldn't risk him leaving me.

Yet Nick *had* left him even though Nick likely believed him quite capable of putting his family out on the street right there and then.

But Nick had put his principles before his fears. And there was nothing to fear, because Bane *wouldn't* put the Fairfaxes out. No matter how much he hated them, because he'd realized something that he should have always known: he *loved* Nick more than he could *hate* anyone.

He *loved* Nick. Yes, that was the truth of it. He *loved* Nick, but it might be too late to actually tell him that and have it mean anything.

It was then that Bane became aware of his surroundings again. The beast had been racing through the woods on silent paws, but now it slowed down and a familiar sound hit Bane's ears. It was the the throaty growl of a *motorcycle's* engine. Bane went cold with shock and fear.

The beast had caught up with Nick.

No! This isn't possible! Nick is safely miles away! Nick is behind doors and locks and lighted corridors that a tiger cannot sneak down without being caught! No, this can't be Nick!

But he *knew* it was.

The beast slowed its run to a stealthy stalk. Nick's clean, woodsy scent washed over them both and Bane felt drawn to it as much as repelled by the idea that he was smelling it while the beast was in control.

Panic flooded Bane's mind and he mentally tried to claw his way

CURSED: BELOVED

into control of the tiger's form, but it was as if he was in a glass prison. No matter where he scrabbled, he could gain no purchase, find no toehold. He spun around and around, but got nowhere. He could *feel* the press of cool earth against the tiger's paws, but he could not move the legs, could not make the beast turn and lope away from where the sound of Nick's motorcycle engine was coming from.

There was something wrong with the engine, too, though he couldn't say exactly what it was. The sounds the engine was making reminded the beast of a wounded animal. The beast's ears twitched and it lifted its head as the engine suddenly sputtered. Bane was on tenterhooks. Was the motorcycle coming towards them? Yes, yes, it was! Could the beast leap out of the woods and take Nick down like a gazelle on the plains? Yes, yes, it could …

The image of Nick pitching sideways on his bike as the beast leaped upon him flashed through Bane's mind. The bike would skid. There would be sparks. Nick's one leg would be trapped between the bike and the road. Nick's jeans would shred then his skin would as his leg was ground against the asphalt. Once the bike skidded to a halt, leaving pieces of Nick scrapped along the road, the greater horror would come. The beast would begin to *feed*, excited by the sight and smell of Nick's blood.

Don't hurt him! Please! He cried to the tiger then he mentally screamed at Nick, *Ride as fast as you can, Nick! Get out of here! Don't slow down! Don't stop!*

The pitch of the motorcycle's engine changed again. Once more, the beast identified it as wounded. More wounded than before. Bane's heart went into his throat as he heard the engine sputter a final time and then fall *silent*. The beast crept out to the edge of the woods and looked down the road. Nick was bringing the bike to a gliding halt on the shoulder. Nick tried the key in the ignition, but the bike's engine just ticked then went silent and did nothing more.

The engine was dead.

Nick, get out of here! You need to get out of here! Bane cried out, but he knew Nick couldn't hear him.

And what could Nick do even if he had heard Bane? The motorcycle was just a hunk of inert metal now. It couldn't fly Nick to safety. And no human could outrun the beast.

It was terribly quiet with the motorcycle's engine off. All the night creatures had gone silent, hiding from the predator in their midst.

Nick cursed and swung his leg over the bike. With the beast's acute eyesight, Bane could see Nick's brow furrow as he checked his phone. Nick shoved the phone back into his pocket without calling anyone.

No signal, Bane guessed. Not that help could have arrived in time anyways.

Nick looked down the road towards Winter Haven and then glanced back the way he had come. There was nowhere for the young man to hide from the beast no matter which way he went, but perhaps the beast would be satisfied if Nick walked back to Moon Shadow. Perhaps it would leave him alone.

It was a vain hope.

Turn around, Nick! Go back to Moon Shadow!

But Nick *didn't* turn around. The young man clearly was determined to get away from the mansion and from Bane. Bane could almost imagine him thinking that there was no way he would consider going back to Moon Shadow and asking Omar for help.

Nick began pushing the heavy piece of metal towards the city. The beast silently stalked after him. It's whiskers twitched and it contented itself with smelling Nick's scent and keeping the young man in sight. Nick took off his jacket and his scent rose up far greater than before. Sweat and his normal clean woodsy scent wafted over to the beast. It was a beloved scent, but it was causing Bane to bleed mentally now. The beast increased its speed. It was then that Nick seemed to sense that he was being followed.

Just keep going, Nick! Ignore this feeling you have. Don't see the beast. Just keep walking.

Perhaps if the beast had not been alerted by Nick's fear, it would have contented itself with merely following him. But the moment it scented that sharp, alarmed smell, it went into full predator mode.

The young man's head turned this way and that, looking for whatever it was that caused the hair on the back of his neck to stand on end. Nick's eyes narrowed as he peered into the forest. The beast was amused by the young man's almost awareness of it. It lowered its massive head and slipped quietly between the trees. The leaves were thick above its location so no moonlight shone down to reveal its presence. But the beast wanted Nick to see it in the end. It wanted him to know that he was being tracked and see what Nick did in response.

It wanted to *play*.

No, no playing! You could hurt him! One swipe of your paw and he could bleed out! Don't you understand? Nick is NOT your toy!

The beast ignored him.

The young man's shoulders hunched and he pushed the bike forward faster. The beast stepped out into the road just then and into a pool of moonlight. Nick froze. He saw the beast for the first time.

Nick ...

Nick's nostrils flared and his eyes widened in fear and shock. The scent of him became richer with these emotions and the beast raised its nose in the air to scent him. What must Nick be thinking to see a white Bengal tiger in the middle of Winter Haven? To see *any* kind of tiger, let alone this *apex* predator, would have been mystifying and terrifying. Those combined emotions were reflected in the young man's eyes, but then there was *recognition*, too.

"Are you ... are you *Bane's*?" Nick asked almost as if he expected the beast to answer him.

The beast let out a low roar to indicate that it was *not* Bane's. It would *never* be Bane's. It was its own. And Nick belonged to it, too.

Nick's shoulders drew up to his ears, cringing in fear, and then Bane saw the young man's eyes dart towards the woods, telegraphing where he intended to go.

Nick, don't run! Don't run! It will chase you and you can't outrun it!

Bane could picture what would happen if Nick ran. Nick would drop his bike and race into the woods. The beast would take off after him. The powerful muscles in its legs would easily allow it to reach Nick before he had gotten far into the forest. It would then leap onto Nick's back and take him down. Nick would fall, crushed beneath the weight of the beast. Again, if the leap didn't snap Nick's neck, what would come next would be worse.

The eating.

The claws would shred Nick's clothes and his back. They would slice into Nick's sweet skin and ...

NO!

Bane didn't know what he expected to happen if Nick didn't run though. For them to stay in this strange, silent tableau until a car came along and its headlights scared the beast into the forest?

And then Nick could flag down that car and escape. Yes, please let that be what happens!

But the beast had determined that though Nick's scent was delicious on the air, it would be even *more* delicious if it could nose and lick Nick's skin. The beast took a single step forward. Bane already knew that silent approach would be too much for the young man. Nick would flee.

NO!

Almost as if mirroring his imagination exactly, Nick let go of the bike, which fell over like a dead mount onto the asphalt. Nick leaped over it like a gazelle and took off into the forest. The beast took off, too. The absolute joy of the chase filled it.

Don't hurt him! DON'T YOU DARE HURT HIM! DAMN YOU!

The beast flew through the woods after Nick. It moved like the wind. The distance between them shrank until Nick was only ten feet ahead of it. The young man was fighting the underbrush that filled his path. He cast a glance over his shoulder only to see the beast *right there*. His eyes opened wider and he gave out an inarticulate yell. The beast did not roar. Tigers did not roar when they hunted.

Stop! I'll give you whatever you want! Just don't hurt Nick!

Nick ran faster. He dodged past trees and jumped over fallen trunks. More than once he nearly fell as underbrush wrapped around his slender limbs. But each time Nick managed to right himself and keep running. But so did the beast. It was loping after him easily, enjoying the chase. At any moment it could have caught him, but it was *playing*.

Nick's scent was thick on the wind now. It was sweet with terror and sweat. Nick's white shirt glowed in the darkness between the trees. It was like a giant neon sign for the beast to follow even if the beast did not have the excellent night vision it did.

The beast could go on forever at this pace. Nick could not. He was slowing. He was starting to wheeze. But, even worse than Nick's failing strength, they were running out of forest. The beast's keen hearing caught the faint sound of running water ahead of them.

The ravine!

Bane vaguely remembered from other jaunts as the beast that there was a steep-sided ravine that cut through the woods at this point. It was impossible for a person to scramble down as the sides were nearly sheer. It couldn't be jumped either as it was a quarter of a mile wide. And then he wasn't just hearing the water, he saw the ravine itself. Trees clung onto the very edge. Some actually leaned forward as if they were about to dive in.

NICK! STOP! THE RAVINE!

Nick evidently saw it as he changed course and tried running parallel to the ravine, but the young man was almost down and out. The wheezing had become gasping. His steps were mostly stumbles.

The beast sensed the play was at an end, too. It put just a little more speed into its run and the distance between them halved. Nick glanced over his shoulder once more and nearly fell as he saw how close the beast was to him. That was when both of them realized that the ravine *curved* left so that it was directly in front of them again. There really was nowhere left for Nick to go.

Bane watched with mute horror Nick jump and catch the trunk of one of the trees that lined the ravine's edge. Nick tried in vain to climb up it, out of reach of the beast. But there were no branches low enough to aid his climb, so he was stuck shimmying up the slick trunk.

But it doesn't matter. Tigers can climb, too.

The beast leaped.

NO CLAWS! DON'T USE YOUR CLAWS!

Bane would have closed his eyes, but he didn't want to miss one moment of Nick's life ... or death. He would use the memory of the moment of Nick's death to give him the courage to destroy himself after this. He couldn't live having done anything to Nick. He just couldn't.

But the beast gently swatted Nick's side and the young man lost his grip on the tree. Nick went crashing down onto the ground on his back. He lay there. Stunned. Felled. Prey.

Nick's face was perfectly showcased in a pool of moonlight. He looked dazed by the fall and was blinking repeatedly. Then Nick's gaze focused on the beast standing a foot away. He started to scramble backwards, but the beast put one paw on the center of Nick's chest as if to say, "Stay."

Nick stayed.

Don't hurt him, Bane repeated this phrase like a mantra over and over and over again.

He was almost numb from the terror he had been under since this all began. His voice petered out as the beast stared into Nick's eyes. The beast just stared with that one heavy paw, claws retracted, sitting on the center of Nick's chest.

Nick stared back.

This mutual staring went on for what felt like an eternity. It may have only been five minutes or five hours. Bane couldn't be sure. Finally, the beast moved. Bane's heart stopped as the tiger leaned down.

And began to lick Nick's face.

CHAPTER FOUR - MOON MADNESS, MOON MAGIC

"Hey! Hey! Enough with the licking! You have tiger breath!" Nick laughed as that rough, yet ticklish, tongue swiped over his throat as if he were a dish of cream the tiger was lapping up. The tiger's breath was rich and heady with wet heat.

He gently reached up and touched the tiger's soft cheek to try and stop the clearly affectionate licking. He could feel the wiry whiskers as well as the impossibly soft fur under his fingertips.

This is surreal. Is this really happening?

The tiger licked Nick's nose this time with abandon and Nick swore that the animal was smiling at him. Nick laughed more. He knew that the laughter was partially hysterical and partially joyous.

The tiger was *not* going to eat him.

At least, not at the moment.

No, he won't hurt me. I can feel it.

That thought was so strong and simple that it lodged deep inside of Nick's heart. The rational part of his mind told him that this was ridiculous. The tiger was a wild animal. Even if it was also Bane's "pet", it wasn't domesticated and *play* could become *violence* in a moment for no reason. Hadn't that magician in Las Vegas, who loved his tigers, ended up being mauled by one of them? That could easily be him. He should be slow and careful. He should stop laughing and try to get away.

But though his rational mind thought all those things, his heart didn't agree. That first strong, certain thought that the tiger would *not* hurt him had taken hold and he couldn't shake it. Also, absurdly, he felt that he would hurt the tiger's feelings if he tried to leave. There was also the issue of that paw on his chest. The beast wasn't putting much weight on him, nor were any claws extended, but it was clearly telling Nick it didn't want him to move.

It placed another lick along his right cheek this time. Another on his chin. And a final one on the other cheek as if to even the slobber out. The tiger then took its paw off of Nick's chest and took a step back.

Nick carefully – and *very* slowly – sat up. Grass blades and leaves fell from his back to the forest floor. The tiger moved in close again, but instead of licking Nick, the animal leaned against him, rubbing its furry cheek against Nick's smooth one. Nick let out a hiccupping laugh. He wrapped an arm around the tiger's chest. It was partially in surprised affection, but also to keep himself upright as the tiger's gentle rubbing was powerful. The animal didn't know its own strength.

Nick had been so afraid of this tiger when he'd first seen it. His heart had been in his throat when the animal had begun to chase him. He'd honestly felt like he was going to die. Yet, strangely, he'd felt it was *fated,* too. He and this tiger had been *destined* to meet. That it was going to end with blood and pain and death was almost *secondary* in his mind.

And now, with the tiger pressed against his side, leaning on him, rubbing on him, practically purring – he was aware that tigers could *not* purr though this one was trying its darnedest to do so – the sense of destiny was so strong that he could almost taste it. There was a sense of familiarity, too. After all, this was the tiger he'd dreamed of for months. A spike of uncomfortable arousal went through him at the memory of the dream where the tiger had lapped at Nick's cock before transforming into Bane.

Bane! A realization zinged through him and he froze. *The tiger is what this weekend must have been all about! Bringing the tiger back when I wasn't around. He knew that I wouldn't approve of him caging the tiger again.*

Nick pulled away so that he could look into the tiger's beautiful, noble face with those Siberian blue eyes so like Bane's. Maybe it was because those eyes were so like Bane's that he decided to talk to the animal as if the tiger could understand him.

"Bane brought you back from the zoo, didn't he?"

The tiger snorted and tossed its head as if the idea of a zoo was abhorrent.

"Bane couldn't be without you, could he?"

The tiger stared back at him without blinking as if willing him to understand something. Only Nick couldn't figure out what that was. Nick patted the powerful neck, curling his fingers in his fur.

"So he brought you back, but hid it from me, because he knew I wouldn't approve of him locking you up again," Nick continued.

The tiger let out a low growl, but it was not directed at Nick. The tiger seemed to understand the idea of being "locked up" and, clearly, hated it. Nick wasn't sure how the tiger could understand such a thing. Maybe the words "locked up" were familiar to it and it associated them with the idea of a cage.

"If he'd told me that he needed you near him so desperately, I would have understood. I would have found a way to convince him to give you places to run and be as free as possible around here." Nick shook his head in dismay. "But instead he made you yet *another* secret that he didn't trust me to know."

The tiger licked his cheek as if it recognized that Nick was upset. Nick turned and put his arms around the tiger's neck and held the animal close. The tiger was so warm. His powerful chest and front paws were solid and hard against Nick's chest. He could hear the magnificent beast's heart thumping steadily. Nick let out a soft breath and the beast curled around him. The two of them stayed like that for long moments. Finally, Nick pulled back and slowly rose to his feet.

The beast let out an inquisitive grunt, which Nick responded to, "We have to get you home. Will you follow me back to Moon Shadow?"

The tiger rose up onto all fours again and took a step towards the highway where Nick's bike lay on its side like a felled gazelle. The tiger looked over its shoulder at Nick expectantly.

"I guess I'm going to follow you," Nick chuckled and walked beside the tiger out of the woods.

A sense of wonder filled him as the tiger picked its way, unerringly, in the deep dark. The beast avoided obstacles that it could have easily jumped over, but would have caused Nick difficulty. The tiger watched Nick negotiate the dense underbrush as if to make sure Nick followed exactly in its footsteps. When they passed out of the line of trees they were only five feet from the motorcycle. It was as if the beast knew that he had to collect his bike before they could go back to Moon Shadow.

Maybe Bane got him from a circus and that's why he's so familiar with human commands. Or maybe tigers are just way smarter than I thought.

He picked up the bike and his jacket. He arranged the jacket once again on the handlebars while the tiger waited beside him. Its Siberian blue eyes swept from the right to the left and back again. Its ears twitched when there was the faintest sound.

It's listening for cars!

Nick was amazed all over again. This tiger could not be a normal tiger. It was an *extraordinary* tiger.

Maybe that's why Bane is so attached to him. Though who couldn't love such a beautiful beast even if he wasn't smart?

The tiger was sitting back on its haunches, tail swishing the ground, stirring dead leaves and the grass like a metronome. The animal looked up at him and there was such *tenderness* in those blue eyes that Nick had to look away. His own eyes pricked with shocked tears. The look it gave him ... it looked like *love*. It reminded him of the look he'd once imagined Bane giving him in his bedroom at Moon Shadow that first night they'd met.

A wash of grief went through him as he thought of Bane. He was going back to Moon Shadow, *beloved* Moon Shadow, and Bane would, undoubtedly, be there. Bane. His Bane. The other half of him. The half of him that he *couldn't* have any longer. Not unless Bane changed. But people didn't change. Seeing Bane again, knowing he couldn't have him, that he would forever be incomplete, would be *hell*. But he had to go back. The tiger needed him.

He cleared his suddenly tight throat and then turned his head to look into those blue eyes again. He got down on his haunches, which made the tiger taller than he was. He knew that for some animals staring them in the eyes was a challenge and a really bad idea, but he felt it wouldn't be taken that way here. Again, this seemed a bit like magical thinking, but it also felt *right*. He cupped the tiger's face, fingers flexing in the fur and whiskers.

"Okay, here's the deal, I'll take you back to Moon Shadow." The tiger's ears twitched and its eyes were intent on Nick's face as if very happy they were going back. "I'll stay –" The beast leaned forward, eyes fixed, not even blinking. "Until I assure myself that you will be taken care of properly. No more cages. No more basement."

The tiger's tail whooshed faster over the ground and those eyes just *sparkled* as if the beast knew *exactly* what he meant. Nick let out a breath and stood up straight again. He let his hands linger on the tiger's head. The tiger half closed its eyes and rubbed its cheek against Nick's hand so like what Bane would have done.

"All right, let's go," Nick said and put both hands on the handlebars.

He and the beast began walking next to one another along the side of the road. The bike that had felt so heavy before when he was pushing it to Winter Haven hardly weighed a thing as they walked towards Moon Shadow. He found himself talking to the tiger about the forest, the sky, the names of the moon depending on the month, and the joy of roses.

He did not speak of Bane. He couldn't. All words about Bane stuck in his throat. He kept talking until his mouth was dry and tacky. Yet he continued to speak, because as long as he talked, he wouldn't *feel*. His grief over Bane would not overwhelm him. The tiger looked up at him as he spoke, making low sounds as if responding.

A sense of unreality filled Nick. He couldn't quite believe he was talking to a tiger that seemed to be talking back. The sky above them was this gorgeous wash of velvety blackness with stars like diamonds sprayed across that vast expanse. The moon was huge, seemingly twice its usual size. The moonlight seemed to caress the beast's white and black fur. It made the night as bright as day.

Moon madness. Moon magic.

They were interrupted only one time in their conversation. It was when a car passed by. Before Nick could urge the beast to hide, the tiger had already disappeared into the forest without a trace. Nick stood there stupidly as the headlights washed over him. The car didn't slow down and, if he weren't accompanying a tiger, Nick would have been annoyed, but now he wanted the car to speed by as fast as possible and not notice him at all.

Yet as he stood there in the wash of light, his eyes searched the forest for the tiger. Because, for one horrible moment, he thought the tiger was a *dream*, that this was *all* a dream, and that he would wake up at Jade's place with an emptiness in his chest where his heart should have been. But as soon as the tail lights were out of sight, the tiger bounded out of the woods, tail high and eyes bright. The animal bumped up against him, rubbing its own length against Nick's leg. Nick couldn't help but reach down and ruffle that soft fur and hug that huge body. The tiger leaned against him. Relieved, Nick started talking about nothing again. The topic this time was about buying expeditions with Jade as they walked mile after mile back to Moon Shadow.

In no time at all, the the gates to Moon Shadow were in sight. The tiger and Nick quickened their pace, both eager to be *home*. Though Nick was quick to remind himself that it *wasn't* his home any longer. Still it was good to be here.

Nick was dying for an icy beer and he was sure that the tiger must be thirsty as well. Nick's stomach gurgled just as they walked through the gate and onto the crushed gravel drive. He was starving. He'd been too nervous to eat before or during the charity event and all this walking had built up an appetite. He was sure he wasn't the only one. A tiger this big needed a lot of food. Hopefully, Omar would have food enough for both of them.

"Does Omar keep large sides of beef for you or something?" he asked the tiger.

The tip of the tiger's tail wagged at the mention of "beef".

"All right then. I'm guessing they have made provisions for you," Nick said. "We'll both eat and drink and be merry. I'm dying to know what Omar will say when he sees the two of us together."

As if thinking the man's name made him appear, the doors to Moon Shadow opened and Omar stepped out into the rectangle of light. He had a flashlight and a long length of chain attached to a massive steel collar. As soon as the beast saw that, it gave a low growl. Nick reached down and petted its head. The tinkling sound of the fountain stopped Omar from hearing that throaty growl.

"Don't worry. No one is putting that on you," Nick assured it.

The tiger glanced up at him and gave him one of those tender, loving looks again. It was then that Omar swung the flashlight towards them and the light struck Nick's face. Nick held up a hand to block out the beam.

"Omar! Sheesh, lower the weapon," Nick laughed. "It's just me."

Well, it's not just me. But I want to see how he reacts to seeing the secret tiger that he and Bane tried to tell me was staying in Europe!

Just the thought of Bane when he was now standing in Moon Shadow's drive caused Nick's heart to twist. Was the big man here? Was he waiting for Nick? Would he apologize? Would he change?

I've been gone just a couple hours and I think everything's going to be perfect? Come on!

"Oh, Nick, thank the gods! It is you! But what are you doing *here*? I *want* you here, but I thought that you were *leaving* and ..." His voice died and Nick knew he had seen the tiger. The cat had literally gotten Omar's tongue. Omar's mouth opened and shut, but nothing came out. Finally, Omar stammered, "N-Nick, you need to -- to step away from the t-tiger."

Nick put the kickstand on his bike down and then sat on his haunches beside the beautiful beast. He slung an arm around the tiger's neck. The beast immediately licked his cheek, making Nick laugh.

"We're perfectly fine, Omar. He's not going to hurt me. The pawing before was an accident. Wasn't it?" he asked the tiger the last bit.

The tiger actually seemed to *nod* and then the beast tenderly nosed his scarred shoulder. Nick blinked. He really was anthropomorphizing the tiger's actions. The tiger couldn't *actually* understand what he was saying. Yet this was the first tiger he'd seen outside a zoo. He didn't know much about them and he was already convinced that this tiger was extraordinary so maybe somehow the animal *did* understand what he was saying.

Nick petted the beautiful beast and kissed its nose, which had the tiger letting out a pleased huff. There was a clanking sound. Nick and the tiger turned to the Indian man. He had dropped the chain and collar onto the gravel driveway in shock. He was staring at the two of them with his mouth open.

"You and the tiger are ... *friends*?" Omar asked weakly, but Nick had this idea that the Indian man was going to say another word, a very different word than *friends*. He remembered how Bane had asked him if he was his *mate* earlier that evening.

"Yes, we are. He found me on the road after ... *escaping* from here clearly. Don't know how he did it, but he did. My motorcycle kicked the bucket. I've just come back here to make sure that you and Bane don't lock him up again," Nick said, his voice sharpening with the last words. "He needs to be outside, Omar. He needs to be able to run and hunt and sun himself. You can't keep him in a filthy cage in the basement. I won't allow it!"

Omar jerked with every word. He started to nod like one of those plastic birds who when you touched their beak to water would continue to dip it in forever. "I understand. I agree with you."

CURSED: BELOVED

"But Bane doesn't?" Nick's voice sharpened even more and a shiver of anger went through him. Anger mixed with pain and longing. "Bane wants to keep him locked up?"

Omar opened his mouth, but then shut it. Nick sensed he had been about to lie, but thought better of it. That was a good thing. Nick would not accept any more lies from Omar or Bane. He was done with that.

"Things are more *complicated* than you know, Nick," Omar finally said. "You have every right to be angry with Bane and me. I would only ask that you let us explain."

"You can explain while getting the tiger some food and water. He's parched and so am I, but I can serve myself." Nick turned to the house and froze. Was Bane inside? Was the big man watching them, hiding behind a curtain and his fall of hair? He felt such longing and anger towards the billionaire at that moment. His heart was falling and rising alternately. "Is Bane here?"

The billionaire's seeming supernatural hearing should have alerted him to Nick's presence. But Omar shook his head.

"No, he is not here," Omar answered, but it sounded like he was lying somehow. Yet Nick sensed that the big man was not in the house. Moon Shadow felt *empty* without him. "He will return ... in the morning."

"Where is he?" Nick demanded to know. "Is he out looking for the tiger?" He rubbed his cheek against the tiger's. "We could just call him and –"

"No," Omar said simply and that somehow stopped Nick cold.

"Is he looking for -- for *me*?" Nick hated the hope that had crept into his voice.

"He *was*, but I told him where you were or where you were going to be," Omar answered.

"So he's at Jade's?" Nick realized that he should call Jade and explain that he wasn't coming back tonight.

When will I be back? But how can I stay here with Bane? My heart can't take it.

But one look at the tiger and he knew he could not leave the magnificent animal until he was sure that Bane and Omar were taking proper care of it.

"No, Bane is not at Jade's," Omar said simply though there was this sense that he could say so much more, but was holding back.

"What aren't you telling me?" Nick asked.

"So much. So very much." Omar scrubbed his face with his hands and even in the moonlight, Nick could see how weary he was. The lies he'd had to tell obviously weighed heavily on him. His next words confirmed as much, "But I do not wish to lie to you any longer. If you stay here until morning you will understand."

"Please tell me that you've only ever lied to me about *Bane's* secrets, Omar. Please tell me that you ... that you ... I thought we were friends," Nick got out, his voice tight with pain.

Omar's expression became almost wild with despair. He clasped his hands together with the flashlight between them, illuminating his face with the beam like kids did when they were telling ghost stories.

"Oh, Nick, I *am* your friend! I begged Bane to tell you the truth. There can be no love without trust! But he would not listen! And I am bound to his service and not to betray him in this."

Nick's anger and hurt bled out of him and his shoulders slumped. Omar was clearly guilt-wracked about lying, but just as equally, he clearly felt he had no choice but support Bane's decision to lie about so many things. The tiger moved closer and rested its furry head against Nick's chest. Nick wrapped his arms around the beast and held it again. There was a soft sound from Omar and a few whispered words that – though Nick didn't know the language or what the words meant – could tell was a prayer.

And then he heard words he did understand, "I knew you were the one."

These words were whispered and half obscured by Omar's sigh but he heard them. Nick wanted to ask what Omar meant, but his stomach gurgled again.

"Are you as hungry as I am?" he asked the tiger.

The tiger let out a huff of air in agreement. He thumped the beast's side like it was a drum.

"Okay, let's get something to eat for both of us and then maybe Omar can answer a few more questions," Nick said.

The tiger huffed again and then headed straight towards the doors of Moon Shadow, slipping inside, tail held high. The tiger was happy to be home. Nick wished he could feel half so joyful.

CHAPTER FIVE - CARE, CUSTODY & CONTROL

❦

Bane felt like he was simultaneously in Heaven and Hell. The beast had *not* killed Nick, had not even *scratched* the young man. The beast's behavior could even be called *gentlemanly*. That was the Heaven part. The Hell? Well, the beast was not ceding control to him and, with the strength of the moon, it felt like the beast *never* would. Panic fluttered within him. The longer the beast was in control, the greater the chance that it would hurt Nick, even if unintentionally.

And what if it finally does give over control and I shift in front of Nick?

Bane shuddered. Other than with Omar and his family, he had *never* shifted in front of anyone else. Well, except for that *one* time in front of his mother, that *first* time ... that first, *unforgivable* time ...

Omar's family had worshipped the tiger spirit since time immemorial. The idea of a man shifting into a beast was not alien to them. They accepted it as part of their worldview. His mother's worldview had *not* included tiger-shifters. After she had seen him shift and attack his father, her mind had given way. She'd regarded him with terror after that. She'd had to be institutionalized for the rest of her very short life.

While Nick was not as mentally fragile as his precious mother had been, Bane was certain that Nick would fear him, might even be *horrified* by him, if he knew the truth. He was absolutely sure that Nick would *never* be with him romantically again, even if he could convince the young man that he was worth loving once more. So somehow he had to convince the beast to leave Nick's presence before the sun rose.

After leaving Nick and Omar at the front of the house, the beast had gone directly to the large refrigerator in the pantry where the sides of beef were kept for it. It sat on its haunches, acting almost like a tame housecat. Omar made a little hop as he and Nick found the beast so primly sitting and waiting for its food.

"The tiger knows where his food is kept," Nick said, sounding slightly surprised.

"Oh, yes, yes, he does," Omar said hesitantly.

The Indian servant moved around the tiger and opened the refrigerator to take out a large vacuum packed side of beef. Normally, Omar cut off the plastic wrapper and tossed it into the cell in the basement. But that was not going to happen this time. Nick was intent that the beast not be chained, which the beast was preening over.

"Let's eat outside on the porch," Nick offered. "Or, well, I'll eat on the porch and the tiger can eat on the grass. He'd probably like that. What do you say?" Nick leaned over the beast, smiling broadly. "Would you like to eat out under the moon?"

The beast's tail whapped happily and it licked its muzzle.

"I believe that is a yes," Omar responded and sounded both giddy and alarmed at the same time. Nothing like this had ever happened before and, clearly, like Bane, he had no idea what the beast was going to do next.

"Sounds good. I'll go grab some food for me. You just take care of him." Nick scritched the tiger on the head, which had the beast's eyes fluttering halfway shut. "Do you want anything, Omar?"

"No, no, I ate earlier."

The young man then went into the adjoining kitchen. Bane could hear the opening of the refrigerator door and the clinking sound of cutlery and plates being brought down as Nick made himself some-

CURSED: BELOVED

thing to eat. Omar took this opportunity to speak to Bane, or, at least, try to.

"Bane," Omar whispered. He leaned down over the beast. The tiger looked back at him, but then looked meaningfully at the beef.

"Bane, are you in there? Can you hear me? One nod for yes. Two for no."

Bane tried to make the beast respond, but he was still in his cage of glass. The beast pawed the vacuum sealed side of beef, ignoring Omar's request. The Indian man looked down at the bag.

"Yes, yes, you are hungry. You shall eat outside just like Nick suggested and *then* maybe you will let Bane talk to me." Omar grabbed a pair of scissors from a drawer and the beef with the other.

The Indian man headed out of the pantry through the kitchen and out onto the back porch. The beast padded out after him. It laid down in the grass at the base of the porch steps and looked expectantly at Omar. He cut open the plastic and upended the package so that the thick slab of raw beef fell onto the ground with a solid thump between the tiger's paws. The beast licked its muzzle, but did not devour the beef. Instead it *waited*. It took Bane a moment to realize that the beast was waiting for Nick to come out with *his* food. They would eat *together*. Omar realized this, too, and his face lit up with wonder.

"Normally, he devours the beef in two gulps. It looks like he is waiting for you," Omar told Nick as the young man shouldered open the porch door.

"I hope I didn't take too long. I'm sure he's hungry. He ran from Moon Shadow to me and back again." Nick smiled broadly.

"He found you." Omar blinked, realizing this for the first time Bane could see the excitement in the Indian servant's faintly quivering form. Bane also noted that Omar was calling the beast "him" and not "it" just like Nick did. He wasn't sure what he felt about that. Omar's voice was soft as he said, "He *sought* you out."

"He did. He showed up right when my bike gave out." The young man sat down on the steps instead of on the couch or chairs. He had a plate with a sandwich on it - fresh turkey, ripe tomatoes, crisp lettuce and havarti cheese, oozing with mayo - and an icy cold Corona. He took a bite of the sandwich, eyes fixed on the beast. He gestured for the tiger to eat, too. "Go on, you earned your dinner."

The beast dove into the tender beef with gusto. Bane felt a surprising sense of satisfaction in ripping through the meat with sharp fangs. The beast though took time between each bite to gaze up at Nick lovingly. Nick, too, watched the tiger, the smile never leaving his face.

"So ... what's his name?" Nick asked Omar.

The Indian man had joined Nick in sitting on the steps. His hands were loosely clasped in his lap. He appeared utterly amazed and joyous. This question though shook Omar out of his thoughts. One of his hands rose to the tiger amulet.

"The tiger has no name. None that we know," Omar answered.

"None that you *know?*" Nick's forehead furrowed. "Did someone else have him as a pet before Bane?"

"What? No! No, not at all. He was ... in the wild," Omar explained.

"But it sounded like someone else had named him."

Omar shook his head. "No, if he has a name, he has not shared it with us."

Nick's expression turned from confusion to amusement. "He is quite an extraordinary tiger. He seems to know what we're saying sometimes!" The young man glanced at the tiger who gave him soft eyes in response. "But he can't very well speak, can he?"

But though Nick's tone was teasing, Omar answered seriously, "No, you are right, he cannot speak to us through our language, but he can communicate in other ways."

Nick turned a speculative glance at the beast. "I can believe that. So do you and Bane just call him 'tiger'?"

Omar's head lowered. "Bane merely refers to him as the 'beast'."

Nick's eyes widened with shock and then anger flashed in them. "*Beast?!* Like he's some kind of *monster* that belongs in the basement? Is meant to be locked up and abused?"

Bane winced at Nick's words. What Nick had said wasn't altogether *wrong*. That *was* how he thought of the tiger spirit.

Nick does not understand what the beast really is! He has no idea that it keeps me prisoner! That it turns me into the monster! And he can never know. I'll have to lie to him some more ...

"Bane is trying not to -- to become attached to him. Giving the tiger a name would cause him to become more than just -- just a *beast*," Omar answered and sounded miserable.

Nick shook his head violently. "That makes no sense! You said the tiger was Bane's sacred charge! What would he treat the tiger so terribly?"

Omar's head shot up and the Indian man looked worried he had said something that revealed the truth. "You are right, the tiger is a sacred charge of Bane's. He is not a pet. Giving him a name would make him more a *pet*. That is what I meant."

Bane wanted to cheer. That was a far better way of explaining it. But Nick was not buying it.

"If Bane truly cared for the tiger, he would give him a name. He wouldn't lock the tiger up in the basement. He would let him run free and understand that he needs to be outside. But he doesn't do *any* of that," Nick objected. "Yet, he made up these elaborate lies to get Jade and I out of Moon Shadow this weekend so he could bring the tiger *back*. He knew I wouldn't approve of keeping the tiger locked up. But Bane brought him back from the zoo anyways as if he couldn't bear to be parted from him. Does Bane care about the tiger or not?"

The beast was keenly interested in what Nick was saying. Its ears twitched and its eyes were fixed on the young man. It had even stopped grooming the blood from its whiskers to pay full attention. The beast turned his attention to Omar as the Indian man answered haltingly.

"Bane and the tiger are ... inseparable. Bane's feelings about the tiger are complicated. These feelings stem from things that I cannot tell you. Only Bane can." Omar's eyes fixed on the tiger, but he wasn't looking at the beast. He was looking *beyond* the tiger to Bane. "He will have to explain himself. There can be no more lies on this matter."

Oh, there can be, Omar! And there will be! I won't have Nick hate me like my mother did! I won't have him fear me and think I am a freak!

But even Bane knew that lying to Nick again would only damage their relationship further. And he couldn't imagine the young man accepting his blanket statement that there were simply certain things that he would not explain.

Nick shook his head. "There's so much between Bane and I right now, Omar. I don't know if I want to talk to him about his *reasons* for anything. I just want him to *do* the right thing in regards to the tiger."

Omar's right hand went to the amulet again. He worried it between his fingers. "I understand. But if anyone can reach Bane, it is you. Especially about the tiger."

"Nothing else has changed, Omar. I can't be with Bane the way he is. I am only going to stay as long as it takes to make sure that the tiger is safe and happy," Nick told the Indian man. The look on his beautiful features was fierce, but Bane could see the pain that lay underneath.

"I understand."

Nick wiped his hands viciously with a napkin and tossed it onto his empty plate. "I'm saying this more for *me* than for *you*."

Omar gave him a sad smile. "I have faith that things will work out."

Nick looked down at the ground. "People don't change, Omar."

I can change, Nick! I've already changed since meeting you.

Omar put a gentle hand on Nick's back. "I do not agree. People change all the time. But if you do not give them a chance to show you then you will not know if they succeeded."

"If Bane won't let my family go there won't be anything he can do or say that will make any difference in my feelings. We'll be over," Nick said firmly. His jaw clenched and he stared angrily out onto the garden.

Words alone will not work with Nick. I must take action. But I cannot. Because I am stuck in this cage! Release me, beast!

Bane angrily looked at the beast, hating it more than ever as he was stopped from acting to fix what was wrong between him and Nick. The beast did not care. It just lay in the cooling grass, grooming itself and gazing at Nick out of hooded eyes. Bane decided that now was the moment to convince the beast that it needed to cede control back to him before the morning light dawned. He forced himself to calm. He stuffed down the anger and frustration. The beast would not respond well to that. He had to be reasonable.

Bane began stiffly, *Thank you for being so good with Nick. For not harming him. For bringing him home safely.*

The beast did not respond to him, but he knew that it was listening.

Something could have happened to him on the road when his motorcycle broke down. He was too proud to go back to Moon Shadow on his own. He would have tried to walk to Winter Haven. But he came home because of you.

The beast's ears flickered.

I can see that you truly care for him. That he is ... is precious to you. He swallowed and added, *I can also see that Nick cares for you, too.*

The tip of the beast's tail wagged, showing its agreement with him about that in any case.

But that is because he believes you are just a tiger. He has no idea that you are a spirit. That you inhabit my body.

The beast stilled.

Do you remember how my mother reacted to you? How she screamed? How she would not look at us ever after that?

The beast remained still.

You do not want Nick to have that reaction to us, do you?

The beast's ears flattened and it let out a nearly inaudible growl. Neither Nick or Omar heard it.

So you cannot allow Nick to see us shift. You need to leave him before the morning's light. You need --

No, the beast suddenly interrupted. Its voice was deep and almost soothing, but its words were not as it continued, *Nick is our mate. He must know the truth. You cannot be allowed to lie to him any longer.*

But by showing him the truth, you risk us losing him forever! Bane sputtered.

Then so be it. For your lies will do the same just as certainly, the beast answered him. *Nick will see and know the truth. You will not stop this.*

CHAPTER SIX - DAYLIGHT

Nick and Omar sat outside with the tiger until near dawn. Nick's jaw cracked from yawning so much, but he had wanted to let the tiger be out as long as possible. But it was the tiger that made the decision to go inside in the end. The magnificent beast rose up after Nick's last jaw-cracking yawn and gently nosed Nick up onto his feet, too, before herding the young man towards the door to Moon Shadow.

"I think he wants to go to bed," Nick laughed as the tiger's nose hit his butt for the second time.

"Yes, so it seems!" Omar agreed, standing up as well.

"Where will he sleep? In the cage?" Nick suggested it but he didn't like the idea at all.

If the beast was placed in the cage then Nick would sleep down in the basement with the sweet animal. Nick had just opened the door as he asked this and the tiger shouldered past him inside and headed towards the stairs to the second floor. The beast paused at the bottom of the stairs and looked meaningfully at Nick. Its eyes glowed with nightshine like twin copper coins.

Omar stepped up beside Nick and regarded the tiger. "I do not think he intends to sleep in the cage."

"No, I guess not. He wants to sleep upstairs with me." Nick felt touched by this.

The tiger looked at him with such tenderness that Nick almost believed the great animal loved him. There were many theories about whether animals could love. Nick was sure they could, but he was still surprised that the tiger seemed so *intent* on him already.

I wonder if he's dreamed about me like I've dreamed about him?

Nick laughed that idea off. He was really anthropomorphizing this magnificent beast.

"I guess I will have a furry sleeping companion tonight," Nick told Omar and his heart twisted a little bit.

Bane should have been the one sleeping beside him, but even if the billionaire had been there, he would not have been in Nick's bed. Nick was likely never to share a bed with the big man again, because people didn't change.

A crushing weight fell on Nick as he realized this. Being back here had made him forget how bad things were. He had to remind himself that even though he was back in Moon Shadow, even though he was going to sleep in his bed, even though he would see Omar in the morning, and even though the day would dawn bright and brilliant as it always did over the roses in the garden, things were *not* the same. The happiness these facts would have normally brought was replaced by grief. Now, it all tasted like ashes in his mouth. But he swallowed down the sadness and tried to give Omar a smile, but it came out more as a grimace from the Indian man's reaction.

Omar put a comforting hand on his shoulder. "In the morning, things will be ... *different.*"

The Indian man squeezed his shoulder and he walked off into the dim coolness of Moon Shadow. Nick stayed a moment in the threshold of the back door, but then he, too, made his way down the hallway towards the tiger. As soon as the tiger saw him moving, it went up the stairs and waited for Nick at the top. When Nick reached it there, the two of them went as one into Nick's bedroom.

The curtains were not drawn. The rapidly lightening sky illuminated his bed. Nick saw the credit card and the cash he'd left for Bane scattered on the floor at the foot of the bed as if Bane had picked these objects up and thrown them down in a temper. That was likely what *had* happened.

Nick swallowed a lump in his throat. He could imagine how upset and hurt Bane must have been when he had realized that Nick had left. Even though Bane had said and done things that were awful that night, Nick still hadn't wanted to cause him pain. He'd left because that was the only real choice he'd had.

The tiger disturbed him from his thoughts as the beast lightly leaped upon the bed and stretched out with its back towards the window. The light streamed in from the window and highlighted the black and white fur. Again, the animal gave him this expectant and *inviting* look. The tip of its tail thumped against the bed in seeming excitement at the thought of Nick lying down beside it. Nick couldn't help but smile.

"Let me just close the drapes and get undressed, then I'll lay down and we can sleep," Nick explained.

He pulled off his t-shirt, toed off his boots and socks, then shucked his blue jeans off. He kept on just his boxer-briefs. Somehow it would have been a little strange to sleep completely naked with the tiger. He glanced up at the beast then and saw the tiger was regarding him out of hooded Siberian blue eyes. Nick swallowed. The regard he saw there was almost *sexual*. It reminded him of how Bane would look at him when he undressed.

They do say that people's pets are like them, but this is sort of ridiculous!

Nick went to the curtains to draw them closed, but the tiger made a low growl and Nick paused. He looked back at the tiger. The tiger had twisted around to regard Nick. There was something in the tiger's expression that made Nick let go of the curtain and allow them to stay open. The morning light would likely wake Nick up, but he didn't have the heart to close out the world if the tiger wanted to view it so much. He imagined that the tiger was anxious not to be cut off from the outdoors even if it was simply by cloth. Nick padded over to the bed and stretched out on his side next to the tiger.

It felt strange yet *right* to look over at the furry face. For one moment though, Nick superimposed Bane's face over the tiger's and his heart clenched. He swallowed down bitterness. It was normal that he was missing the billionaire. Being here naturally made him think of Bane and what could have been. After all, it had only been half a day since he'd decided to end it. Less than twenty-four hours ago, he and Bane had been happy together. If he'd been at Jade's it wouldn't have been so hard to forget that he and Bane were through.

Speaking of Jade, I didn't call her. It's way too late to do so now. I don't want to chance a text waking her either. She probably figures Bane and I are talking or something. I'll call her first thing when I wake up.

The tiger suddenly leaned over and rubbed its cheek against Nick's. A large paw slid over Nick's side and around his back as if the tiger was *holding* him. Nick let out a startled huff of laughter. After a moment, his arm slid around the tiger and he held onto the soft, yet muscular form.

Perhaps it was something about being held, even by a tiger, that caused his eyes to burn with tears. Maybe it was the beast's size that reminded him of Bane. Nick swore he could still smell the billionaire's scent of sandalwood and cinnamon in the tiger's fur.

Bane must have petted him earlier and left his scent behind.

The thought of Bane giving comfort to the tiger caused another wave of pain to go through Nick and his breathing hitched. Why did things have to turn out like this? Why did Bane have to be so impossible? Why couldn't they have had their happily ever after?

Because of secrets and lies. It wasn't just Bane lying, but I did, too. I didn't tell him until it was too late that I wanted my family free of the deal. I should have done it right from the beginning. Instead, just like Jade warned me, I gave my heart to a man who shattered it.

"Bane," he found himself whispering.

Some tears squeeze out of his eyes and he rubbed his face against the tiger's soft chest. The beast let out a sound more like a purr than a growl and he felt the gentle lapping of the tiger's tongue on his bare shoulder. The beast was grooming him in an attempt to soothe him.

Nick held onto the tiger tighter. He felt warm and safe and, strangely, *loved*.

CURSED: BELOVED

Nick pressed his ear to the tiger's chest, listening to the steady thump of the great beast's heart. It was calming and his tears soon dried, but sleep remained elusive. The night sky turned slowly to day. The first rays of the sun hit the tiger's coat and the magnificent animal let out a soft sigh.

Nick slowly tried to rise, thinking that he could close the drapes now. It was the only way he would get to sleep. The tiger's one paw though was still around him. He was just going to slip out from under it, close the drapes and snuggle back down when he met the tiger's blue-eyed gaze.

The tiger's eyelids were halfway shut. Nick was transfixed by them. There was so many *emotions* in them. There was so much *intelligence*. His heart rate sped up. He felt like he was looking into a *human's* eyes.

I feel like I'm looking into Bane's eyes. I can almost hear his voice. And it sounds as if he's begging me to look away. Why would I imagine him saying that?

There was no chance that Nick would look away. As the sun rose further above the horizon, its rays streamed into his bedroom and illuminated more of the tiger's coat. Nick saw dust motes dancing in the air above the beautiful beast. A few stray tuffs of the tiger's fur joined them and they did a lazy waltz in the sunlight.

The tiger's eyelids lowered more as if *exhausted*. Nick reached out and ran a hand along the beast's side, resting his hand midway down the large body. His hand rose and fell as the great animal breathed. Nick had a momentary worry that the beast was sick, because of the lethargy.

Maybe he's just falling asleep finally.

And then something very strange began to happen. The hand Nick was resting on the beast's side started to *tingle* as if a low current of electricity were running through it. He quickly drew it back and started to flex his fingers. The moment he wasn't touching the tiger any longer the tingling stopped. He frowned.

That was when he saw a *mist* begin to curl around the tiger's body. It wrapped around the powerful limbs. It coiled around the tiger's strong middle. The black stripes almost disappeared completely beneath this soft, silent white mist. Soon, only the tiger's head was visible, but then the mist surged up and covered that, too. Nick gasped, but found himself unable to move. The tiger's blue eyes could still be seen, looking into his with such intensity that Nick couldn't look away.

Then the mist dissipated.

Instead of the white Bengal tiger lying there, a very naked Bane lay on the bed beside him, those same blue eyes staring into his.

"N-Nick." Bane reached a shaking hand towards Nick.

Nick jerked away in surprise and Bane's hand fell back to the mattress. Bane didn't try to touch him again. The big man curled into a fetal position, arms curling around his magnificent body. Nick swallowed, unable to speak. He wasn't even sure he was *thinking* at that moment. There had been a tiger in the bed then there was Bane in his place.

Just like before. Bane and the tiger are ... one.

Things that hadn't made any real sense before clicked into place. The tiger hadn't escaped from his cage and found Nick's bed a month ago. Bane had *shifted* into the tiger, likely by accident. Bane had taken off to Europe because he thought he'd hurt Nick when he was in the tiger form. The tiger and Bane had the same eyes, the same eyes that looked at Nick with such love, because they *were* the same. And the full moon was this weekend. Bane had been desperate to get Nick and Jade out of Moon Shadow because he would *have* to shift into his tiger form.

Werewolves are said to shift on the full moon. Maybe were-tigers do, too.

Nick covered his mouth with one hand as hysterical laughter threatened to pour out. He looked over at Bane, not wanting the big man to think he was laughing *at* him. He was shocked. Beyond shocked. His worldview had just changed radically. Omar had told him that morning would bring clarity and it certainly had! Were-tigers were *real* and Bane was *one* of them.

More things slotted into place. Bane's story about being cursed by an Indian priestess for killing a sacred tiger was the *truth*. What else could be real? Elves? Vampires? Werewolves? Magic? It was almost too much to take in. But then he realized that Bane was shaking.

That snapped Nick out of his shock. Bane was ... *crying*? Silent tears were pouring down Bane's cheeks and the big man was trembling. Nick realized that he had withdrawn from Bane and was saying nothing. He had been in shock, but Bane thought it was *rejection*.

Nick gently touched Bane's shoulder. He was real. He was there. Human skin was beneath his fingers. Nick squeezed that solid flesh and saw Bane's head shift a little so that the big man could look up at him through a fall of tangled hair.

"Bane," Nick breathed. "Oh, my God, Bane, *this* is what you were hiding. That you're a -- a *tiger-shifter*?"

Bane's Siberian blue eyes searched his face, for what, Nick didn't know. "Nick, don't be afraid of me. *Please*."

Nick blinked. Bane hadn't needed to use that super-powered word. Fear had actually been the *last* thing on his mind. "What? No, I'm not ..."

Bane sat up. He moved so fast that Nick drew back and, immediately, Bane cringed. "I'm sorry! I didn't mean to move so quickly. It's part of ... of *what* I am."

"*What* you are? You're --"

"Awful. Hideous. I know. I'm a monster. But I won't hurt you! The beast and I made an agreement and --"

"You're *magic*, Bane," Nick interrupted, which stopped the flow of self-loathing words that were spilling out of Bane's mouth. How could Bane think he was a *monster*? He was *incredible*!

"Magic? No, I'm *cursed*," Bane corrected and his face fell.

"You're beautiful. You're ... *amazing*."

"Aren't you afraid of me? You ... you are *not* afraid," Bane answered his own question. That answer though seemed to shock and confuse him.

Bane lowered his head, but Nick put his fingers beneath Bane's chin and forced Bane to meet his eyes. Nick then carefully moved the hair out of Bane's face to see the scar. He stretched his own hand out so that his hand overlaid the handprint burned into Bane's face. The big man sat very still as Nick did this. Nick brought his hand down.

"I'm not afraid of you. I could *never* be afraid of you," Nick found himself saying. "Even when you *pawed* me." Nick touched his scarred shoulder. "I wasn't afraid. Just surprised. I knew it was an accident the moment it happened."

"Y-yes. The beast took over. Normally, I only have to shift at the full moon, but with you … the beast likes you," Bane muttered and looked away from Nick.

"Why do you call the tiger 'the beast'?"

"Because that is what it is!" Bane's jaw clenched.

"No, Bane, he's *not*," Nick objected. "He's a part of you and there's no *beastly* part of you. He was as gentle and loving and amazing as you are." His lips twitched into a smile as he added, "And he's as ornery as you, too."

Bane opened his mouth, but then shut it. He just shook his head as if he couldn't believe *anything* good about it. Nick's head was spinning. He rubbed his face. All the tiredness had left him. He felt like he would *never* sleep again. He had to know *everything* about this from Bane. He wanted to hear every little detail.

"Would you …" Nick began and paused, but then charged on, "Would you tell me about the tiger and all the rest of this?"

Bane looked up at him and, though his expression was unreadable, he nodded. "Yes, Nick. I will tell you anything you wish to know."

CHAPTER 7 - FRAGILE

Bane felt fragile as he pulled on his dress shirt. His body *hurt*. The soft cotton seemed like sandpaper and he shuddered with every brush of the material over his skin. But he continued to put on the light weight suit. He didn't stop until he was dressed impeccably.

He then went to brush his hair. His movements were slow and jerky. There was none of his usual grace in them, but he persisted in this, too, even as the bristles felt like knives scraping across his scalp. He did this because the suit and the grooming reminded him that he was a *man* and not a *beast*.

When he was done he put the brush down on his bathroom's vanity. The faint clicking sound it made was like cymbals crashing to his sensitive ears. He leaned on the cold marble countertop with both hands and stared at himself in the mirror. Even in the shadowy room, he could see the haunted look in his eyes. The scar was a livid red and pulsed with pain. He dragged his long hair over it, blocking it from sight.

He hadn't turned on the lights. The only illumination came through the open bathroom door. The curtains in his room were only partially closed and sunlight - bright and golden - streamed inside.

His eyes stung and watered even with this faint illumination. He turned away from the mirror, determined not to look at himself again for a very long time.

Normally, after a shift he would stay in bed. His body had to readjust to being human again. For days after the full moon it would feel like his bones weren't quite right. That was true of this time, too. In fact, he felt worse than normal, but he had gotten up anyways. And, somehow, he had to be *clear* mentally as well. If he was to win back Nick, he had to be his absolute best even if he felt his absolute worst.

The young man was downstairs in the kitchen with Omar. Nick had wanted to stay with Bane while he dressed, but Bane had urged him to go. Though, things were not good between them, Nick still cared for him. Nick had seen that he was struggling and wanted to help. Even though Bane had tried to hide his weakness from the young man, Nick had sensed it anyways. Bane had convinced him though that he would be fine alone for a little while. So Nick had reluctantly left him.

But there had been no kiss before Nick went downstairs. No press of hands. No embrace. Bane didn't know if that was because he was a monster or if it was because Nick was through with him for what he had said about the Fairfaxes the night before. Maybe it was a combination of both.

Yet the fact that Nick was still there at all was a *good thing*. No matter the reason for his presence, it gave Bane the chance to put things right. He had to find a way to do that. He loved Nick more than life. He prayed that Omar was right and that Nick was *different*, that he could *accept* Bane and the beast, as well as forgive him for all the bad things he'd done. Putting it like that though made it seem impossible. Nick was not a *saint* and perhaps only a saint could accept him.

But he'd promised Nick answers no matter what. So Bane left his bedroom and headed downstairs. He felt like a newly born fawn taking his first steps as he took the stairs slowly, one at a time, with his right hand securely on the banister in case he stumbled. His eyes watered as he neared the sunlit first floor. Sunlight streamed through

CURSED: BELOVED

the front doors' stained glass panels and jewel toned splashes played across the oriental carpet at the bottom of the stairs. Slowly, his eyes adjusted and as he took that last step, he could see clearly. He stood there in the red, green and blue light.

It will be all right. I am a man. Not a beast. I am ...

The beast lifted its head from where it had been curled in sleep. It scented Nick. Its tail began to thump eagerly.

No, please, I need to be able to speak to him. I have to explain. Don't take over from me.

The tail wagging reduced in speed. He was surprised when the beast lowered its head upon its paws. Its eyes closed halfway. It would be able to see Nick and that was enough. For now.

Bane drew in a shuddering breath and smoothed his hands down the front of his suit coat. He walked down the hallway to the kitchen. Nick and Omar's voices drifted out towards him. He paused as he heard what they were talking about: him, of course. But also about Omar's history.

"So your ancestor is the priestess who put the tiger spirit in Bane's body?" Nick sounded boggled.

"Yes, Abinisha was my great, great grandmother. No one knew how old she was ... or *is*," Omar added that last part with a note of wonder in his voice.

I never knew the priestess' name. I never asked Omar. Never thought to make her a person, Bane realized with a start.

The beast let out a snort. He wondered it if were in reaction to his thoughts or if the beast was just settling. Yet it had sounded like a *derisive* snort.

Forgive me if I did not care to know the name of the woman who cursed me!

The beast merely yawned at him and settled its massive head down on its paws.

"What do you mean? She can't *still* be alive. The British Raj was over one hundred years ago!" Nick protested.

"Bane is still alive," Omar pointed out.

"Holy shit, you're right," Nick breathed. Bane imagined Nick sinking into one of the chairs around the butcher block island in shock. "Bane's over one hundred years old! I teased him when he would say things about his youth like it was so long ago. But it *was!*"

"Yes, but he has adapted to the times surprisingly well for someone so *stubborn.*"

"Yeah, yeah, he has!" Nick let out a laugh. Bane was sure that Nick was raking a hand through his hair now. Those platinum locks were undoubtedly standing on end and adorably mussed. He wanted to see them, but the moment he stepped in there, they would stop talking and he would have to start. "Bane definitely doesn't seem a man out of time."

But am I out of time with you, Nick?

"No, indeed not. But as to Abinisha, I cannot tell you that she died, because the last anyone saw of her was when she went into the jungle one day and never returned," Omar explained. There was the bright smell of oranges and a grinding noise of a motor. Bane realized the Indian man was juicing fresh fruit. "Some foolish people thought she had been killed by animals, but the animals saw her as one of their own. They would never hurt her. Others thought she had gone out to die in the jungle, sensing it was her time and wanting to give herself up to nature. And others claimed that she was not actually human at all, but the eternal Earth Mother who had deigned to grace us with her presence in the flesh for a short time before withdrawing to the world of the spirits."

"So you could be the descendant of a goddess?" Nick didn't sound so much disbelieving as amazed at the idea.

"Well..." Omar dithered. "I suppose if the last is true then *yes*, but I am very much a man and not a god myself. I am not special."

"You most definitely *are* special, Omar," Nick replied quietly.

Bane thought of how he had dreamed of Abinisha for years and how he had seen her in his bedroom at the condo. She was more than human. She was something completely beyond understanding.

"One thing I can say," Omar responded, "Because of Bane and the tiger spirit, I have had the privilege of knowing that the world is a magnificent, mysterious place where there is much we do not see."

"Did Abinisha ever come to see Bane after -- after what happened?" Nick asked. "I mean he and the tiger spirit are *one* and she was close to the spirit."

"Not that I know of. But others went to him. Another relative of mine came to him after the tragic accident," Omar said quietly.

Bane found himself stepping into the doorway then. If anyone were to tell Nick what had happened after he was cursed, it would be him. He saw that his vision of Nick and Omar's positions and activities in the kitchen were correct. Omar was standing by the counter juicing oranges. Nick was sitting on one of the chairs at the butcher block island. The young man had on a pair of his favorite pale yellow shorts that were a little frayed around the edges and a soft white t-shirt with the ripped collar. His hair was standing up from when he'd raked a hand through it. Bane didn't think Nick could have looked more beautiful. The beast's tail thumped appreciatively and its Siberian blue eyes widened in pleasure as did Bane's. If he had a tail at that moment he would have been wagging it, too. Last night he'd feared he'd never seen the young man sitting in the brilliant sunlight in Moon Shadow's kitchen again. But there he was.

Still here. I still have a chance.

"Bane," Nick said.

The tone of the voice calling his name held a mixture of emotions: surprise, pleasure, suspicion, and hurt. It was amazing how one word could hold all of that. Nick slipped off the chair and stood, but came no nearer.

"Nick. Omar," Bane responded with a formal bob of his head like he was a marionette. His body still did not feel like his own. His scar burned.

Nick's hands awkwardly swung at his sides as if he wanted to reach out to Bane, but wouldn't let himself do it. Bane yearned to close that space between them and engulf the young man in his arms. But he did not.

I have no right to do so. Nick left me last night. He is not back for me now. He is here for explanations.

"Bane," Omar said brightly. "You must be hungry. Sit. Sit!"

Omar gestured towards the butcher block island where two place settings were already out. Bane took a step towards the island and he nearly stumbled. Nick caught his arm. Bane closed his eyes, relishing that touch.

"Whoa! Are you okay? Let's get you to a chair," Nick said and helped him sit.

"I am fine. Thank you." As soon as he said "fine" he saw the faint frown that crossed Nick's lips. It was a *lie*. Nick thought this was a sign of what was to come. He had to fix this. Now. "I am a little uncertain on my feet. It is always this way after the shift. It's almost like my bones and muscles aren't quite *right*. Aren't quite *human*."

"Oh." That frown left Nick's face. "I can't even imagine how that would feel."

"It makes me *clumsy*." Bane gave him a small smile. "But it's nothing life threatening. It normally passes within a few days." But it would be longer than that since he had agreed to give the beast freedom for *three* days rather than the usual one this month.

Except it broke our agreement so I don't have to honor my part of it.

The beast stared back at him without blinking. He couldn't read its thoughts at all.

Nick's answering smile was still a little uncertain like he didn't know how to talk to Bane any longer. But, again, Bane didn't know if it was because of their breach or Nick's knowledge of what he was. A flash of his mother's terrified face when he'd shifted that first time in front of her went through his mind.

But Nick hadn't been driven to madness by witnessing the shift, but to *wonder*. Yet that did not make speaking easier. How to explain what he was suddenly overwhelmed Bane. How to start this conversation with Nick about what and who he was? And how was he going to heal the breach between them?

He was saved by the sound of sizzling. Omar had put thick slices of maple smoked bacon onto a searing hot skillet. There was a cracking sound as fresh eggs were split on the side of the skillet and then a popping sound as the soft insides cooked in the hot bacon fat.

Omar sprinkled salt and ground fresh pepper on the eggs. He slid slices of the dense bread from a bakery that Bane loved into the toaster. Butter was already softening on the island as well as a pot of homemade marmalade. The rich, buttery, eggy, yeasty smells were delicious and his stomach rumbled. As soon as Bane was safely settled on a stool, Nick got back up on the stool opposite him.

Bane kept his eyes on his plate. He wanted to look at Nick. He wanted to memorize every line of that face, the curve of those lips, the tousled hair and elegant eyebrows. He saw Nick's faint reflection in the white plates, but it was nothing distinct, but it did show him that Nick was stealing glances at him, too.

"Do I look the same to you now that you know what I am? Or are you trying to find some differences?" Bane kept his voice low so that Omar wouldn't hear it over the sizzling of the bacon and eggs. He chanced one glance up at Nick. Sunlight caressed the side of the young man's face.

Nick's lips were slightly parted. Catching Bane looking at him, he blinked and stammered out, "You -- you look the same." He paused and then added, "But *different*, too." Nick shifted under his gaze, giving him a small smile. "Maybe it's me. Maybe *I'm* different because I know now."

"You know *some* of it. But not *all*," Bane said. His fingers danced over the silverware. He wished he could reach out and cover Nick's hands with his. But he didn't. He had no right to touch.

But then Nick reached out and touched him. Just a brief brush of fingertips over the top of his right hand. "I *want* to know. I have no *right* to know. But I want to. If you want to tell me."

"I think I owe you that. If there is to be a relationship between us." Bane saw Nick's eyes immediately flicker away from him. "I know there's so much else that's wrong." Bane lowered his head. "Perhaps *unfixable*, but you have to know this if we are to even *try*."

Omar came over and loaded their plates up with food and put a basket of warm toast between them. "There! Perfect!"

"I don't see a plate for you here, Omar," Nick pointed out. He gestured towards the island.

"I already ate earlier," Omar said, but then seeing their twin disbelieving expressions, he added, "Besides, the two of you must talk alone. Do you not think so?" The two of them flashed a glance at one another, but then they both nodded, understanding reached. Omar bowed. "Then I will leave you and when I come back, things will be *different.*"

But does different mean better? Things are not good now and that is different than before. They must get better. Or they must end. Bane couldn't think of those last words without his heart threatening to shatter. *But there's still a chance I can turn this around. If I'm honest. If I tell him everything. If Nick is as strong as Omar thinks he is.*

He is our mate, the beast rumbled. It seemed completely unconcerned that his revelations to Nick would only drive the young man further away from them. He hoped that it knew something he did not.

They both watched as Omar left the room. They were silent for long moments. Their eyes met and they both smiled nervously. How to begin this? Bane opened and closed his mouth half a dozen times. Nick nervously shook one of his legs. There were so many things to say that they stuck in Bane's throat. He looked down at the food and realized there was *something* he could say while he was figuring out what to say.

"We should eat before this lovely food gets cold. Omar puts so much effort into this meal it would be a shame to waste it." Bane picked up his fork and gestured for Nick to do the same.

"Right. Yeah. Good idea."

The young man cut into his perfectly done over easy eggs. The yellow yolks spilled over the plate like a sunrise. Bane buttered a piece of toast with ridiculous thoroughness as if missing even a bare edge would cause the bread to be inedible. He did the same with the marmalade.

Without taking his eyes from his toast, Bane asked, "How do you feel, Nick? Are you any worse for wear after having the beast chase you through the woods?"

He nearly held his breath as he waited for the answer to that.

"You didn't hurt me, Bane," Nick said, setting down his fork, so that he could give Bane his full attention. "I was perfectly safe."

Perfectly safe? Good God, he has no idea.

The beast's sleepy eyes were fixed on Nick. It gave out a low huff of air at his words as if to say to Bane, "You are a fool."

We were lucky last night. Things could have gone quite a bit differently.

Another huff and then a contented shutting of eyes as Nick continued to gaze upon them. Bane realized he had been silent too long as Nick's staring turned from curiosity to concern.

"It wasn't *me* in control last night, Nick. It was the beast. I would *never* have approached you like that if I had been the one in charge. It's not safe." Bane crushed the toast. Sticky marmalade and slippery butter coated his fingers. He gave out an exasperated sound as he went for a napkin to clean his hand. Nick though reached across and grasped his dirty hand. Bane stilled. "Nick, you shouldn't touch me. I'm -- I'm *dirty*."

I'm cursed.

"I don't care about that," Nick said and when Bane met his eyes he saw that Nick meant more than just getting his hand covered in butter and jam.

"You don't *know* everything," Bane found himself saying.

Nick squeezed his hand. "Then tell me. Please."

"You claim that word is a super power in *my* mouth, but you have *no idea* what it's like when it comes out of yours," Bane murmured.

Nick was still holding his hand. He let out a deep breath. "So I already told you about how I came to be cursed by the priestess, but you don't know what happened afterwards when I returned home. You see, when I told you that my father was dead and that my mother committed suicide, I omitted the most important fact, which is that I was responsible for both of those things."

CHAPTER EIGHT - FIRST FULL MOON

Over one hundred years ago in India during the British Raj ...

BANE'S SKIN prickled and his bones felt *wrong*. He rubbed his arms to stop the almost tickling sensation. He then turned his head from one side to the other to pop his spine back into alignment for what seemed like the millionth time that day. It was as if his body wanted to fit into a *different* shape.

He was out on his bedroom's balcony, leaning against the railing. He found that he liked to be up high. It allowed him to be able to look down on things. It made him feel ... *safe*. He'd wanted to be on the roof, but when Tarun had caught him going into the attic and asked, with a very strange look on his face, where he was going, Bane hadn't been able to answer so he had gone back into his room and out onto the balcony. He couldn't explain himself, not in any way that would make sense to anyone else.

They were all looking at him with alarmed expressions these days. Ever since the incident with the priestess, it seemed that they didn't *trust* him. His mother, Tarun, Nadal, and even his father acted like he might *do* something. What that something was he didn't know. Maybe they didn't know either. So they were watchful, careful, suspicious of him. He didn't blame them for being worried. He wasn't the same as he had been before the hunting trip. It wasn't just the terrible scar that marred his face. It was ... *everything*.

His hearing, vision and sense of smell were all extremely acute. Even though his mother was in her studio floors away, he could hear the faint rasp of her brush against the canvas. If he concentrated even harder, he could hear every person's heartbeat on the estate. That told him where everyone was. For instance, Nadal was washing his mother's brushes in the sink outside of the house. The Indian servant's heart was steadily thumping as he hummed a tune under his breath.

Tarun was in the kitchen, flirting with one of the kitchen maids. Tarun's heart galloped along as he laughed and joked with her. In contrast, his father was in his study, drinking, a black mood settling over him like a cloak. His father's heart had a dull, thumping beat that reminded Bane of the coming of a black horse. He withdrew his senses into himself to escape that sound.

Bane looked out onto the front yard. He could see the individual blades of grass that poked out between the flagstones of the path that wound around the house. He saw black beetles swarming around a small dead mouse at the base of a tree. He smelled the sweet rot of that decaying body, too. But then the scent of flowers burst over him like fireworks, overwhelming the stench of death. He could also smell the raw, earthy smell of the horse's manure. He could almost taste the sweat of the stable boy as he mucked out the horse's stalls.

Bane could spend hours parsing out the individual sights and smells and sounds. In fact, he had done just that. It was fascinating and frightening to be able to do this. While others saw him simply sitting or leaning, completely still and silent, he was really and truly a part of the world, connected to everything around him, more so than all of them were. But his super attuned senses were not all that was different about him.

He was also stronger and faster than before, too. *Preternaturally* fast. Just the other day, Nadal had dropped a glass of wine that he was handing to Bane's mother at dinner. Bane had caught it before it hit the floor. *More* than that, he had caught it *without* spilling a drop. Everyone had gone silent at that, even his father. Bane had excused himself from the dinner table soon thereafter. He rarely took meals with them now.

The priestess said I was cursed. But how? It is not just the scar on my face, is it? Though that is a heavy burden indeed.

He never looked at himself in the mirror any longer. He was growing his hair longer so that it could cover the scar. And he, rarely, left the estate. He felt more than scarred. He felt *marred*.

He glanced back over his shoulder into his bedroom. He had felt eyes looking at him. Siberian blue eyes to match his own. The white Bengal tiger's skin was at the bottom of his bed, covering the floor. Despite worshipping the beast, the villagers had sent the skin to him with the head stuffed and glass eyes set inside; eyes that matched the tiger's in life and were eerily similar to his own. It was beautiful work. Yet it caused him to shudder.

He quickly looked away from it. He'd told Tarun the beast would make a fine rug and it did, but he couldn't stand the sight of it. He had thought of burning it, but couldn't actually bear to be parted from it either. He should want to forget what happened, but, perversely, he went over the experience with the priestess again and again in his head. He especially remembered her hand on his face. Beyond the pain, there had been images that had flashed through his mind before he had fallen into unconsciousness. They were images of stalking two men in the jungle. The two men were himself and Tarun.

Did the beast know what would happen that day? That I would kill it? But why would it want to die? And what of the priestess' words that I must live two lives? What does that mean?

He had many questions for the priestess, even as he loathed her and never wished to see her again. But whether he wanted to see her or not, it wouldn't have mattered. His father had taken a group of men to look for the villagers and the priestess. Despite his pleasure at Bane's disfigurement, Lord Richard Dunsaney was still angry. No one else got to break what was *his*. But there was no sign of the village in the valley. It was as if they had disappeared. Or been hidden beyond anyone's reach.

I should just forget it all. Forget everything.

Bane's scar ached as if to tell him that he *could* never forget. He would never be *allowed* to forget killing the tiger spirit's form. He reached up to touch it before stopping himself. It hurt more when touched. He quickly put his hand back down onto the cool stone railing.

Will I ever heal? It's been three weeks and the scar looks worse than before. I swear it is changing with the moon!

The full moon was that night and it seemed to him that as the moon had blossomed, the strangeness in him had grown. Had his experience somehow unhinged his mind slightly? Was he now like one of those lunatics whose every mood was determined by the lunar cycle? Or was it magic? He'd seen the mud bubble around the priestess' hand. He had no explanation for how that had happened.

At that moment, there was a snuffling sound in the long grass that bordered the side of the house. Bane's head snapped towards the sound. His eyes narrowed and he focused in on a spot where the grass shifted. His nostrils flared and he took in a deep breath. It was a pig.

Bane's mouth began to water. He opened his mouth and breathed through it, trying to draw the very essence of the pig into himself.

I should call for Tarun to get me some food. Yes, that would be --

But before Bane had finished that thought he had leaped on top of the railing. He was balancing there with absolutely no effort and no desire to get down. The pig snorted and rooted around some more in the grass. Bane found himself skinning back his lips from his teeth. The pig started to turn away, to move deeper into the long grass. Bane *jumped* off of the balcony towards the earth below.

He landed nearly soundlessly in a crouch on the flagstones. His legs trembled beneath him, not because of the effort of the jump or pain from the impact, but *shock*. He was perfectly fine. He looked up at the balcony above him. How had he survived such a fall without injury?

And why did I jump in the first place? I couldn't stop myself. I --

The pig let out another snuffle. Bane whipped around in a fluid movement. He drew in another breath of the pig's scent and his mouth started salivating again. He heard the pig's heart, too. Thump. Thump. Thump. Bane started loping towards it. His feet made hardly a sound as he raced over the gravel path and then onto the grass.

The pig did not hear him until he was upon it. His hands reached for its neck and it let out a high pitched squeal of fright as his right arm wrapped around its plump body. But it was that squeal that had Bane, once more, coming back to himself. The pig thrashed to get away from him. He let it go and stumbled back into the drive while the pig ran into the grass.

What was I about to do? Snap its neck and bite into its flesh like a wild beast?

"Sahib? What are you doing out here? I thought you were in your room," Tarun's voice came from behind him. It was filled with that questioning, uncertain, almost alarm that seemed to always fill others' voices now.

Bane turned around too fast to face him. He knew from Tarun's disturbed expression - and how the man half put up his hands as if to ward Bane off - that the Indian servant had noticed it, too. Bane knew he should say something to calm Tarun, offer some explanation as to why he was down here, what he had been about to do to the poor pig that was running away as fast as its legs could carry it, but his heart was pounding so hard in his chest and his blood was whooshing so loudly in his ears that he felt incapable of speaking. He and Tarun just stared at one another for long moments.

"Tarun," Bane finally said, sounding breathless, "I was about to come get you. I'm ..." He licked his lips. "I'm *hungry*. Very hungry."

Tarun gave him an uncertain smile. "Of course, sahib. Is there anything that you desire specifically?"

Bane licked his lips again. "*Pork*. I would really like some pork."

* * *

THE KITCHEN WAS able to honor Bane's request and he had devoured piles of roast pork until he was unable to force down another mouthful. He'd eaten alone in his room, feeling as if the act of feeding needed to be done solitarily. With his belly full, he curled up in a ball on his bed and slept, dreaming of running through India's thick jungles where he hunted eternally.

"-- should be down here! Why does our son not eat with us?" his father hissed.

Bane's eyelids shot open. He no longer woke groggy and uncertain like he had in the past. Instead, he snapped to full alertness.

"He is not well, Richard," his mother responded almost wearily.

"You molly coddle him, Mary!"

Bane's sensitive hearing tuned in further to their conversation. His parents were in the dining room. He could hear the clink of silver and the ting of china as they ate and spoke of him.

There was a pause, a very pregnant pause, and then his mother said, her voice low and filled with concern, "Haven't you noticed the changes in him?" She paused again, her voice dropping even lower as she added, "Sometimes when I look into his eyes I think I see *something else* looking back at me"

"*Something?* That's ridiculous!"

"The priestess did more than just burn our son. She -- she *changed* him. She made him almost ... *wild*." His mother sounded distressed.

"You would give him any excuse to avoid his responsibilities. And he is *weak* because of it, Mary," his father muttered.

"Why must you always find fault, Richard? Why can you not just *see* beyond your prejudices? Your son is *not* weak. He's strong. He's so strong. Stronger than he should be," his mother's voice was strained as she tried to explain her feelings. "Tarun found him on the front walk today after he'd seen him -- him *jump* down from his room. *Jump*, Richard. From the second floor."

Richard grunted. "That's not an impossible feat, Mary. Maybe for a *woman* --"

"Would you do it?" she cut him off, her voice incisive. "I am telling you that our son is not himself. Not like anyone else either. I'm worried about him. So worried."

Bane winced, his shoulders curling inwards as he heard her true thoughts about him. It was one thing to guess that she felt differently towards him, but another thing altogether to hear it from her lips.

"Bah! He's the same as he ever was! Now the scar on his face has given him an excuse to dream his life away in his room! He needs to be a *man* and face things!" Richard growled. The disdain ran deep in his voice, but so did the drink. There was a slur underlying his words.

Bane could hear his silverware clanking on the table as his father slammed it down. There was a sloshing sound and Bane smelled the peaty scent of whisky.

"He's already faced plenty," his mother responded coldly. "You should know that most of all."

"*I* should know that? I know *what*? Do you want him to be a nancy boy, Mary? Perhaps you want to be the only woman in his life?" his father spat the words and Bane heard him drinking deeply. More whisky. More black anger. "I want to *whip* it out of him."

"You want to whip it out of *yourself*," his mother's voice was soft.

"What? What did you say?" his father's voice was low and dangerous.

Bane found himself out of the bed and at his door. He stole on silent feet out of his bedroom and down the stairs. Nadal was in the doorway to the dining room. His face was a picture of agony for his mistress. Bane came up behind him and touched the man's shoulder.

Nadal let out a shout, but Bane covered his mouth with one hand before the shout escaped. He held Nadal in place and raised a finger to his lips with his other hand. The man's brown eyes were huge, but he gave a jerky nod and Bane removed his hand. He gestured with his head for Nadal to stand back from the door. The servant nodded and retreated while Bane took his place.

"Richard, you think I do not know what was between Alastair and you before our marriage?" his mother's voice was strong, stronger than he'd ever heard it. He realized then that everything that had happened since Alastair had come back into their lives had changed his mother. She was no longer willing to retreat into her painting.

Bane glanced into the dining room. His mother sat at one end of the table and his father at the other. Candles lined the center of the table along with vases filled with white roses, which were his mother's favorites. The French doors that made up the left wall of the dining room were open. The bone white moonlight streamed into the room from there. Bane flinched away from even looking at it. His bones seemed to go *soft* and want to *reform* in alien ways the longer he gazed into the silvery light. He drew his focus back to his mother and father.

His mother was wearing a pale green dress and a simple emerald on a long silver chain around her delicate throat. She looked thinner than before and Bane frowned. Her face was narrower and there were dark circles under her eyes that not even the forgiving candlelight could hide. Her fingers moved restlessly over the napkin she'd picked up from her lap. She hadn't looked so pale and wan before his incident with the priestess. Worry for him had transformed her into a ghost of herself.

His father was a hulking presence at the other end of the table. His back was to Bane. He was wearing black and when he ate his massive shoulders rose and fell making it seem like he was devouring his prey.

"You need to watch your tongue, Mary," his father's voice sounded guttural

"Or what? You will hurt me? You do that anyways. Besides, I do not care about myself any longer, but I do care about my son. Your behavior towards Bane has to *stop*," she said. Her right hand fisted in the napkin.

"If Bane starts to act like a *man* --"

"He *is* a man! A *good* man!" Her knuckles knocked on the table. She took a breath to recover herself. "Your actions are -- are *poisoning* him. Making his world smaller and smaller until there will be no room left for him! And the truth is that when you go after him, you are doing so because of your hatred towards *yourself*."

"Mary," her name was said as a warning.

"You *loved* Alastair, but you *married* me for *money*. You've never felt a moment's passion for me or -- or *any* woman," she said.

Bane nearly gasped as his mother exposed this part of his father so bluntly. Richard had gone very still.

She continued, "I think you were born like this. No one would choose to be so -- so *isolated*. So *outcast*. To constantly have your heart want what society would condemn you to have. Bane is the same as you. He feels that same pain. You could *help* him. He could *help* you. Instead of condemning him, you could embrace him."

Her words were so *kind*, so *understanding* that Bane thought - for a moment - that his father might confess his feelings, that he might admit that he was in *pain* because he desired men, but could not have them.

That was a *vain* hope.

"I am *not* a sodomite. How *dare* you suggest such a thing!" His father rose from his seat.

Mary leaned back in hers. Her hands were trembling slightly. "Richard, we both know the *truth*! Why are you denying it? Why keep --"

She got to say nothing more. Richard had lunged across the table towards her and his hands were on her neck. She let out a strangled cry.

Bane did not remember going after his father. He only became aware that he'd moved when he'd thrown his father against the wall. Richard hit the wall so hard that he was stunned and slipped down to the ground to sit there, shaking his head, like a befuddled beast. Bane turned back to his mother. She was leaning forward in her chair, clutching her throat, breathing raggedly in between pained coughs.

"Mother! Are you all right?" Bane got down on his haunches before her and tenderly touched her face. Already, he saw bruises blooming on her tender throat and rage burned inside of him.

"I -- I am all right, my son," she gasped out.

"He is a *monster*. He is a *beast*," Bane hissed and his vision blurred for a moment.

He spun around to face his father. Richard was slowly staggering to his feet. They were both bathed in moonlight and that *softening* of his bones sensation went through him again, yet Bane, conversely, felt stronger. His father's eyes focused on his and his expression *twisted* as he realized what had happened, who had bested him.

"You!" Richard growled, his voice almost bestial. He stripped off his dinner jacket and tie, ripping open the collar of his shirt as he did so. "You will regret this, boy. You will regret this once and *for all!*"

Richard brought up his fists in a classic boxing stance. He looked huge, hulking, as he advanced. His right hand, bunched into a fist, shot out towards Bane's chin. Even drunk, his father was fast, but not as fast as Bane. It seemed like time slowed down as Bane simply *stepped* out of the way of his father's fist and watched it miss him. His father then jabbed with his left. Bane easily bobbed down and his father missed him again.

His father's lips writhed back from his teeth. "What the hell is wrong with you? What is *wrong*?!"

"Nothing is wrong," Bane laughed, a tinge of hysteria to it. "Nothing at all. Let me show you."

The moonlight made him feel *invincible*, almost *mad*. He danced towards his father on light feet as he raised his own hands. With sizzling speed, his right hand caught his father in the jaw. Richard let out a pained groan and jerked back, hitting the wall once more, and sending pictures falling to the floor. The glass shattered and it sounded like music to Bane's ears. He hit his father in the ribs. Right, left, left, right. A rat-a-tat-tat of jabs.

"You'll never touch her again!" Bane hissed. "Never. Never. NEVER!"

His father lurched away from the corner where Bane had pinned him and out of the French doors into the courtyard. Bane followed him. Moonlight skated over his skin and, suddenly, there was the sense that a million tiny needles were pushing through it from the inside. He looked down at his arms and he saw white hair - *no, fur* - covering his arms.

And then, he had the strangest experience. He *saw* a tiger in his mind's eye. The one he had shot. It was *inside* of him. It had been curled in a ball, sleeping, but now it was roused. Its expression was alert. Its Siberian blue eyes intent. He thought, just for a moment - an insane moment - that it asked him, *Hunt?*

His father took advantage of his shock and hit him hard in the face. Bane felt his nose spurt blood as he staggered back. He should have fallen, but he somehow caught himself and dropped into a crouch before Richard could get in any more blows.

His mother's voice rose up behind him in a wail, "Stop! Stop! Please!"

His father's face looked slashed open by his smile. Blood stained his teeth black in the moonlight. "You both need a lesson. I'm going to beat you, Bane, and then I'm going to beat your mother --"

He'll never stop. Not until Mother and I are dead, Bane realized as his father made dark promises of pain and retribution as he rolled up his sleeves. His father's big, beefy hands flexed as he prepared to make those promises a reality. *Or ...* The moonlight seemed to penetrate his skin then, seep all the way down to his bones. *Or ... I stop him.*

Hunt? That soft voice asked.

"I'm going to make you *pay*, boy," Richard growled and he was advancing on Bane.

He looked at the moonlight playing over his strangely hairy skin. It looked like tiger's stripes, white and black.

The tiger ... The tiger's spirit.

"Richard, no!" Mary screamed.

"Boy, accept your punishment." His father grinned at him.

Bane looked up into his father's eyes, which had no mercy, no love, nothing but blackness inside of them.

I have to stop you. You've given me no choice, Bane thought.

The tiger seemed to ask again, *Hunt?*

And Bane answered, *Yes.*

His father took a step and then hesitated just as Bane felt his skin *peel* off of him. There was a scream from his mother, but he could not respond to her. His mouth wouldn't move to form words. Only growls and snarls. His father fell back, a look of horror on his face.

"What -- *what* -- *are* you?" Richard rasped out.

Bane suddenly fell to all fours. His bones melted and reformed inside of him. He saw his hands - no, *paws* - on the ground before him. Tiger's paws. There was a small pond in the courtyard. He moved towards it on four legs. He looked at his reflection in the pond. He was the white Bengal tiger. The same one he had shot.

Two lives. I must live two lives. Now I understand, Bane murmured. He was in shock. He knew that. This couldn't be real. But it *felt* real.

"Bane?" it was his mother's voice that called to him.

He turned his massive head towards the doors where his mother stood, swaying, one hand tentatively outstretched towards him. His father had joined her. Both of their faces were white. He took one step towards them. His father grabbed his mother's arms and held *her* in front of *him*. He was using her as a *shield* against Bane. Her mouth opened in an "O" of terror as Bane's ears flattened and he let out a low growl.

"Get back!" Richard's voice was high and shrill. "Get back!"

Bane snarled.

"B-Bane?" his mother stammered. Fear was so huge in her eyes that it looked to swallow her whole.

"Stay back!" his father cried.

Bane hesitated then his father wrapped his arm tighter around her throat. *He'll never stop. He'll never stop. Until I stop him.*

Bane's front lowered while his back lifted. He leaped.

Bane's paw hit the side of his father's neck. Blood poured out of the wounds. His mother screamed though, too, as he nicked her shoulder. But the desired result happened from his attack: his father released his mother. Richard sprawled on the table. Bane heard shrill cries from his mother as she fell to the floor and curled into a ball. But he had no time to comfort her. His father had to be *stopped* and *he* would *do* it.

He put both paws on either side of his father's head and leaned down so that they were practically nose to nose. Richard let out a fearful cry. Bane *roared*.

And then ...

And then ...

He ripped his father's throat out.

* * *

SIX MONTHS LATER IN ENGLAND ...

BANE STOOD OUTSIDE of his mother's room in the sanitorium, looking in at her through the glass panel. She was sitting by the window, staring outside at the front lawn and the rain. It was so green here. The green was almost *blinding*. Bane took in a deep breath.

"Lord Dunsaney," Dr. Berkhoff called to him.

Bane turned too quickly and he saw the doctor's momentary confusion. Bane dug his fingernails into his palms.

I must move slowly. I must keep my temper. I must remember my strength and speed and hide them.

Those had been part of the instructions Jalal had given to him after he had recovered himself in India. After he had awoken in the jungle with his father's blood smeared on his face and his father's flesh between his teeth. Jalal had come to the house the night of the full moon, but he had been too late to stop what had occurred there. It turned out that he was related to the priestess who had cursed Bane, and now, he had come to offer his service to protect the tiger spirit inside of him.

Although he had come too late to save Richard Dunsaney, with Nadal and Tarun's help, Jalal had managed to cover up the truth of what had happened. The story was that a tiger had gotten into the house and killed Bane's father. Bane had gone after it into the woods to shoot it. His mother's mind after seeing her husband killed had ... given way. So no one listened to what she said about her son *shifting* into a tiger. That was, of course, *absurd*.

It was a terrible, terrible tragedy.

"Dr. Berkhoff, forgive me, I didn't hear you coming. I was just ... just going in to see my mother," Bane said and a brittle smile appeared on his lips.

Dr. Berkhoff looked at him through his gold-rimmed spectacles with a kindly, sympathetic smile on his face. He was her doctor. He knew best of all what happened when Bane visited her and why Bane might not be eager to go inside.

"I do apologize for sneaking up on you," Dr. Berkhoff replied. He looked through the window at Mary, too. "She's having a good day. Perhaps ..."

Bane wondered what he was going to say. Was it perhaps it would be best if Bane didn't ruin it by going in? Or was it, perhaps she wouldn't scream and call him a monster? But Dr. Berkhoff didn't finish his sentence as his mother had turned towards the door, hearing their voices. She caught sight of Bane.

Both of them froze. Her eyes were fixed on his face without blinking. Finally, one of her hands rose, shaking, to her mouth as if to cover it, as if to stuff back a scream. But then it extended towards him, still shaking, to point an accusing finger directly at him.

"Beast," she whispered. *"Beast."*

Bane retreated a step for every time she said that word until his back hit the opposite wall. Dr. Berkhoff gestured to a nurse to come and see to the patient while he grasped Bane's arm and led him away.

Bane allowed himself to be blindly guided for some time, without speaking himself, and barely registering Dr. Berkhoff's prattling words about how his mother's mind had been *fragile* for some time. He might not have noticed this. Was she often ill? Weak? Yes, well, this last shock had just shattered that last bit of sanity she was clinging to.

Bane suddenly stopped dead when he realized that they were going to Dr. Berkhoff's office and not the front entrance. Dr. Berkhoff vainly pulled at his arm for a few moments before giving up. When Bane didn't want to be moved, no one could move him. Not anymore. He was too strong for any human to overcome.

"I thought we could have a cup of tea in my office and discuss your mother's treatment," Dr. Berkhoff said.

"Whatever you think is best do it," Bane answered almost mechanically. "I won't ... I won't be coming back."

"Well, perhaps today is not a good day --"

"Ever," Bane interrupted him.

He felt so sick. He felt like he was empty at the same time. Except ... except there was a tiger that he envisioned in his chest, like it was an egg about to hatch. It looked at him out of Siberian blue eyes. It wanted to get out again and hunt. This new green place intrigued it.

No, never. I will never let you out again, Bane told it.

It merely stared back at him with unrepentant tiger eyes.

Dr. Berkhoff stammered, "T-today was a bad day, Lord Dunsaney. With time, we can --"

"Dr. Berkhoff, it should be as clear to you as it is to me that my mother's mental health is *adversely* affected by my presence. Therefore, I must *stop* seeing her no matter how much -- how much it pains me," his voice cracked a little on the end.

"Like I was just saying, perhaps after further treatment she will improve enough to see you without causing you both distress."

"Yes, perhaps," Bane said, hating that word. *Perhaps* was *never* in this case. He would never torture his mother with his presence again "Good day, sir."

He spun on his heel and headed towards the exit. He would never see his mother alive. The next time he heard from Dr. Berkhoff was when the good doctor contacted him to tell him that Lady Mary Dunsaney had taken her own life.

And as the doctor's letter had dropped from Bane's numb hands, he'd thought, *I did not just kill my father that day. I killed my mother, too.*

CHAPTER NINE - SHARING A LIFE

Nick leaned against the massive oak's trunk. He was sitting in the corner of Moon Shadow's back garden. Sunlight filtered through the trees and dappled the grass. He plucked one of the blades up and sucked on it. Green juice coated his tongue. The wind, warm and sultry, blew over him like a hundred hands caressing his skin. The ever-present scent of roses - that heady, sweet scent - bathed his senses. It was a perfect summer day, but Nick didn't see it or feel it or even acknowledge it as he normally did. His mind was elsewhere, thinking about a night in India over a hundred years ago when Bane had been put in an impossible situation and had to make an impossible choice.

Add to that tiger shifting and ... God, I don't even know how he handled it at all! Nick spit out the piece of grass with disgust at himself. *Just like when I questioned him about Alastair, I had no idea what I was actually asking him to remember!*

Nick brought his knees up against his chest and rested his chin on them. He should get his cell phone out of his shorts. He'd come out here to call Jade, but his thoughts were still reeling. Yet he needed to tell her at least where he was, if not why.

And whether I'm staying or leaving. This choice was awful last night, before I knew the truth, but now? How can I leave Bane when he's in so much pain?

Now that he knew Bane's secret, his anger had melted away at the big man. There was still the very big issue of his family and Bane's hold over them, but, other than that, Bane had very good reasons for acting as he had.

This is such a big secret. Tiger shifting, curses, immortality? If the wrong people were to find out about what Bane is, he could be in real trouble. They'd want to run tests on him, cut him open, maybe kill him. The less people know, the safer he is.

But the thought of lying to Jade made him feel sick to his stomach. Yet, just as Omar had said, it wasn't his secret to tell. He could have asked Bane to give him permission to tell Jade the truth, but he knew that the billionaire was in no fit state to defend himself from any of Nick's requests. The devastation of Nick leaving him was huge in his eyes. Nick was pretty sure that Bane would do *anything* to make him happy at that moment even if it was detrimental to the billionaire.

Like telling me about his parents. God. Nick closed his eyes. *His father had it coming. Bane did the right thing. His mom's mind just snapped. That wasn't his fault!*

But it didn't matter what the facts were. Bane still blamed himself.

The tinkle of ice cubes had Nick opening his eyes swiftly. Omar was approaching him with a tray laden with a pitcher of lemonade and two perspiring glasses. His mouth immediately began to water and he grinned at the Indian man.

"Omar, it's like you read minds," Nick said and hopped to his feet to help Omar with the drinks.

"It is my secret gift. Tell no one," Omar chuckled.

The thought of secrets had Nick's grin dying. He helped Omar set the tray down on the grass. He was pleased when the Indian man sat down beside him in the shade. Omar poured out the tart lemonade for them both. Each took sips and savored the sweet and tart taste. They both looked out at the garden and said nothing for a long time.

"Bane still in his office?" Nick asked. Bane had retreated there after finishing the story.

The big man had said to him, "I can tell you need time to -- to *process* what I've told you. No, Nick, don't deny it. *Please*. Take that time. We can talk later."

"I'm *not* afraid of you, Bane. I *don't* blame you for ending the life of a monster. Your mother's death *wasn't* your fault either. I *love* you." Those were all the things that Nick had *wanted* to say at that moment, but they had stuck in his throat. He had been too stunned to speak and Bane had interpreted it as rejection once more.

The big man had gone to his study and shut the door while Nick had walked dazedly outside to this tree to curse himself. He needed time to formulate the right words. To really know what he felt. To know what he was going to do. But his mind was still muddled.

"Yes, I have heard him talking to people on the phone. He must be doing something important to be working now," Omar answered. "The shift makes him very tired and with everything *else* going on, I am surprised he is risking speaking to anyone. His temper is always worse around the full moon as you have seen. He is fighting for control of himself during this time."

Nick's heart ached. He lowered his head. "Maybe he's finding solace in working. It might be allowing him to *not* think about things."

"Yes, that is possible. I had not considered it that way." Omar nodded and sipped his lemonade.

The silence fell again, but it was not comfortable.

"Was I wrong to leave him, Omar? Am I wrong not to just patch things up now?" Nick swallowed and asked, "Or ... or should I leave? The deal with my family means that things can't work between us long term, but ... oh, God, Omar, I don't know what to do!"

The Indian man blinked rapidly as if surprised by the questions. "While I want both of you to be happy, I do not think you were incorrect in leaving, Nick. And though Bane has finally revealed the truth about himself, he only did so because you *caught* him, so to speak. Plus ... there is the very real issue of your family. Even if you could forgive him for keeping secrets about the tiger spirit, your family is a different matter."

Nick's hands tightened around the perspiring glass. He and Bane hadn't talked about his family and the deal yet. How could they after Bane had told him about the deaths of his own? In some ways the possible fate of his family seemed minor in comparison to what had happened to the Dunsaneys, but it wasn't. It was huge in its own right.

"I can't just *leave* him. I *do* forgive him for the lies he told about the tiger spirit. I get how *huge* a secret that is. I'm sitting here trying to figure out what to tell Jade."

"It is a difficult thing ... to lie to a friend." Omar stared straight ahead.

Nick slung an arm over Omar's shoulders and hugged him hard for a moment. "I understand why you couldn't tell me, Omar. I so get it now."

The Indian man lowered his head and let out a relieved breath. "I urged Bane to tell you. I told him that you would understand. That you were different."

"I'm not sure how that conversation would have even started." Nick raked a hand through his hair. "Actually, he did *try* and tell me once, but I didn't realize he was being *literal* when he said he was cursed."

"He is *not* cursed. He is *blessed*." Omar's right hand rose to the tiger amulet around his neck. "He has the opportunity to live *two lives*. One as a man. The other as a tiger. He can live and learn and love through the ages eternal. Yes, he is *separated* from other men, but there is so much he has been *given* in return. Only, he will not see it that way."

Nick was quiet for a moment, letting Omar's words sink in. "It's because of what happened with his mother. I think he would have come to *accept* who he is, but for her reaction and death."

Omar nodded slowly. "Yes, but she was already ill with ... with, well, there is no shame in it though some people still think so. She had neurosyphilis."

"What?" Nick turned fully towards the Indian man.

"He did not tell you this?" Omar rubbed his hands together. "No, he would not. He would protect her *honor*, even though, as I said, there is no *shame* in it. And she, undoubtedly, contracted it from her husband." Seeing Nick's confused look, Omar asked, "Do you know this disease?"

"I've heard of syphilis before. Is neurosyphilis a form of that?" Nick asked haltingly. Omar nodded. "Al Capone died of it, didn't he? Went sort of mushy brained first though. It's an STD, right?"

Omar nodded again. "It is a form of syphilis. It has many terrible symptoms, but among them are changes in mental stability and even psychosis. The doctors *told* Bane this after her death, but --"

"He likely thinks that accepting the diagnosis would be avoiding responsibility for what happened to her," Nick filled in the end. "But dammit, he's not to blame!"

Omar put one of his hands over both of Nick's. "I am so glad that you believe it, too. I have told Bane this over and over again, but he thinks I am just trying to get him to accept the spirit!"

Nick chewed on this. *Accept the spirit?*

"Omar, Bane thinks of the spirit as ... *separate* from him, doesn't he?" Nick asked.

Omar nodded. "Yes, he does. He calls it a 'beast' as I told you.'"

"Yeah, I heard him call it that too." Nick raked his teeth over his lower lip. He had heard the *loathing* and *fear* in Bane's voice as he spoke of the spirit. "But I could *see* Bane in the tiger's eyes, Omar. I could *feel* him. That's why I stopped being afraid of him."

"The spirit is fond of you, too, I think."

Nick felt a wash of *pride* at that. A spiritual being that *liked* him, maybe even more than liked him was amazing.

Like Bane more than likes me. The spirit treated me with such tenderness, such care. He would never hurt me. He is the farthest thing from a beast anyone could be.

"If Bane had someone *other* than you showing him that the spirit *isn't* a beast, might he learn to accept it?" Nick asked.

Omar's thoughtful gaze landed on him. "Perhaps. I do not see that it could hurt him"

"I keep imagining what the tiger's life is like. Bane keeps him bottled up inside all but one night a month, right?" Nick confirmed.

Omar's head lifted. "Indeed. He fights the shift, too, trying to stave it off until the last moment."

"So the tiger gets only one night a month, only twelve nights a *year*, and Bane keeps him in the basement, too, during those times out, too?" Nick's heart clenched as he asked that.

"Yes." More shame in the Indian man's voice.

"Over a hundred years stuck inside Bane then in a basement ..." Nick shuddered. "It's horrible. The spirit is a wild animal. He needs to be outside."

"I have tried everything to change the spirit's circumstances, but ... I have *failed*. I have failed Bane *and* the spirit," Omar sounded miserable.

Nick gripped the Indian man's shoulder. "You haven't, Omar."

"Both Bane and the spirit are in pain, Nick. They are as far from peace as possible. I do not understand my ancestor in choosing this course. Why did she not pick someone from the village to host the tiger's spirit? Someone who would have welcomed this union?" Omar shook his head.

"It has to be more than to punish. I mean, why would she punish the *spirit* as well as *Bane*?" Nick asked.

"I do not know. I have puzzled on this for as long as I have known the secret," Omar's mournful voice broke off in a sigh.

"Your ancestor was a -- a *wise* woman, wasn't she? She might have even been a -- a goddess."

"Oh, yes, she was full of wisdom!" Omar confirmed.

"Then she must have known something we don't. She must have understood somehow that the *best* place for the tiger spirit to be was with Bane and for Bane to be with the tiger spirit," Nick said.

Just saying this out loud made him realize what he wanted to do. He wanted to stay. He wanted to help Bane and the tiger spirit learn to coexist. Was it totally delusional to think that he could help Bane when Omar and all his ancestors hadn't been able to? Probably. But Nick had to try.

He found himself saying, "We've just got to make Bane see that he and the tiger spirit are *fated* to be together."

"But how?"

"By making him see that the tiger spirit *isn't* a beast, isn't a *monster*. And that *he* isn't either." Determination filled Nick. They could do this. The two of them together could reach Bane.

"You have a plan?"

Nick opened his mouth and then shut it and then opened it again. "No, not yet. But I think it starts with no more cages and letting the spirit out much more often."

"My understanding is that Bane made a -- a deal with the spirit that if it did not harm you that he would give it three nights of freedom this month." Omar gave him an uncertain look as if he wasn't sure how Nick was going to take the terms of that deal.

"That's why Bane needed Jade and I gone this weekend?" Nick realized.

Omar nodded. "Yes."

Nick's forehead furrowed as he considered this. "So Bane's already agreed to let the spirit out some more. Has the spirit seen daylight in over a hundred years?"

"I do not think so. Bane is only *required* to cede control of his body to the spirit on the full moon, but he could do so *willingly* at any time in my understanding," Omar explained.

The plan started to form. *Bane has to share his life with the tiger. He has to start to see it as a part of him. Then it won't be a battle to keep control. How to do that?*

Both he and Omar were silent for a long time. Bane had to see that the tiger spirit would not harm anyone if let out. The tiger spirit had to be allowed out by Bane instead of forcing its way into control. The two of them likely distrusted one another deeply. But if there was a mutual show of trust ...

Nick got up and dusted off his shorts. "I think I know what we should do first."

"What?"

He offered Omar a hand as the Indian man was struggling to his feet. "I'm going to ask Bane to cede control of his body to the tiger during the day. The tiger spirit will then show him it can be trusted. That will be the first step to his accepting that he *shares* a life."

Omar looked uncertain, but then he said stoutly, "I believe if anyone can do this, you can, Nick."

As they walked back to the house, Nick texted Jade. He couldn't lie to her so this controlled communication was the best.

He typed, *Sorry didn't contact you sooner. I'm still at Moon Shadow. Bane's not feeling well. I'm staying until he gets better. Will talk soon. Love you.*

He then turned off his phone. He didn't want to chance her contacting him back and asking him questions that he wouldn't be able to answer. Now he had to fully focus on Bane and Bane alone.

CHAPTER TEN - INSIDE OUT

"Sloan, are you clear on what I want you to do?" Bane asked into his cell phone.

He could picture his attorney sitting behind her sleek glass and steel desk in her downtown Winter Haven office even though it was a Saturday. As a lawyer, she believed it was her duty to always be on call. He heard the soft touches of her fingers on the keys of her MacBook as she typed out his instructions.

"Yes, you want me to draft up a document returning Fairfax International to the Fairfaxes, no strings attached, for a Monday morning meeting with Charles Fairfax?" Her voice was crisp and professional. To the average listener there appeared to be no feeling behind it whatsoever, but to Bane's keen ears, he heard *relief*.

"This is what you thought I was going to do when I came into your office last week, wasn't it? What you *hoped* I was going to do?" Bane realized as he interpreted the reasons for that relief.

She had expected him to immediately end the deal because he and Nick were in a relationship, but he had arrogantly - and *wrongly* - told her that Nick was *separate* from his family, that Nick *hated* them just as he did, and would, essentially, not care about the deal.

A stray beam of sunlight crept between the curtains. His light sensitive eyes immediately stung and he raised a hand almost as if to ward the light off. He stumbled to his feet and closed the curtains tighter together. Blessed darkness, except for the muted light of the green shaded banker's lamp, fell upon him.

"Can I speak plainly, Bane?" she asked.

"Yes, always." He paused and then said, "I *do* mean that, Sloan. I *do* want to hear what you have to say."

"I appreciate that, Bane. Sometimes my clients want to hear anything *but* what I have to say, especially considering this is about your personal life. Yet we're ... *friends*, but I know there's a line," she admitted.

Friends? Are we friends? Have I treated her as such? I do not treat her as Nick treats Jade, but ... I do appreciate her.

Bane realized though what she was going to say, "The issue here is that I was *combining* my business and personal life, wasn't I? I thought I could act as I wished in *business* with the Fairfax family and that it would not affect my *personal* life with Nick, didn't I?"

Bane winced at the arrogance, at the sheer *thoughtlessness* of what he had done. He had put Nick in an impossible situation and, the truth was, that some part of him had known it. He hadn't separated the two things because he'd wanted to keep Nick with him and his family's fate would be a good motivator for Nick to stay. He felt sick just thinking about it now.

"You're always risk averse, Bane," Sloan said simply, acknowledging what he had been doing in that clinical manner of hers. "You hedge your bets. Did something happen with Nick over this deal?"

Of course, she understood him. And, of course, she knew what had happened. The grapevine would have reported his argument with Nick. That's why she was such a good attorney.

"Yes, it did. He wanted me to end the deal and I wouldn't. I said *things*, unforgivable things. He would have left me ..." *Except for the beast interfering, but not even I can tell her that.* "I don't know if I can get him back, but regardless, I need to release the Fairfaxes from this deal. It was a terrible idea from the get go. I should never have done it."

But I wanted Nick. I had to have him. Even now I feel like I'm dying at the thought of not being with him.

"I'm a lawyer so I'm a realist, Bane, but ... maybe I'm a bit of a romantic, too. I know that people are run far more by their emotions than their rational brains," Sloan said, her voice growing warmer. "I saw the looks Nick gave you even when you *weren't* together. The two of you ... the two of you are *meant*. That's my hope, anyways."

Bane gave a weak smile. "Thank you, Sloan. That is my hope as well."

"Are you going to tell Nick about this?" she asked.

"No, I cannot make this seem ... *quid pro quo*. Do you understand, Sloan? Seeing Nick hurt caused me to understand the wrongness of my actions, but I cannot expect him to be with me simply because I've finally done the right thing," Bane answered her. "I do not know if that makes sense."

"It does in a way. But I think you should tell him. I think it will matter to him very much. But that's all I'll say on that point." She was all business again as she added, "I'll have the paperwork ready for you by tomorrow. That will give you time to read it over before you sign it."

"Thank you, Sloan. I'm sure it will be fine," he said and they rang off.

He went to the address book on his phone and contemplated calling Charles to set up the meeting, but he abruptly changed his mind and simply sent an email. Charles would make himself available no matter what else the elder Fairfax had planned. Besides, he couldn't quite bear to talk to Charles that day. He was still too raw. It seemed the safest bet to simply set up the meeting. Less than thirty seconds after he had sent the email, Charles had accepted the request and asked how he and Nick were doing.

Bane,

You and Nickie left the party pretty quickly. I hope that you're both feeling all right. All of Nickie's photographs sold! In fact, I've gotten requests from a half dozen people for Nickie to do commissions for them. Can't wait to talk to you on Monday. Though feel free to contact me at any time!

Charles

Bane turned off his phone in case Charles decided to follow up the email with a phone call. He let out a breath and leaned forward, resting his elbows on the desk. He closed his eyes, suddenly feeling so very tired.

Memories of his parents, of his mother and father, flashed behind his closed eyelids. His father's wide eyes as he ripped out his throat. The taste of blood on his tongue. His mother's accusing finger. Her calling him a monster, a *beast*. He opened them just as quickly as he had closed them. His eyes burned as if they had sand in them, but he would not let them close again. Too many memories threatened to overwhelm him.

The beast regarded him carefully. It was not sleepy. Its body did not ache. It wanted to be free again. It was eager to play with Nick. He clenched his hands into fists and let out a low growl. He bit the sound back as there was a soft, uncertain knock on the door. He straightened up and smoothed his hands down his front. His hands shook. He hid them beneath the desk.

"Come in," he said, hoping his voice sounded authoritative, but fearing it came out as shaky, too.

Nick's head poked in and Bane's heart leaped. The beast's tail whapped the ground eagerly and it lifted its head.

"Are you busy? I don't want to intrude," Nick asked tentatively.

"No, not at all. I finished what I had to do." His heart beat faster, almost guiltily, as he thought of his conversation with Sloan. But he had been doing nothing wrong. He simply didn't want to use the one good thing he'd done to get Nick back. It felt dishonorable. "Would you like to sit?"

He gestured to the seat opposite him, half rising from his chair as Nick came inside and closed the door of the office behind him. Nick wiped his hands on the fronts of his shorts before he perched on the edge of the visitor's chair opposite Bane. Bane's own palms began to sweat and he found himself twiddling with a pen and straightening random things on his desk to keep his hands busy. He feared that they might shake noticeably otherwise. Nick coming in like this likely meant the young man finally wanted to *talk*. Whether that *talk* would be about his being cursed or the end of their relationship, neither would be good. He cleared his throat.

"So ... what can I do for you?" Bane asked, his tone formal as if Nick was a business associate that had dropped by. He internally cursed himself.

Nick, though, did not seem to notice his awkwardness. The young man kept shifting in his seat, head slightly lowered, gaze unfocused, but not on Bane. He clearly wanted to talk about something and wasn't sure how to begin. Bane was the one that had caused this awkwardness between them. It wasn't just the curse, but what he'd said and done the night before. Nick was going to leave him for that. Perhaps that was what Nick had now come to tell him. Perhaps he should be the one to start the conversation. Bane's throat was so dry and tight it might have been made of sandpaper.

"Are you here ... do you want ... do you want to leave?" Bane asked. "Is that what you are here to tell me? I've answered your questions about my *condition* --"

"What?! No!" Nick's head jerked up. "I don't want to leave! Unless ... do *you* want me to?"

Bane could have almost cried out in relief, but he managed to get out a choked, "No, of course not. I *never* want you to leave." They were both silent then as if recovering from that emotional ordeal until Bane said, "You did come in here for something, Nick. What is it? Tell me. Please."

Nick nodded and bounced one knee. "It's not about us. I mean it *is* about us, but ... but not the parts about my family and stuff like that. I still feel that you can't hold my family hostage and expect us to be together, but that's not what I'm here about."

"I understand." Bane wanted to tell him then that he was in the process of unraveling the deal, but then Nick was speaking again about something unexpected.

Nick's gaze had dropped down to the tiger rug by the fireplace. "Is that ... is that the tiger spirit's body? What's left of it, I mean?" Nick pointed to the rug. His finger shook a little bit.

"Yes, it is."

Bane didn't look down at it. He didn't have to look at the beast's corpse on the floor when it was eagerly kneading the interior of his chest, anxious to get out and be with Nick. He was sure if he were to look down at his front, he would see the claws stretching his skin.

Nick shocked him when he dropped to his hands and knees on the floor, and reached out to the beast's old head and cradled it in his lap. There was such a look of sadness and tenderness in Nick's expression that left Bane temporarily speechless. Nick's elegant, artistic hands stroked over what had been the back and paws. Nick stared into the glass eyes that were the same Siberian blue as the beast's and his own.

The beast had gone completely still in his chest and was watching Nick intently. Nick continued to pet and look meaningfully at those glass eyes and then back up at Bane.

"Nick, what are you doing?" Bane finally was able to say, his tone a mixture of affection and bewilderment.

"Do you feel pain when you look at the rug?"

"Do I feel ..." Bane blinked. "No, no, Nick, there is no pain looking at that unless it is the psychic pain of a bad decision."

"What about the tiger spirit? Does he feel pain when you look at his old skin?" Nick asked so very earnestly.

At first, Bane was inclined to quickly tell Nick that, of course, the *beast* didn't feel anything. He would, also, say "beast" instead of "spirit" and he would say "it" instead of "he". Or, at least, that's what he *would* have done in the past. But that's not what he did this time. He looked at the rug and opened himself to what the tiger spirit was feeling.

There was a remembered flash of hunting through the jungle, completely free, under sun and moon. It remembered lapping at cool pools in the jungle's heat.

"It remembers --"

"*He*. He remembers," Nick corrected gently.

Bane gritted his teeth, but then he simply nodded and agreed, "He remembers being free. The jungle's heat. Bathing and drinking from cool pools. The taste of fresh kill on his tongue. The soft earth beneath his paws."

The memories were so *real* that he had to touch the top of his desk to center himself in the present.

"He misses having a body that he could be free in?" Nick guessed.

"Yes, yes, he does."

With such intensity that it nearly burns me. He regarded the tiger. *I did not know.*

The tiger answered him, *You did not try.*

No, I did not.

Guilt had Bane slumping in his chair. Nick gently put the pelt down on the ground and crawled over to him. He settled between Bane's legs, still kneeling on the ground. Arousal immediately spiked in Bane's body. Nick's hands settled on the tops of his thighs as he gazed up at him.

"Nick, what are you doing now?"

Bane framed the young man's beloved face with his hands. He could not help himself. To be near Nick was to want to touch him. If Nick didn't want his touch, he shouldn't have come so near. Nick did not draw away from him, but actually turned his head into the right palm, but, almost immediately, stopped himself. His eyes though were luminous.

He still loves me.

"I'm just ..." Nick paused, swallowed, then went on, "There are so many things that I wanted to say to you after you finished telling me about your parents and I -- I --"

"You don't have to," Bane quickly said. He could almost imagine the horror Nick must have felt hearing about him feeding on his own father's corpse and causing his mother's fragile sanity to snap. He didn't want to actually hear it.

"No, you don't understand," Nick was adamant and Bane braced himself. "I can't imagine what you went through with your father. I thought I hated him before, but now ..." Nick shook his head. "You did the right thing. You did what you had to do."

"He would have killed her, and I needed to stop him, but how I did it --" Bane's mouth went dry and he couldn't go on.

"You did the *right* thing," Nick repeated.

"My mother ... my mother did not think so," Bane whispered.

Nick opened his mouth as if to say something, but then shut it again. There was a pause and he finally spoke, "I think your mother wasn't -- wasn't *herself*, Bane."

He knows. He knows about her illness. Omar told him. Of course, Omar told him. But that isn't the reason her mind snapped altogether. No, I was the cause of that.

Nick's luminous eyes fixed on his. His artistic hands covered Bane's on the arms of his office chair. "I know you blame yourself ... and the tiger spirit."

Bane shifted uncomfortably. How could he explain to Nick the *change* in him when he had become the tiger? He had become a beast himself. After that, he had fought against the shift every single time it happened. He never again allowed himself to merge with the beast like that again.

"That was the one and only time I have -- have *willingly* worked with the beast, Nick, and look what I did! What *we* did together?"

"You might not have been able to stop your father without shifting, Bane. The spirit was trying to save your mother and you, wasn't he?" Nick pressed.

Bane was speechless this time. Could that be true? Had the beast wanted to save them? Looking back ... yes, that was what it had been. The eagerness had not been to take over Bane's body and kill, but to transform and *protect*.

The beast was looking at him.

You tried to save us both, didn't you? Bane confirmed. *You did what I asked. Gave me the strength I needed.*

It simply regarded him quietly.

He focused on Nick's face. His fingers feathered through Nick's soft, platinum hair. "Perhaps it -- *he* was. I know he was. But it just shows that, even with the best of intentions, the beast -- the *spirit* - is dangerous. As am I," he added.

"Isn't everyone when it comes down to it? You're just stronger and faster than most, but it doesn't mean that you are necessarily *more* prone to hurting people. You just have the *potential* to be, but only if you choose it," Nick contended.

Bane turned his head to the side. "I might not choose it, but the -- the *spirit* is a wild creature. It -- *he* -- knows only to kill or be killed. He's a predator, Nick," Bane explained, but then shook his head. "But why are we talking about this? Is it just something *general* you wanted to say or --"

"Not just general," Nick quickly said. "I mean, *yes*, I wanted to tell you that you were right in what you did. But there's more." The young man licked his lips. "I'm not sure how to begin this. I'm not sure I even have the -- the *right*. But I believe that you will be happier - that the spirit will be happier - if ..."

"If what?"

"If you make peace with him," Nick said. "If you *share* your life with him."

"W-what?" This echoed words that the priestess had said to him over and over. He had understood what that meant the night of his father's death, but he had rejected it. He couldn't accept the beast again. Could he?

Nick's hands tightened over his. "You need to stop fighting the spirit and keeping him inside or locked in a cage when he's out. You have to live *both* of your lives, Bane."

"What are you suggesting?" Bane definitely had an idea of what Nick wanted. And he was thinking himself about the beast's memories of being free.

So he wasn't altogether surprised when Nick said, "I think you should let the tiger out. Not just on the full moon. Not just once a month. A lot more actually. And I think ... I think you should let him out during the *day*."

Bane could feel his heart thumping quickly in his throat. "When are you suggesting this daylight shift take place?"

"Today. Now, actually."

CHAPTER ELEVEN - MERGE

"*N*ick, *no*. It's not possible." Bane shook his head. Nick felt the big man tense at the very thought of shifting voluntarily.

"But it *is* possible. You're just *afraid* to do it and I get why," Nick responded with earnestness. "But it will be okay. We could go to the glade where we had lunch. That would be the perfect spot for you to shift. It's private, but will give the tiger sun and trees and plenty of room to play. I know he likes being petted --"

"Petted?!" Alarm sprang large in Bane's Siberian blue eyes. "And where would you be during all of this romping in the forest and petting?"

"I would be doing the petting and maybe some of the romping. You're really quite cuddly when you're in tiger form." Nick purposefully grinned at him then. He wanted to show Bane that not only was he *not* afraid, but he was looking forward to this experience.

Bane, of course, looked horrified. "Nick, you must take this seriously!"

Nick squeezed his hands. "I *am*. You're not going to hurt me, Bane."

"I thought I hurt you last night. Didn't I? Weren't you leaving me because of how badly I treated you? How terribly I *hurt* you?" Bane's eyes searched Nick's face.

Nick flushed and looked away, but only for a moment. He didn't want to think about last night. The fact that Bane was bringing it up showed just how scared he was of shifting. He was trying to push Nick away, but Nick wasn't going anywhere. He was staying. He was going to help Bane whether he wanted it or not, because Bane *needed* to be helped.

"*Physically*," Nick finally clarified. "You would never hurt me *physically*. And you didn't *mean* to hurt me in any other way either."

"My intentions are *nothing*. I *can* hurt you both physically and emotionally no matter *what* I intend." Bane tried rising up from his chair, shaking his head the whole time. "Nick, I know your heart is in the right place, but this is a *curse*."

"It could be a *blessing*." Nick caught his hands and pulled him back down. "Bane, you can become a *tiger*. A freaking tiger! That's the stuff that *dreams* are made of! There's a spirit inside of you that's existed for who knows how long. Imagine what he knows! Can't you see how *beautiful* that is?"

Bane stilled. His Siberian blue eyes were the only things moving. They flickered over Nick's face. "You think ... you think it's *beautiful*?"

Nick couldn't help himself. He reached up and trailed his fingers down Bane's high cheekbones. "*Everything* about you is beautiful."

Bane turned into the touches. There was such a needy, almost starved expression on his face that Nick felt guilty for withholding any touch from him. Yet their relationship was such a mess right now. Bane still hadn't said anything about letting his family go. And what if the billionaire *never* did? What if Bane determined that his family failed and turned them out into the streets like he'd threatened that first time they'd met? After all, Bane felt that punishing the Fairfaxes was a *good* and *right* thing.

Nick shook those thoughts away. He and Bane had to talk about that stuff, but what was more important at this moment was freeing the spirit. That took precedence and he believed, unlike about his family's fate, that Bane would listen to him about this.

"What do you think letting the spirit out like this will accomplish?" Bane asked, his breath puffing against Nick's right palm. "What do you hope for?"

"Your happiness."

"Nick --"

He held up a hand to stop the flood of Bane's objections. "Imagine that you were imprisoned for all but one night a month. Imagine that during that one night you're locked up in a basement cell. Imagine that you haven't seen the sun or felt the wind or rain on your skin, or haven't run free for over a *hundred* years. What would that do to you?" Nick asked. "What would you feel?"

Bane shuddered after each statement. He finally whispered, "It would be hell. It *is* hell."

"Yeah, it is." Nick was thrilled that Bane recognized what he was doing to the the spirit. He had only spent one night with the spirit, but he *felt* the being's pain and could almost hear the spirit telling him what it wanted. "You've imprisoned the spirit and yourself, Bane. Your life changed that day the priestess merged you and the tiger spirit into the same body, but you're still trying to act like *nothing* happened. You're not a normal man any more, Bane. You've got to accept that and live the life you have now."

Bane leaned forward. His hair fell over his face in a waterfall of dark waves. "I understand what you are saying, Nick, but I do not know how to do that."

"First step, is letting the spirit out. You've got one body. You have to *share* it. And that can start right now. *Today.*"

Nick held his breath. He could tell from Bane's thoughtful expression that the big man was considering it. But what decision would he make?

Bane slowly began to shake his head, almost regretfully. The regretfulness gave Nick hope even as Bane continued to object, "It's not safe, Nick."

Nick pressed, "What would make it safe? In your mind, at least? And you can't say not doing it or locking the tiger up in the basement. That's not happening any more. That's not a shared life."

"It's not?" Bane's right eyebrow lifted even as a half amused smile graced his lips.

"It's *not*. You know it hurts the spirit. And it hurts *you*." Nick brushed the hair out of Bane's eyes. The scar almost called him to touch it, but he didn't.

"You're putting restrictions on me --"

"Yes," Nick admitted unrepentantly. "I am. You've been dealing with this for over 100 years --"

"Yes, I have."

"And what you are doing is *not* working. You're miserable. The spirit's miserable. So why don't we try things *another* way? What do you have to lose?"

This was really the crux of his argument. Bane's way of dealing with the spirit had been to *not* deal with it. It hadn't worked.

"You getting hurt. I couldn't *bear* that. I couldn't *live* through that."

Bane's voice was a rough rumble. It skated down his spine. Mix that with the look of love on Bane's face and both had Nick wanting to fall into the big man's arms and just *be* there, where it was safe, where he was *treasured*. Where he was *loved*. Nick blinked, forcing himself to focus.

"I'm safe with you." Nick gripped Bane's nearest forearm as if he could imprint those words physically on the big man. "I know that down to my *bones*. But ... if me being there means you won't shift then I'll stay away so long as you *promise* to let the tiger out."

He ached at the thought of not seeing the beautiful white Bengal tiger again. But he'd do whatever it took to free the spirit and Bane, especially, if all it took was denying himself the pleasure of seeing the lovely animal once more.

"The spirit would only come to you anyways, Nick," Bane said with a laugh.

"He would?" Nick didn't believe that Bane and the spirit were as separate as Bane liked to think. It meant that no matter what form Bane was in, he still cared for Nick, longed for Nick.

"Oh, yes, he's quite ... in love with you." Bane turned his head away, staring into the unlit fireplace. Long moments passed before he said, "Omar must be there with my rifle."

"You mean there when ... when you shift? In the glade?" Nick's heart slammed against the inside of his chest. Had he actually convinced Bane to do this? It hadn't been easy, but it hadn't been as hard as he'd feared. "You're going to do it?"

"Yes, Nick, you have *won*. Though I do not believe this will lead to the rapprochement that you hope it will between the -- the *spirit* and myself." Bane wearily ran a hand through his thick hair. Nick noted that the scar was raw, but not so raw as it had been just moments before.

"I don't think it can make things worse between the two of you, can it?"

Bane's mouth opened and then closed. He finally admitted, "Probably not."

"Then let's do this."

Nick got up from his knees to his feet. Eagerness to start what he hoped would help Bane and the tiger spirit co-exist raced through him. Bane got up as well. Nick linked their fingers together. He went to draw Bane to the office door, but Bane drew them over to the gun rack on the wall where his rifle hung. He took it down.

"Bane, that really won't be necessary --"

"This is my *one* condition, Nick. You have won, but I won't have you there without protection," Bane answered and his tone brooked no argument.

"Okay. But Omar won't need it. It's going to be great. I'm telling you that the tiger and you are going to love sunning your fur," Nick told him.

Bane let out a laugh after tilting his head to the side as if listening to something only he could hear. "The beast -- *spirit* agrees with you. He is quite excited about the prospect. He wants you to pet him behind the ears. I do not know if I want you to get that close."

"But it felt nice, didn't it? When I petted you behind the ears last night? You felt that, didn't you?"

Bane lowered his head and looked at Nick through his lashes. "I did and, yes, it was quite pleasurable. You are a good petter."

Nick grinned. "You were very soft. Fluffy even."

Bane rolled his eyes. "Fluffy, indeed."

"You did have cat breath though and you had to do your business in the rose bushes. Tiger poop in the house would not have been cool."

"Tiger poop." Bane snorted. "At least, it will fertilize the roses. That's somewhat good in any event."

Nick grinned. He and Bane then walked to the kitchen where Omar was preparing something tasty for lunch. Bane's steps were reluctant but he wasn't holding back.

"Omar, we need you. Can you take a break?" Nick asked. His heart was racing and he knew he was smiling too brightly.

"Of course." Omar wiped his hands on a towel and turned towards them. "What can I help you with?"

Bane handed the confused Indian servant the rifle. "You need to keep Nick safe."

"Against who? Against what?" Omar asked. He held the rifle with surprising confidence and familiarity. Nick had assumed wrongly that the Indian man would have no knowledge of guns, but, clearly, he did.

"Me," Bane answered simply.

Omar's eyes went huge. "You would never hurt Nick!"

"See?" Nick grinned. "Omar knows you would never hurt me either!"

Bane gave him a bland look. "I am going to ... *shift*, Omar."

"He's going to transform in the glade! In the sunlight! Right now!" Nick found himself enthusing.

In contrast, Bane looked rather gray and sweaty. Nick's enthusiasm dimmed. He put a comforting hand at the base of Bane's spine. Bane gave him a wan smile.

"That is wonderful!" Omar's eyes widened even more. His shocked and pleased smile was as bright as the sun.

"You didn't think I could convince him?" Nick grinned at the Indian man.

"I admit I believed that Bane would put his ears back and act more like a donkey than a tiger at your suggestions," Omar answered, but looked utterly pleased to have been wrong.

Bane glanced between the two of them. His Siberian blue eyes narrowed. "You've been planning this together?"

"This is Nick's plan. It is a *good* one and I am in complete agreement with it. I am happy to assist in any way I can," Omar explained.

"The only reason it's my plan is because you wouldn't listen to Omar about this. I'm just glad you're willing to give it a try for me, at least." Nick couldn't resist the urge to lean against Bane's big body. "Okay, we ready to go?"

"Absolutely!" Omar grinned.

"As ready as I will ever be," Bane said again with that wan smile that projected how little he believed this would accomplish.

The three of them walked together to the grove. The day was brilliantly hot and fine. Sunlight streamed down on them in unending golden waves. Sweat was already trickling down Nick's spine and sticking his t-shirt to his back. Omar had the rifle slung over his shoulder and a small smile on his lips, looking remarkably crisp and cool despite the heat. Bane was staring down at the ground. His lips were pressed together and he looked rather like a man going to the gallows. Nick hoped he was right to suggest this.

Well, we're doing it so I guess I'll find out soon enough.

"We're here," Nick said unnecessarily. His voice seemed to echo.

They had arrived at the glade far faster than he and Bane had for their picnic. Nick rubbed suddenly sweaty palms against the front of his shorts and turned to Bane. How to begin this?

But he needn't have worried. Bane already had it in hand. The big man was stripping off his clothes. Nick glanced at Omar as color rose in his face. The Indian man quickly turned his back and appeared to find the trunk of one tree just *fascinating*. Nick couldn't look away even though he knew he should. He'd broken things off with Bane.

He had reasons to do so. So he didn't have the right to stare at Bane naked. But he was doing it anyways.

Bane's perfectly cut muscular form was revealed to him inches at a time. The big man had slipped out of his loafers and socks. His belt was coiled neatly on top of them. He undid the pearl buttons of his button down shirt with practiced ease before neatly folding the shirt and placing it on the grass.

Then his hands went to the button and zipper of his pants and Nick's breathing hitched as they slid down Bane's powerful thighs and calves. Bane's muscles bunched and released under silky looking skin as he removed them. When Bane stood up fully and turned to face Nick, the young man had to yank his gaze up from the big man's perfect cock and balls. No blush appeared on Bane's cheeks. Instead, his mesmerizing eyes hooded and he stared at Nick without blinking. It was the stare of a predator, Nick realized, and a shiver of *pleasure*, not fear, went through him. Nick found himself stepping *towards* Bane, but the big man held up a hand.

"You need to keep away, Nick. You can't physically touch me when this happens." Nick was going to open his mouth to object, but Bane said firmly, "Not *just* because I'm worried about hurting you. Most often the shift is *violent*, and also because it will be too hard for me to *let go* if you're near me."

"All right," Nick nodded slowly. He was a bit worried about the word "violent" that Bane had used to describe the shift. He hadn't considered that it might *hurt* Bane physically to shift. The rest he could understand. "How far away do you want me?"

Nick really didn't want to go that far away, but he would give Bane as much space as he needed to give this transformation a real shot. The freedom that shifting on demand would give to *both* Bane and the spirit would be unfathomable.

"Go about twelve feet away." Bane gestured with his chin towards a spot on the grass that was just by the treeline. "Omar, stand by Nick. Have the rifle ready to fire. Keep it pointed at me."

Omar began, "Bane, I --"

"No questioning, Omar. This is how it *must* be. Please honor my wishes," Bane commanded.

The Indian man nodded. He and Nick went to stand where Bane had indicated. Bane, himself, went to stand in the very center of the glade where the sun shone brightest. He stood with legs shoulder width apart and head tilted back. Bane closed his eyelids and let the sun bathe his skin. The scar on his face was almost invisible. Nothing happened for an awfully long time and Nick dug his fingernails into his palms as if he could will the shift to happen.

You can do this, Bane. I know you can!

Finally, wisps of mist appeared on the ground beneath the trees. They flowed out into the glade, glittering in the sun. Nick pointed down at them.

"Omar, look! It's the mist! This happened before when Bane shifted," his voice was just above a whisper and filled with awe.

Nick held his breath as the mist reached Bane's feet. Bane's eyelids remained closed, his face was still tilted up towards the sun. The mist swirled up over Bane's feet then ankles then calves then knees then thighs. It wrapped around the older man like a silken cloak. It was up over his pectorals and then obscuring his neck. All Nick could see was Bane's beautiful face. And, finally, the mist flowed over the top of Bane's head, covering him completely.

Nick waited.

And waited.

He thought his fingernails might draw blood from his palms.

The tower of mist glittered and then, suddenly, it collapsed. Nick gasped. He couldn't see Bane or the tiger. The fallen mist obscured his view. For one frightening moment, Nick thought that both had simply disappeared altogether. He waved a hand in front of his face to part the clinging fog.

And then he saw something *move*.

He drew in a sharp breath as a massive white Bengal tiger appeared out of the mist.

CHAPTER TWELVE - REVELATIONS

The spirit blinked as sunlight streamed down upon it. It turned its gaze up to the blue sky, squinting, unaccustomed to the golden light that bathed it. Grass tickled its paws. It kneaded the rich earth as if it had never seen or felt it before. Green juices burst from the torn grass and the scent of growing things flooded its nostrils. A sudden delirious happiness filled the spirit and it rolled over onto its back, all four paws waving in the air, worshipping the sunlight. In contrast, Bane felt a stab of guilt go through him. It was deeply apparent that the spirit had been starved for light, air and the outside.

And it was *his* fault.

The spirit wiggled against the grass, tail swishing, paws flexing, making happy grunts and other tiger sounds. The spirit finally closed its eyes as it concentrated on sunning its thick, white coat. Bane could still see the red-orange glow of the sun through its eyelids. The spirit's joy was so *sharp* that Bane actually *hurt* as he experienced it, too.

I didn't know you missed the sun and earth so badly. Why didn't you say something? Bane asked the spirit.

Would you have listened?

Of course! Bane protested.

But would you have done anything about it?

Bane was silent at this. If he were honest with himself, he wouldn't have done anything. He would have justified his inaction with the thought that it was too dangerous to let the spirit outside at all, let alone in daylight. So what would have been the point in the spirit saying anything? There wouldn't have been one.

"Omar, *look*! He's so happy!" Nick said, his voice filled with awe and a little bit of heartbreak.

"You are right! He is practically smiling! Oh, Nick, this is such a *good* day!" the Indian man responded.

Bane flinched. Nick had known immediately how cruel it had been to chain the spirit and never allow him to see daylight and the outdoors. But then Nick was always thinking of others while Bane, more often than not, thought only of himself.

I am sorry, Bane began again, *that I did not consider how you were feeling when --*

You believed that it was your life alone that was ruined when we merged. I lost the jungle. I lost my freedom, the spirit interrupted him.

Bane did not respond for, at that moment, he realized he had defined himself as the *sole* victim of the curse, but what about the spirit? The spirit had lost its very body that day. Bane had wanted its pelt as a rug. And because there was nowhere else for the spirit to go, it had been placed inside an alien form that had become its virtual prison for over a hundred years. A prison that *Bane* had made for it.

So who really was the victim here? Bane had a terrible idea it wasn't him.

Why did the priestess put you in my body? Could not another in the village host you? They would have been happy to, Bane argued weakly.

She thought you would come to want me. She thought you would come to an understanding, and so would I. She was wrong. The spirit paused before asking, *Wasn't she?*

Bane, of all people, could make her wrong or *right*. He alone would determine the spirit's happiness.

Live two lives. I need to live two lives, he murmured to himself.

The spirit cracked an eyelid and turned its massive head towards Nick and Omar. Its tail immediately began to thump against the grass as it glimpsed the young man kneeling down on the grass. Nick's thighs were spread apart invitingly. His golden, muscled arms and beautiful face glowed in the sunlight. Bane was slightly disturbed by how happy and *aroused* the spirit became seeing the young man.

Mate, the spirit corrected. *Our mate.*

He is my mate. I mean ... he is my lover. Or was. It hurt to use the past tense.

He is ours, the spirit said with a regal tone.

You think Nick is romantically in love with you? Would have sex with you in this form? Bane scoffed.

The spirit though wasn't at all repressed by Bane's disbelief. It answered with a simple confident, *Yes.*

Bane let out a strangled sound. *That is ONE thing that you will never do with Nick!*

We would pleasure him. You would like it, too, the spirit sounded amused.

That is beastiality! He would never - I would never ... But then the memory of licking Nick's cock in the tiger form in his dream flashed before his mind's eye.

You would enjoy it, the spirit repeated and Bane could feel the great beast smiling.

That was ... that was before I really knew Nick. And I thought it was a dream!

Now you play the gentleman, the spirit huffed amusedly. *But our mate would enjoy our tongue.*

I AM a gentleman.

Then as if Fate decided to play games - and test just how much of a gentleman he really was - Nick got down fully on his hands and knees and slowly approached them in a sensual crawl. Not that Nick had any idea that what he was doing was sensual. He likely did not know the image he presented to them as he stalked through the long grass all golden limbs and flashing gray eyes.

Beautiful. Our mate is strong and graceful and beautiful, the spirit rumbled, its eyelids hooding.

Yes ... yes, he is, Bane murmured then sharpened his tone, *You are not doing anything sexual with him!*

The spirit snorted. *Priest is here. Later we will love Nick. When we are alone. I am a gentleman, too.*

The priest, or rather *Omar*, Bane noted, had the rifle still slung over his shoulder, clearly forgetting that he was supposed to be protecting Nick with it. The Indian man looked utterly amazed and in awe of the tiger. The spirit could have leaped upon Nick and disemboweled the young man before Omar could have gotten the rifle into position.

Bane's annoyance with Omar almost immediately faded away. There was no need for the rifle. Nick was perfectly safe. He could sense that. Other than the spirit's *teasing*, Bane knew, without a doubt, that the spirit would never, ever hurt Nick as the spirit had opened all his thoughts and desires to Bane.

Why are you showing me all of this? Bane asked as he realized just how open the spirit was being with him.

So you see that there is no reason to fear.

Why didn't you do this before? He demanded.

The spirit huffed, *Because you would not have listened! And ...* There was a slight bit of shame here, as it added, *I wished you to be afraid of me. It was the only defense I had with you.*

Bane heard the sadness in those words. This royal spirit had been his prisoner so, of course, it had tried to behave like it was big and mean. If he'd only allowed himself to truly know the spirit's thoughts earlier, all this angst could have been avoided. But then he'd have been forced to *share* his body with the spirit. And if he had been willing to do that, he couldn't have cast himself into the role of victim any longer.

You clung to being seen as a beast while I clung to being a victim instead of a villain, Bane said.

Yes, now we see each other clearly.

Nick was now only six inches away from the tiger.

Nick, Bane murmured.

He was filled with longing and a strange grief. Understanding, it seemed, came to Bane much too late. Or maybe it was simply that he was a selfish being like many had said before. He hadn't wanted to share his body with the spirit and he hadn't wanted to give up his revenge against the Fairfaxes. For these acts, he had lost everything.

It is not too late, the spirit told him. *Nick is still here. Still loving us. You can make this right.*

Nick reached out one hand towards them. That hand hovered just an inch above the white fur. The spirit regarded that hand, anticipating the pleasure,

"Can I touch you?" Nick asked the spirit. "You look so soft."

The spirit immediately nosed Nick's hand to encourage the young man to touch it. Nick petted its massive head first. The spirit closed its eyes in pleasure as that hand scratched between its ears, which flickered in response.

"You're so beautiful," Nick murmured.

The young man's hands then flowed over its belly and rubbed its paws. Nick was laughing as the spirit reached up and licked his face with its large pink tongue. Bane had *wanted* to do that and the spirit had *done* it.

Not you or me, but ... us. We're doing this together, Bane whispered, shocked and amazed that he and the spirit were of one mind and one body for one moment.

"At least you don't have terrible tiger breath. You haven't eaten yet today ... as a tiger anyways," Nick chuckled before kissing its nose and then that soft spot right between its ears where he had scratched earlier. The spirit's tail wagged every time Nick's lips touched its fur. "He's so fuzzy, Omar! Bane's going to *kill* me for saying that."

I am not going to kill you, Nick. Just give you a hard time for treating us like a giant stuffed animal, Bane thought with amusement.

The spirit though was acting like a very large stuffed animal or more like a tame house cat. It was practically *preening* with every exclamation Nick made about how beautiful and soft its coat was, how big its paws were, and how adorable its tail was. Nick would "capture" the tail and the spirit would whip it away from him. Nick kept reaching for it and the spirit would keep the fluffy length of fur, muscle and bone just out of reach.

"Omar, you've got to get in on this!" Nick enthused.

"Oh, I don't know. Bane might not like it." Omar though put down the rifle and started to advance towards the tiger even as he dithered. "And it *is* the tiger spirit. He is sacred and he may not wish me to -- oh, he is looking at me! And thumping his tail!"

"He totally wants you to pet him," Nick assured the Indian man.

Omar got down on his knees on the other side of the tiger from Nick. He drew one hand along the the spirit's back. Now both Nick and Omar were stroking and ruffling the spirit's fur. Bane found himself relaxing under the gentle, loving touches from the two people in the world he knew loved both the spirit and him.

"You do not think that Bane will find this ... *objectionable* for me to be touching him like this?" Omar's eyes went from the their face to Nick's.

"Oh, no. I'm sure he won't." Nick paused then added with laughter in his voice, "I can't quite imagine us doing this together though when Bane is in his *human* form, but when he's fluffy all bets are off."

"Indeed! I do not imagine that Bane would show his belly like this under any other circumstances. He is not normally this trusting."

Nick snickered. "You're so right about that."

You're the trusting one, Bane noted in amusement to the spirit.

The spirit huffed, *You are the one eager to roll us fully on our back so that they can rub our belly more.*

Maybe. Bane hadn't been aware that he had been urging the spirit to expose more of their soft underside.

We must show them that we are only trusting because we are the king, the spirit informed him.

Bane's eyebrows rose. *The king? Aren't lions supposed to be the king of the jungle?*

The spirit made a disgusted noise. *Human nonsense!*

To protect their dignity, the spirit rolled to its side and then rose up, shaking off the petting. The spirit nudged Nick with its nose to walk with it as it started to investigate the clearing. Nick put one hand on the tiger's back, his fingers catching and releasing the fur. The spirit investigated every flower and sniffed every tree.

That's a tree. That's another tree. It's the same as the last one, Bane muttered in half frustration and half amusement. But he didn't try to stop the spirit from doing whatever it wanted.

The spirit ignored his grousing, even going so far as to *return* to a tree it had just sniffed, to sniff it again for good measure.

"Does that smell different to you? These woods are far different than the jungles in India, I bet," Nick remarked indulgently.

The spirit wagged its tail and then buried its face in the long grass around the base of yet *another* tree. Bane sighed, but he was smiling on the inside. More sniffing ensued and Bane almost would have dropped off, but then the spirit suddenly *moved*. More like *leaped*. Very high up into one of the trees that had gotten sniffed multiple times. Nick and Omar both gasped. Bane did, too. The tiger form's sheer power was never something he'd ever had a chance to enjoy other than that first night.

Do you wish to know it now? The spirit asked him.

You would let me ... let me control this form for a moment? Bane asked.

I did earlier. We shared.

Yes, you did. Bane paused and then said, *Why don't we try sharing again? Working ... together?*

All right. Let us show them our balance. Walk along the branch and then jump to the neighboring tree, the spirit instructed.

Bane felt how they used their tail to balance themselves as they lightly stepped along the thick branch just until it was nearly bending under their weight. Then they launched themselves from the one branch to a close by trunk of another tree. Their powerful claws dug into the bark, cutting through it as easily as a knife through butter on a hot day. Their claws caught and they had a firm hold on the other tree.

Let's do it again! Bane's excitement threaded through his voice.

Though his human form was strong and capable, there was something so much more powerful about the tiger form. He had never allowed himself - not even during that first shift - to truly feel or understand that difference, let alone indulge in.

Yes, we will go around the whole clearing without touching the ground, the spirit agreed enthusiastically.

To Omar and Nick's delight, they jumped from tree to tree around the entirety of the clearing without a single paw touching the grass. Finally, they leaped down onto the ground and Bane got his first taste of controlling the tiger's form *running*. They raced across the entirety of the clearing, turned on a dime, and raced back the way they had come.

I want to run in the fields. Imagine all the golden wheat and corn waving all around us, Bane told the spirit.

Yes! We need to run and run and run! But, first, a drink, the spirit suggested and pictured the hose in the back garden.

Their mouth immediately watered as both Bane and the spirit imagined lapping up ice cold water.

And some food! Omar has a leg of lamb for you. For us, I suppose, actually, Bane corrected himself with a laugh.

Do you not want to shift back into human form? The spirit regarded him carefully.

Do you?

The spirit seemed to shrug, but clearly was waiting for Bane's answer.

Bane had them turn towards Nick who was watching them with a huge, satisfied grin on his face. Nick knew he had done something *good* that day.

Look at him, Bane said to the spirit. *His expression is solely filled with happiness. When he looks at you ... at us ... in the tiger form there's no complications for him. No regrets. No pain. He's not thinking of what I did last night, of the things I said, of the things I meant.*

The spirit regarded him sadly. *I understand. But we cannot hide from this forever, Bane. This must be fixed.*

I know. But you deserve this day ... so many days, countless days, and I ... I don't know how to fix this with Nick, Bane admitted then realizing fully what he had said, what he had determined since shifting into the tiger form today, he added, *I don't even know how I can apologize enough to you either.*

You thought you were cursed, the spirit whispered and Bane could hear the hurt in the spirit's voice. He recalled then blaming the spirit for his unhappiness.

But I'm not, am I?

Only if you perceive yourself to be, the spirit answered carefully.

I don't want to be. I want us both to feel ... blessed, Bane said and swallowed. Could the spirit feel blessed to share a human form, which was so alien to what the spirit was accustomed to? Could he make it so the spirit felt that it was *their* forms and not just *his*?

If you wish to share with me then I would feel more than blessed. Together ... we would never be alone, Bane, the spirit answered.

Bane felt a tightening in their throat and tears prickled their eyes. *We wouldn't be, would we?* He quickly said, *We'll devise a schedule so that you always have equal time in control as me --*

He felt a paw against his chest. *No need for schedules. We will know when it is right to shift. We will listen to one another.*

We will. Bane paused and then added, so softly, *Thank you.*

We are in this together, the spirit answered and a rush of warmth flowed from the spirit to Bane.

And, for a moment, it felt like they were completely *one*.

Nick was suddenly crouching down in front of them. His expression was slightly concerned and Bane realized why. While he and the spirit had been speaking, their form had stopped moving and was staring off into the forest.

"Everything okay?" Nick asked.

They let out rumbling sound and rose up. Everything was better than okay. They went over to where Bane's clothes were folded, before leaning down and taking the shirt in their jaws. They held it out to Omar.

"Oh, my, what is going on here?" Omar cheerfully asked as he took the clothes from Bane's mouth.

Nick was frowning, but then his expression cleared. "I think he wants to go back to the house."

And, indeed, that was exactly what they wanted. After Omar had collected all the clothes and the rifle, Bane and the spirit led the way back to Moon Shadow, tail held high. They went right to the hose and batted at the faucet handle to turn it on. That had Nick laughing again. The young man held the hose out so that they could lap at the cold water. Nick didn't start to spray them playfully with it until *after* Omar had gone inside to get lunch for everyone.

They spent the entire day in the tiger form being petted, running, chasing Nick or Omar or both men, then lazing on the porch as the sun slowly set. Nick sat beside them on the porch steps, their head in the young man's lap as the stars wheeled overhead and the moon beamed down upon them.

"His eyes are closing. I think he's going to sleep," Nick said softly, his fingers pausing in their stroking of the thick fur.

"It has been a long, wonderful day," Omar remarked.

"It really has been," Nick agreed softly. His eyes were shining as he stared down at them. "I wasn't sure this would work. But I think it has."

Omar held his tiger pendant and his expression was serene. "They are at peace, Nick. I can feel it down to my bones."

Do you wish to shift back into our human form? The spirit asked.

Nick won't let us sleep with him if we do that, Bane pointed out.

Then we will not shift until the morning, the spirit agreed. *But, Bane, we must fix this.*

I know. I swear I'll think of something - I'll do anything - to make this right, Bane assured it.

As Nick rose up, they did as well. The young man held the door open to them. They loped inside, down the hall and up the stairs before pouncing on Nick's bed. They looked back eagerly at the young man who just shook his head in amusement.

"You better not be a bed hog like last night," Nick laughed.

They scooted over and looked at him meaningfully, but that just had Nick laughing harder. But then he was stripping off his clothes down to his underwear and lying beside them. After Nick's breathing settled into the rhythm of sleep, they put a protective paw over his back and gently nuzzled his hair.

Our mate, the spirit murmured.

Yes, Bane agreed. *Our mate.*

And, hopefully, in the morning, something would come to Bane to fix the damage his selfishness and blindness had caused.

CHAPTER THIRTEEN - CONTRACT

The doorbell to Moon Shadow rang, echoing throughout the mansion.

"I'll get it!" Nick called out as he took the stairs two at the time from the second to the first floor.

Even though he wasn't the closest to the door he knew that Omar was in the kitchen preparing lunch while Bane was in his office working. Nick had just been reading in his room. He wondered if the billionaire really had some *crucial* work he had to do on a Sunday. His father and brothers worked every weekend, but Nick knew that was because they *liked* working, not because it was *necessary*. But in this case Bane had good reason to avoid him and pretending to work was a convenient excuse.

When Nick had woken up that morning, he'd found that Bane had shifted into his human form sometime during the night. A very *naked* and *beautiful* Bane since the billionaire was stripped of his fur. Nick was transfixed by him.

He stared at Bane as the man slept, itemizing the billionaire's features as if they were treasures. The aristocratic nose. The full, kissable mouth. The strong jaw. The sensitive forehead. The acres of muscles covered by silky skin. Bane was simply breathtaking.

The big man was sprawled out over most of the bed *and* most of Nick. Nick had rooted against Bane's massive chest and the billionaire had wound around him like a vine as they had slept. They had sought each other out in slumber, unable to deny what they felt when their subconsciouses ruled. Their current positions also meant there was no way for Nick to get out of bed without waking the billionaire.

And I don't really want to get up. I have an excuse to be near him like this for now. But, once he wakes, it will be over.

In order to get himself to move, Nick reminded himself of Bane's sneering words about his family. Not to mention the utter disregard that the billionaire had shown for the impossible situation he'd put Nick in by keeping the deal going after they'd begun dating. But it was hard to look at that sleeping, beautiful face and keep being angry.

Instead, he felt a sense of grief as he realized, once more, that *anger* wasn't what was keeping them apart. It was something far more *bitter*.

I know Bane cares for me. But not enough to let go of his desire for revenge on my family.

That agonizing reminder had Nick sliding out from underneath the big man. Bane immediately woke up, not like a human wakes with confusion clouding his senses, but as a beast might into full awareness. Upon seeing Nick, a smile - slow and sensual enough to melt bones - crossed the billionaire's face. But when he saw Nick's frozen expression in return, that smile became questioning and then died as Bane clearly remembered too that they were no longer together.

"Forgive me," Bane muttered, head lowering, even though there was nothing to forgive. Both of them had turned to each other for comfort in sleep.

The billionaire quickly slipped out of bed before Nick could move a muscle. And he was out of the room before Nick could say a word. Since then Bane had locked himself up in his study.

As Nick was about to open the front doors to Moon Shadow, he tried not to look down the hallway towards the office to see if that door was cracked open, but he looked anyways. It wasn't open. It was shut and perhaps even *locked*.

Now that we aren't together, it's not like I should expect to have any of his attention. I should actually be glad he's staying away. It will make it easier when I do leave.

Not that these thoughts helped soothe the pain in his heart. Nick had even started to wonder if that departure should occur sooner rather than later. Yesterday, the spirit and Bane had seemed to be in complete sync and at peace. Omar had even chirruped that morning that Bane had told him that the basement would be gutted and transformed into a play area for the tiger. No more cages. No more chains. And the spirit would only be relegated to the basement for when they could not be outdoors.

"Bane's feelings towards the spirit have completely changed. It is like night and day, Nick! And it is all thanks to you!" Omar had enthused, eyes filling with happy tears while he clutched his tiger amulet. "He even asked me how my people atone to the spirit."

"That's ... that's fantastic, Omar," Nick tried to sound enthusiastic, but his heart had fallen into his feet at the Indian man's assessment..

"Nick? What is it? Why are you not happy?" Omar studied his face.

Nick scuffed a foot over the kitchen floor. "I *am* happy. Really. It just means that there's no longer a reason for me to *stay*."

Understanding flashed over Omar's face and he grew grim. "You think you are not needed here any longer?"

"Pretty much. I'm going to hang around for a little while to make sure Bane doesn't change his mind about the spirit, but I think that's more for *me* than for *Bane*," Nick admitted.

Omar put a hand on his shoulder. "Nick, Bane *cares* for you --"

"But not enough," Nick's voice was anguished and he quickly left the kitchen.

Bane didn't change his mind. Bane was a man of his word. Which meant that he would be good to the spirit from now on. And he would destroy Nick's family for their transgressions.

The doorbell pealed again and, with a heavy heart, Nick plastered a smile on his face and opened the front doors. Sloan Wu was standing there in one of her impeccable black skirt suits. The only thing she carried was a sheaf of papers. He would have expected someone like Sloan to come with a high end bag, if not a fashionable briefcase, to hold her legal papers in, but she had nothing. She gave him a smile.

"Ms. Wu, isn't it?" Nick asked.

"Yes, it is, but please call me Sloan," she answered and her smile grew more genuine as she added, "It's good to see you again, Nick. I can call you Nick, can't I?"

"Of course." He shrugged. The only "Mr. Fairfax" in his opinion was his father.

"I hope you are doing well," she said, searching his face for something.

The first - and *last* - time he had seen her was during that ill-fated weekend with Dean Kettering. The skin between his shoulder blades still crawled a little thinking of the red-faced former football player, but not as much as it had when he'd seen the man just a day or so ago at the art gallery. Had it been such a short time? It felt like ages to him now. So many worse things had happened since then.

He had no real impressions of Sloan, though, because it had seemed to him that she had hidden behind her cellphone and work. He really couldn't blame her considering the odious people there that weekend. He'd tried to hide in his work as well, which had led to the terrible sunburn and the revelation of Bane and his feelings for each other.

"I'm fine," he answered her after the silence had gone too long.

"I'm sorry we didn't have more of a chance to talk last time I was here. Have you fully recovered?" she asked.

Nick blushed as he wondered what she must think of him passing out because of a sunburn. He must have seemed the lamest damsel in distress ever. But her dark eyes seemed to show true concern.

"Oh, yeah, I'm completely healed up. The burn even turned into a pretty damned good tan. Best I've ever had." Feeling a little foolish doing it, but doing it anyways, he gestured towards his golden arm.

She blinked as if totally confused, but then her brow cleared. "Oh, yes, I'm glad you're over that as well. I was referring to ... well, I don't wish to bring up that terrible time with Dean Kettering - the man does not deserve the breath one would use to speak of him - but I wanted to say how sorry I was about everything that happened."

"It wasn't your fault," he assured her. He ducked his head. Being Dean Kettering's intended rape victim made him feel lamer than the sunburn had, even though he knew he should not be ashamed.

"I'd heard things about him. I should have *warned* you. Warned *Bane*, at least. But I normally don't gossip, if I can help it. Yet, in this case, *not* saying something did more harm than good." He quickly looked up into her face. Her expression was pensive. She bit her lower lip and he heard a slight crumpling of the paper in her hand. "Sometimes, it is *much better* to tell."

"Seriously, this is not your fault. No one could have known what Dean was going to do," Nick assured her.

"Thank you for saying that." Her eyes lifted to his again and she smiled, confidence suddenly restored, as if she had made a decision about something. "May I come in?"

"Oh, yeah, please." He quickly stepped aside to let her pass. "Sorry about that. Wasn't thinking. You're here to see Bane about some business, right? He's in his office."

The reason for her being there was just a guess. Sloan was Bane's friend so the billionaire *could* have called her over to commiserate about what had happened with them. But the thought of Bane speaking to Sloan about his love life seemed highly unlikely. Omar was the only one Bane would open his heart to, otherwise, the billionaire kept his feelings to himself.

It used to be Omar AND me that Bane confided in. But not anymore.

"Yes, I am. I have something for him to look over." She waved the sheaf of papers in the air as if it were an exhibit. She dropped her tone conspiratorially and asked, "Would you mind if I used the ladies' room first before you took me to Bane?"

"Of course not. I can take you there, too --"

"Oh, no, I know the way. If you could just wait for me here?" She put her sheaf of papers, typed side *up* on the table that usually held a giant vase of flowers. The vase had been smashed the night before and the florist hadn't been called back yet to replace it. The white papers against the black table was very stark. "I'll be right back."

Sloan smiled at him almost encouragingly and then she quickly walked away towards the washroom. The tap-tap-tap of her heels echoed in the house.

At first, Nick tried not to look at the papers. They were, undoubtedly, about Bane's business. They were, *definitely*, private. But then he wondered why she had asked him to wait for her when she knew the way to Bane's office. And why would she bring *paper* to Bane? Whatever this document was, it could have much more easily been emailed than hand delivered to him. And it was completely careless to not have the papers in a briefcase or, at least, in a folder. Anyone could read them easily. None of this seemed *normal* for a capable attorney like Sloan. He then remembered the look on Sloan's face when she had said that maybe it was better to *tell* sometimes.

Could she want me to look at the papers? But why? I guess the only way to know is to look.

With a quick glance down the hallway to assure himself that she wasn't coming back just yet - in case he misread her altogether - he sidestepped over to the table and bent down to read the first page. It only took him a few moments to understand *why* Sloan Wu had wanted him to see this document. It was a contract giving Fairfax International back to his father and brothers. Nick flipped through the pages quickly. Even with the legalese, the terms were quite clear. The Fairfaxes got their company back with no strings attached. Bane would have no hold over his father and brothers as soon as this document was signed.

Nick stood there, stunned, as he read and re-read the document. He knew he had been reading far longer than it should have taken Sloan to go to the washroom and come back. But he couldn't seem to put the papers down. It changed everything.

Why didn't Bane tell me he was doing this? Doesn't he understand that this is the only thing keeping us apart?

Sloan cleared her throat. Nick spun around to face her.

"Sloan!" Nick swallowed and colored. It was obvious that he'd been reading the very private contract, but then he reminded himself that someone as together as Sloan Wu wouldn't have left this contract here unless she *meant* for him to see it. "Did you ... did you draft this at Bane's direction?"

She gave him a brilliant smile. "Every word."

Nick felt a grin breaking across his own face that almost hurt with its intensity. "Oh, that's ... that's ..."

She checked her phone, or pretended to anyways, and said, "I'm late for another appointment. Perhaps you could bring the contract to Bane for me?"

"Yes, absolutely. I can do that." Nick's heart soared.

"Thanks for the help." She tucked her phone into the pocket of her blazer and moved towards the front door.

He called out to her, "Sloan, did Bane ask you to keep this secret?" He touched the contract.

"Yes, careless of me to let you see it, wasn't it? Yet, somehow, I don't think Bane will be too angry at me about it. He told me he didn't want to take advantage of finally doing what he termed the *right thing* by telling you about it. But as *I* was the cause of you knowing, his honor is intact." Another smile crossed her face.

"It absolutely is. And I'll make sure he *thanks* you and gives you a bonus or whatever special things one does for attorneys," Nick told her.

She gave out an almost girlish laugh. "Bane already *owes* me. This one's on the house." She looked at him with a gentle expression. "You're the first person I've ever seen Bane lose his head over. I know he's done some very foolish things, but he cares about you."

"I care about him, too," Nick answered and *that* felt like the understatement of the universe.

She gave a nod. "I'm happy for you both."

And then she was gone, leaving just a trace of her perfume.

Nick closed the doors after her, feeling almost numb. He stood there for long moments. His mind was blank. But his heart knew *exactly* what it wanted. And he found himself walking then jogging then all out *running* to Bane's office. He burst through the door, catching the billionaire leaning over his desk.

Bane straightened and turned towards him, eyes wide with love and worry as he said, "Nick, is everything all --"

That was all Bane got out before Nick grabbed him and kissed him until they both couldn't breathe. When Nick pulled back, he rested their foreheads together. Bane's arms were tenderly around his waist. The contract was crumpled in one of Nick's hands between them. He figured Sloan could email Bane a clean copy anyways. She probably already had.

"Nick, what has happened? Are you all right? Not that I am *complaining*," Bane's voice was low and sensual, but the way he held Nick - as if he were a treasure that might escape his grasp - had Nick's heart hurting.

He wanted to let everything he thought and felt just tumble out, but all he managed to say was, "Sloan stopped by."

"She -- she did?" Bane sounded uncertain. He glanced down at the crumpled paper between them and frowned.

"She wanted to hand deliver a copy of a *contract*." Nick lifted the crumpled contract as an exhibit.

Bane took it from him and smoothed it out. Understanding and alarm flittered through those Siberian blue eyes as he glanced over the contents. Bane's lips pressed together as he put the contract on his desk. "Did you read it?"

"Yeah, I did. A bunch of times. She left it for me to see. And can I just tell you that Sloan is the best lawyer ever!" Nick laughed.

"Letting you see this is hardly what a *good* lawyer would do --"

"I said the *best* lawyer, Bane." Nick grinned. His stomach was fluttering. All the pain and anguish he'd been keeping inside of him was draining out. It almost made him feel lightheaded. "Why didn't you want me to know about this?"

Bane's forehead scrunched and he looked almost guilty. "I did not wish you to think I was releasing your family *solely* because I wanted us to be together."

Nick's eyebrows lifted. "You realize, don't you, that *this* thing with my family was the only thing keeping us apart?"

"I wanted to show you that I understood what I had done was *wrong* and that I was not just undoing it to get you back." Bane ran his fingers lightly through Nick's hair, sifting the fine strands. "I hoped it would make you see me in a kinder light again. But even if you didn't come back to me, I told myself that I *must* do it, because it was the right thing to do."

Nick's expression softened. "I thought that you wanted revenge on my family more than you cared about me."

Bane shook his head almost violently. "No! *Never*. It was *my* selfishness again. I thought I could have *both*."

"Both?" Nick let out a sad laugh and shook his head. "Yes, Bane, that I can believe of you. You always want to sweep the board."

Bane scrubbed one hand over his face. "I know how awful it sounds. How awful it *is*. I didn't consciously realize that was what I was doing."

"It's hard sometimes to really know what our motives are," Nick agreed.

"And there is one more reason ..." Bane looked down, appearing ashamed. "I was afraid you would leave me and your family's fate would be one more reason to stay."

"Bane, that's --"

"Awful. Horrible. Terrible. Yes, I know."

Nick framed Bane's beautiful face and made the billionaire look him in the eye. "No, I mean *yes*, in some ways. But the truth is that it makes me *sad*."

"Sad?" Bane's forehead furrowed.

"That you would be so afraid of losing me." Nick nodded.

Bane's arms flowed around him once more, pulling Nick close. "You are the most important person in my existence. To be without you is -- is to *hollow* me out. I would be a husk of a person without you. But, ironically, by keeping the deal alive I *ensured* you would leave me."

"Bane, you are your own worst enemy."

"I know that now."

Nick rested his chin on Bane's shoulder and closed his eyes. Being in Bane's arms was where he belonged. His body had actually *ached* for this.

"How did you intend for me to find out about the deal being over?" Nick asked after a long moment of just being held.

"I imagined your father would contact you to crow about it," Bane admitted with a shrug.

Nick laughed rather bitterly. "You're assuming he would have *bothered*. Once he has what he wants, he doesn't bother with the niceties. You see with Fairfax International back in his possession, he wouldn't need me to keep you happy any more. He wouldn't need *me* at all. So he might *never* have called."

"Nick …" Bane's voice sounded wounded for him.

Nick allowed himself to truly feel the hurt. It was the truth. He hadn't wanted to fully admit it. Or maybe it was that he had never wanted to fully *deal* with it. Nick thought of how his father and brothers had treated him up to the moment they sold him to Bane to fix their own mess. He thought of Jade's disdain of them. He even thought of Bane's indictment of them. He considered his own certainty that his father would have disowned him for breaking it off with Bane.

His family did *not* love him. Not the way he *ought* to be loved. And he'd taken it for far too long. That night, the night of the deal, was the first time he'd ever taken action against how his father and brothers treated him. He had intended to chose art and *himself* over them.

I might not have had the courage or strength to truly go through with it then. But I do now. Bane isn't the only person who has been acting out of fear.

He pulled back from Bane's massive chest. "When are you having the papers signed?" "Tomorrow. At my office," Bane answered.

Tomorrow. Am I ready for this? Am I ready to change, too?

Nick bit his lower lip, but then said, "I'd like to be there if that's all right."

"Of course, you can be there. You *should* be there." Bane framed his face with those large, but gentle hands. "I promise you that I'm not going to change my mind and withhold the company from them again."

Nick turned his face into Bane's left palm. "I know that. I'm not worried about it. There's just something I want to ... to *say* to my family after you free them from the contract."

Bane paused before saying, "Whatever you want is fine with me."

"Thank you."

Nick curled against Bane's chest again. The billionaire's arms flowed around him fully. Nick had never felt so safe. He'd never been so *certain* of a decision before. He thought that Jade would be proud of what he was determined to do.

His family would be free of Bane.

And Nick would be free of his family.

Just how it should have been when I came to their offices the night this all began.

CHAPTER FOURTEEN - SUNLIGHT

Bane buried his face in Nick's hair. He took in deep breaths of his mate's scent. A shiver of pleasure and *rightness* ran through him. Not touching Nick, not having Nick's scent in his nose, and not feeling Nick's love had been agonizing.

"My Nick," he whispered.

Mate, the spirit murmured.

"I missed you so much. Even though we were together, it felt like … well, seeing you and not being able to be with you was -- was *awful*." Nick laughed. "Damn, I'm not saying this right."

"Everything is right now that you are in my arms. That's all that counts."

The spirit did a little spin of delight in his chest. It made him laugh out loud to see the massive tiger dancing about like a kitten.

"What are you laughing about, huh?" Nick affectionately kissed his temple.

"The spirit is dancing. If only you could see him like I do now. Well, you *will* see him later. He promises to put on an encore performance for you," Bane's voice was thick with emotion. The spirit curled around his spine, loving him, loving Nick, and offering its soothing presence.

"I'd like to dance with you, too, Bane." Nick gave him a slow sensual smile. His fingers were now in Bane's hair, carding through it. "A slow dance under the moonlight?"

"You shall have whatever you want, Nick," Bane promised.

"The way you say that sends shivers down my spine."

Nick pulled back. It took all of Bane's willpower not to draw him close again. He wanted to practically weld them together if he could. But Nick was insistent. His mate framed his face with his hands. Nick's right thumb lightly brushed beneath the scar. His scar didn't hurt. He hardly felt the burn mark at all.

"I want ..." Nick paused and licked his lips.

Bane cocked his head to the side. "What do you want? I did *mean* it, Nick: whatever you want is *yours*."

What could his mate want that he was too shy to ask for?

"I want *you*," Nick answered in a throatier tone than his usual one.

"You have *me*," Bane assured him.

A flush covered Nick's cheeks, pinking his silken skin. "No, I mean ... in a *physical* way, Bane."

The spirit's tail which had been thumping with happiness froze in mid-air. Bane, too, froze, not certain he understood what Nick was asking for. He had expected his mate to be *tentative* with him, wanting to re-establish their relationship slowly with Bane having to earn every kiss, touch and pet. He expressed this to Nick in halting sentences.

Nick grinned. "Oh, I'll want the you-*earning*-it-part with romance and all that! I can't wait for it, actually. But ..." Nick's expression went serious and he curled one hand along Bane's powerful jaw. "But thinking we weren't going to be together just about *killed* me. So I *need* to know you're mine and I'm yours."

"How would we do that?" Bane murmured. His hands slid around Nick's waist.

"Now that *I* know about the spirit and *you* know he's not going to hurt me ... there should be *nothing* holding us back from being fully together, right?" Nick leaned his front against Bane's. "We can -- can *make love*."

Make love? Finally ... yes, we can.

The spirit quivered.

Bane did not answer Nick with words. Instead, he lifted the young man up into his arms. Nick let out a surprised shout, but soon settled himself. He wound his arms around Bane's neck.

"You really take a guy up on an offer!" Nick laughed.

"You are *everything* to me, Nick. Everything to *us*," Bane corrected as he felt the spirit knead his chest. "So I would give *you* everything."

Nick's pupils expanded with desire. "Oh."

"Indeed, *oh*."

Our mate! the spirit enthused as Bane carried Nick out of his office and down the hall. *We shall be with our mate! Where shall we take him? Which will be our den? His room or ours?*

Bane paused at the bottom of the stairs and asked, "Which bedroom, Nick?"

With no hesitation, Nick said, "Yours. I've had fantasies about you and me in there since we first met."

Bane let out a rumbling laugh. "You must let me make some of those come true."

"You carrying me in there and ravishing me is one of them."

"Your wish is my command." Bane captured Nick's mouth in a fierce kiss that did not end until they were both breathless. When he pulled back, his eyes were hooded and he felt the spirit looking out at *their* mate with desire and possessiveness. "And, Nick? It is *our* bedroom from now on. Not just mine."

A smile dawned on Nick's face that was slow and sweet. He leaned up and kissed Bane. It was as gentle and filled with *thankfulness*. They were in this together. They were in this for the long haul. For a moment, Bane had a fleeting regret. Nick would grow old. Nick would *die*.

And when he does ... I wish to go with him.

The spirit lowered his head. It was immortal. And it had a duty to all the other tigers in the world.

I understand, my friend. You have a duty to them and I have one to you. If only there were a way for Nick to be with us forever ...

"I don't like that thoughtful, sad expression on your face, Bane." Nick stroked his cheeks. "It looks too somber for this moment."

Bane forced a smile on his lips. "You are right. I was thinking about … well, something that doesn't need to be thought of right now. Not for a long time."

Nick furrowed his brow in confusion, but he smiled brightly again, intent on not letting whatever it was ruin their time together.

I need to stay in this moment. Doing that will make my time with Nick feel like forever.

Bane carried Nick the rest of the way to their bedroom - or den. He shouldered open the door. The bedroom was bathed in golden sunlight that streamed in from the open windows. He could just glimpse the rose garden - a riot of color - spreading out into the distance. The alluring, seductive scent of roses curled around them.

The king-sized four poster bed was awash in the sun's buttery light as well. Bane reverently placed Nick down in the center of it. His mate stretched his arms over his head and pointed his toes as he let out a cat-like sound of satisfaction. Bane remained at the bottom of the bed just looking at him.

Nick's long legs were tanned and muscular. The shorts were old and worn and *very* short, showing off Nick's ass. The t-shirt was soft from countless washings. It rode up to expose a strip of delectable stomach. His platinum hair was practically white from all the time he had spent out in the sun this summer. The spirit's eyes hooded and its tongue snaked out and licked its chops as if Nick was a delicious piece of meat.

Don't even think about it, Bane told him, but then grinned as he realized the spirit was playing with him.

The spirit let out an amused huff of air and reminded him of his own actions in using Nick's cock as a lollipop.

Your desire. Not mine. Though he was tasty, the spirit informed him archly.

I think we both want to devour him now. Figuratively, of course.

"Aren't you going to do anything? When is the ravishing going to happen? Or are you just going to look? Not that I couldn't do something with you just looking." Nick drew a hand down the center of his chest and let his fingers linger on the button and zipper of his shorts.

Bane gently pushed that teasing hand away from the shorts. "You are *mine*, Nick. I get to take my time with you now. And I will be the one to expose your beauty."

Nick's pupils went wider and the musky scent of his arousal spiked the air. His mate was barefoot, but he couldn't help but run his fingers up the soles, which had Nick pointing them again and biting his lower lip to stop from laughing.

"Tickles," Nick admitted.

"Mmmm, that is good information to know. I intend to understand every inch of you *intimately*. What makes you *laugh*. What makes you *sigh*. What makes your toes *curl*." His own lips curled into a tigerish smile. "What makes you cry out for more."

Nick's thin shorts were quickly tenting as he spoke. His mate put a hand over his eyes for a moment. "Listening to your voice *alone* could just get me off. I love you ... and your voice."

"More good intel."

Bane's large hands skimmed up Nick's legs from his slender ankles to his taut waist. His thumbs dipped down between Nick's thighs, exploring the silken inner confines of those limbs. Nick's hands left his face and he gripped the comforter. Bane's fingers slipped up under the hem of Nick's shorts and stroked the soft flesh there. Nick let out a gasp and was biting that plump lower lip again. Bane teased it out from beneath those white teeth.

"Do not deprive me of your cries, Nick. They are *addicting* to the spirit and I."

Nick's eyelids, which had shut as Bane explored, opened to show that his pupils were blown completely wide except for a thin ring of blue. "The things you *say*."

Bane grinned.

His fingers abandoned the bottom of Nick's shorts and they went to the button and zipper. Nick drew in a sharp breath. His stomach retreated from the warmth of the backs of Bane's hands. Bane undid the fastenings and with a fluid movement pulled the shorts off of

Nick. He was reminded of shucking corn to see the sweet kernels within. Nick's cock and balls bounced with the movement.

Nick was completely erect. Precum already slicked the pretty pink head of his cock. Bane's mouth watered at the sight of all that lovely cream. He dipped his head down and lapped at Nick's slit. His mate let out a strangled moan. Bane lapped again and then fastened his lips around the spongy head. Nick's heels beat a tattoo on the bed as Bane *sucked*.

"Fuck, fuck, you keep doing that and I'll cum!" Nick whined. "Your mouth ... your *fucking* mouth!"

Nick's fingers threaded through Bane's long locks and he tried to pull Bane off. Bane did not allow himself to be moved off. Instead, he sank down lower on that delicious shaft. He knew that Nick was on edge. He would take that edge off by making him cum once now and then *again* when they were mating.

"You bastard! Oh, God, oh GOD! I love you!" Nick cried out as Bane's tongue pressed against the vein that ran the length of Nick's cock.

Bane devoured the whole of Nick's shaft. He only stopped when he felt Nick's furry, hot, balls pressed against his lower lip. Then he rose up an inch before sinking back down. He would draw up a little more each time before sliding right down to the very bottom again. Nick was no longer fighting him though his fingers were still entangled in Bane's hair. Now Nick was simply trying to hold onto his sanity as Bane sucked him dry.

Bane slid his right hand upwards and pushed the t-shirt that Nick wore up to his armpits. He traced the mountains and valleys of the muscles in Nick's chest. When he found the peaked nubs of Nick's nipples he *twisted* them so that the pain caused the pleasure Nick was feeling to spiral up to greater heights. Nick bucked in response and gave out a shout that he could not hold in.

The heady, musky taste of Nick's flesh and seed filled Bane's mouth. He longed for the spurt of hot cream to slid down his throat and pool into his stomach. Both he and the spirit *hungered* for this completion. He sucked and licked and *rasped* his teeth lightly - oh, so lightly - along Nick's shaft.

His own cock was a heavy bar in his pants. He would be ready to enter Nick's body almost immediately after Nick came. He would *need* to be in that hot tightness, to feel that full physical *connection* between them before he spilled his own seed.

Nick's hips rose off of the bed when Bane tried to withdraw off that beautiful cock again and Bane knew his mate was on the cusp of cumming. Nick pulled on Bane's hair *harder* this time. Bane's fingers rolled Nick's balls and the whine that left Nick's lips told him that the rush of earthy cum was soon to be his. Bane sank all the way back down on Nick's cock. He felt the cock *plump* further and the balls draw tighter to Nick's body.

And then there was the explosion of semen. The earthy, salty taste filled his mouth and flowed down his throat in spurt after satisfying spurt. Nick's body collapsed fully into the bed and his eyelids closed as his cock let out the last of its seed.

Bane nursed on that tender, softening cock until Nick moaned softly in distress. He drew off knowing that his mate was too sensitive for more touches of his mouth, teeth and tongue. Bane shifted so that he was lying on the bed with his head pillowed on Nick's stomach. He let his own eyelids fall shut and drifted in a state of contentment. His cock still throbbed but he could ignore it with the satisfaction of semen in his belly. His mate's completion was his own.

Slowly, Nick began to card his fingers through Bane's mussed hair. Petting him. Loving him.

"I want you *in* me now, Bane," Nick murmured. "It's my turn to pleasure you."

CHAPTER FIFTEEN - ONE

Nick felt a full body shudder go through Bane at his words. He wanted this badly, too. In some ways, it felt as if he had been waiting for Bane all his life. Nick was no virgin, but he felt very *new* and *nervous,* as well as, *excited* and *eager* for what was to come. Bane was a shifter. He was *more* than just a man. When they made love it wouldn't just be him and Bane, but him, Bane *and* the tiger spirit.

Bane rose up off of him and the loss of him made Nick *yearn*. The big man's eyes were hooded and seemed to *smolder* with desire. His large hands rose up to undo the buttons of his shirt. They were shaking slightly and Nick's heart ached a little bit, because nervousness was not something one associated with Bane. It was so intimate to see Bane's burning desire for him tempered with the utter care he was showing.

Nick sat up in the bed and helped Bane with the buttons. His body was still languid from his release. Electric shocks ran through him so his hands were none too steady either. Yet he was already half hard again though he couldn't remember cumming so hard before.

With the unbuttoning finished, Nick pulled the tails of Bane's shirt out of his pants. Bane shrugged the shirt off of his broad shoulders.

Nick couldn't help but drag his fingernails over those beautiful arms. Bane was so very *big* and *masculine*. Everything about him screamed alpha male. Nick felt *small* in comparison. But Bane was utterly gentle with him.

Nick's hands fell to the button of Bane's slacks. It was the *final* button. He saw Bane shift his legs and realized that the big man had slid out of his shoes and socks. Nick's fingers fumbled with the button and zipper much like Bane's had, but he managed to finally undo them.

Bane wore no underwear and his thick cock sprang out into Nick's hands as soon as the zipper was down. Nick's stomach flipped at the sheer *size* of it. He'd seen it before, but now it was going to be *inside* of him in a few moments and that changed things. The head was the size of a plum and dusky rose in color. The shaft was a good eight inches. The balls were covered in fine hair and felt heavy with seed.

"Your breathing has increased as has your heart rate." Bane drew a finger over the center of Nick's chest.

Nick dragged his gaze away from that lovely cock up to Bane's beautiful face. He licked his lips nervously, but managed to say, "I'm just imagining this monster inside of me."

Nick squeezed Bane's length with both hands. It was like hot velvet between his palms. Bane grunted in pleasure. He drew that finger from Nick's cheek up to his chin so that Nick remained looking up into his eyes.

"We will *only* do what you want, Nick. We don't have to --"

"I *want* you to make love to me," Nick assured him even as his stomach kept doing acrobatics. "I want you so badly. I just have to be *prepared* for you and the tiger."

He drew his hands off of Bane's shaft and crawled over the bed to the nightstand where there was a tube of lubricant. He popped the top of it open and squirted a copious amount onto his fingers. Setting the tube back down on the bed for easy access, he looked over his right shoulder at Bane.

The big man had pushed his pants down his legs and stepped out of them. Nick let out a shuddering breath as he let his gaze trace the big man's body from head to toe. Broad shoulders. Defined pecs and abs. A narrow waist leading down to long, muscular legs and rather elegant feet. And Bane giving him that *smoldering*, half-wild gaze through his long hair.

Nick had to look away from this beautiful man as he positioned himself on the bed on all fours or he'd cum again. He spread his legs as wide as he could and still keep balance, while he stretched his slick hand back towards his ass. He was *presenting* himself for Bane. He could *feel* Bane's eyes on him as his fingers drifted up between his own ass cheeks and found that tight pink swirl of muscle, his anus.

He drew his middle finger lightly over that 'O' of muscle. He found himself clenching down as all those nerve endings seemed to come alive with that one brief touch. He took in a deep breath to try and relax himself. Right now it was going to be a struggle to get *one finger* inside of himself let alone Bane's cock.

Nick pressed his pointer finger against his opening, pushing it slightly inwards again and again. His anus relaxed and he was able to thrust the tip of his pointer finger inside of him. He moaned softly as he couldn't help but think of being *pierced* by Bane's cock later. Soon they would be joined together. He heard a soft intake of breath and then *felt* an exhale of hot air against his bare buttocks. Bane had gotten on the bed without him noticing. The big man had moved with the jungle prowl of the tiger. He was very close, so close that Nick could feel the soft brush of his hair against his thighs. He was watching Nick stretch himself.

Got to give him a show.

Nick pushed that finger deeper into his himself, keeping up a steady pressure so that his anus swallowed it down to the knuckle. He let it remain in there, motionless, for long moments, just adjusting to its presence. He found himself bearing down on it slightly and shivered with pleasure. He would do that to Bane soon. He would hold that massive cock inside of him and never let it go.

He slowly wiggled that finger around inside of him, gasping a little when he just barely brushed his prostate. He rested his forehead against the mound of pillows as arousal cascaded through him. His finger though had a mind of its own and kept *moving*, kept *rubbing*. His cock was already standing at attention even though he had cum not all that long ago.

Bane's mouth was suddenly *on* his ass. The big man was kissing, licking and *biting* him. The bites were gentle with only the slightest *burn* of pleasurable pain. Nick's finger started to *thrust* in and out of his hole as he realized that he'd cum soon just from this wild kissing-licking-biting thing Bane was doing. The big man was almost growling-snuffling as he did this. It was such an *animal* thing - a *tiger* thing - that Nick's heart began to hammer in his chest.

Nick thrust a second finger inside of himself. His ass eagerly swallowed both. He wanted to add a third almost immediately. He scrabbled for the lubricant, but Bane got it from the folds of the comforter before he could. The big man squirted more lubricant on Nick's fingers and Nick pushed three fingers inside of himself. He ached for a moment, especially when he *spread* those fingers apart as he drew them out before thrusting them back into his opening almost immediately.

"Let me. Gods, let me be in you," Bane murmured.

His breath was hot and heavy against Nick's opening. Nick pulled his fingers out and Bane's thicker fingers replaced them. The big man thankfully started with only *two*, but he scissored them open with every outward pull. Somehow, he managed to brush Nick's prostate with every inward thrust as well. Nick's hands were now clutching the comforter even as he lifted his ass higher into the air. He bit the topmost pillow beneath him.

Because they were Bane's fingers instead of his own, he never knew where they would go next. How deep or shallow they would delve. How fast or slow they would thrust into him and pull out. Whether they would pull apart or slide in together. He felt as if his body was being played like a fine instrument. He *sensed* Bane was studying his reactions just like he'd promised.

Everytime we make love, he'll know one more part of me. How I love him!

Nick's body felt like it was filled with heat radiating out from his own cock and balls. He was already leaking precum onto the comforter. Bane added a third finger. When those three agile fingers sank all the way up to the knuckle in Nick's ass, Bane held them there. Nick felt himself *breathing* around them.

Bane rubbed a circle at the base of his spine. "Relax, my mate. Relax and let me in."

Nick shivered at the use of the word "mate". Not human. More than human. That's what this was. They were bonded. Nick found his body responding to Bane's urging and he did relax. He had clenched around those fingers, but now Bane could move them in and out of him easily.

He heard the snap of the lubricant opening again and felt the nozzle pushed into his opening and the coolness of the gel squirting inside of him. Bane then went back to stretching him. Bane's mouth was also back to kissing and licking and biting him, not just his ass cheeks though, but up his *spine* where Bane fastened onto the skin at the very top and bit down hard enough that Nick knew he would be marked for *days*. And he *loved* the idea of it. This moment would be written on his skin for others to see. Bane was his. He was Bane's.

Bane lapped at the area he had bitten, soothing away the slight pain. The big man's body was now above his. Bane's fingers were in his ass, but also, Nick felt Bane's stomach and chest skimming along his back. That magnificent cock painted precum on his skin. Bane's long hair brushed over his shoulders as he continued to kiss every inch of Nick. Nick arched up against him, wanting to *feel* Bane fully against him. This caused Bane's fingers to move deeper inside him. Nick moaned and his cock jerked.

"I need you in me," Nick's voice was a hoarse whisper. "I *need* you, Bane."

Bane let out a growl so near to the tiger's that Nick could almost believe that the spirit was about to mount him. Bane's fingers came out of his ass with a wet pop. Nick groaned again, but this time with emptiness. He was *empty*. He needed to be *filled*. He heard the snap of the lubricant being opened one final time, followed by the squish of the gel spreading onto Bane's palms, and then the brisk movement of Bane's slick palms along his shaft.

"Do you want me to take you like this, Nick?" Bane's voice was almost guttural with need. "On your hands and knees?"

Nick wanted to respond, "Yes!" But all he could manage to do was to nod and present himself even more for Bane's use.

He planted his forearms against the comforter and spread his legs wide. Fine tremors went through him as he awaited the press of that bulbous cock head against his opening. Bane shifted on the bed and his hands were suddenly on Nick's hips, positioning him and holding him steady at the same time. Nick breathed to center himself.

"We will be one," Bane murmured.

Nick nodded again, wanting that more than anything, but still without the ability to speak. Bane's cock head was against his opening. It felt so big. It was going to stretch him to the breaking point. There would be blood, but he didn't even care. He wanted them to be *one*. Nick though clenched his anus without meaning to. Bane rubbed his thumbs along Nick's hipbones to calm him. Nick let out a breath and his ass muscles relaxed again.

Bane squeezed Nick's hips in warning as he started to press inwards. The big man simply used his body weight to slowly, but inexorably part Nick's tender tissues. There was pain though Nick had been loosened considerably. He dug his fingers into the comforter in reaction, but the pleasure that accompanied it had him breathless and trembling. He was glad that Bane didn't stop and start. That would have been an agony. Instead, Bane slid in all the way to the *hilt*. Only then did he stop and rest.

Bane's body curled over Nick's. The big man's mouth was on his shoulder, biting down then kissing then licking. He was still though other than that. His cock - thick and long and bulbous at the head - was not moving inside Nick's tender back passage. Bane's hands kept Nick still. Nick breathed into the stretching pain until it disappeared altogether then he bore down on that hot shaft and demanded that Bane *move*.

"Take me, fuck me, love me. *Now*," Nick said.

Bane let out one of those rumbly growls of his and did just as Nick asked. He straightened, his large hands completely controlling Nick's hips, and began to pull out and thrust back in. Nick shuddered with each inward thrust. The sheer power of Bane would have had him falling flat on his face if not for Bane's hands holding him up. The pull outs grew longer even as the thrusts seemed to go deeper. His prostate was brushed with every movement causing Nick to babble about dark stars over endless jungles. He had no idea what he was saying, but he kept seeing tigers slinking through trees that were endlessly tall.

Sweat slicked Nick's body, trickling down his sides, as Bane pounded into him. The rhythm would be incredibly punishing for anyone other than Bane to accomplish, but the big man was more than human. Nick found himself letting out a cry of pleasure every time Bane's balls *slapped* against his ass.

The big man lifted Nick off of the bed and pulled him on top of his lap. He then lifted Nick up and down on his cock like it was a pogo stick. Nick's cock and balls bounced. Bane wrapped one arm around his waist to keep up the movement while his other hand grasped Nick's shaft and began to stroke him with a firm grip. Nick yelled out his pleasure, unable to hold it back.

Nick's whole body felt like it was set aflame now. There was no part of himself that was not *tingling, burning, aching* with this fierce loving. Bane's mouth was on his shoulder and throat again, leaving a line of scalding kisses, licks and bites in a chain. Bane's teeth grazed his collarbone and Nick reached back and buried his fingers in Bane's long hair. He tugged at it mercilessly, which caused Bane to growl in pleasure.

Mate, Nick thought he heard in his head in a voice that was and was *not* Bane's. *Want you. Need you. Love you.*

Bane repositioned Nick again, this time on his *side*, with his top leg pushed up almost to his chest. This allowed Bane to go even *deeper* inside of him. Nick no longer felt like he had higher brain functions. There was only the hot, magma-like pressure in his cock and balls and a lightning storm of pleasure in the rest of his body.

Bane's thrusts were shorter and stronger now. He ground his front against Nick's ass so that he could get as deep as possible. Nick mewled and he clutched onto one of Bane's arms, kissing the palm of Bane's hand almost frantically. He was moments from cumming. He felt it building up inside of him and there was nothing he could do to stop it.

Bane's cock plumped further inside of him. The big man's breath caught. Nick knew then that Bane was just as close as he was. Nick clenched his ass muscles around Bane's cock when it thrust in that final time, keeping it deep within him, near to the very core of his being. Nick's eyes shut tightly as pleasure that had been wound tightly inside of him suddenly unspooled. Cum spurted from his cock in long, creamy streams, painting the comforter and Bane's hand as he put it in front of Nick's cock to catch some of the semen.

Bane brought that hand to his lips and licked it. One taste sent the big man over the edge. Nick let out a cry as he felt Bane's cum coat his insides. It felt hot. It felt like he was being *marked* with it. That seed was *planted* inside of him. His own cock gave out another small spurt of cum in response.

Bane's mouth closed on his. He'd grasped Nick's chin and drew it around so that they were face to face even as Nick's body went limp and unresponsive - tingling and electrified by his release, but out of his control. The kiss *seared* him. Nick would swear he could still feel that kiss hours afterwards.

Their tongues tangled languidly as the aftershocks of pleasure radiated through them both. Bane kept his cock inside of Nick. It still felt hard to him. Nick did not want it gone. This sense of connection was stunning. It was like nothing he had ever felt before.

Bane was kissing his cheek and neck when Nick's eyes began to close of their own accord, but instead of the darkness he expected to see, there was *light*. It wasn't the light streaming from the windows he saw, but light filtered through massive jungle trees. It had a green-gold quality that was strange yet familiar to Nick at the same time.

He was sitting cross-legged in a glade surrounded by those huge trees. He felt afraid for a moment to be in this *wild* place without Bane.

This must be a dream. I'm dreaming.

But it felt real. It felt more real than anything before it.

His head lifted for at that moment, he heard the softest step. A white Bengal tiger stood at the forest's edge. Those stunning blue eyes he would know anywhere looked back at him with such *love*. Nick opened his arms even as he got up on his knees to reach for the tiger. He didn't have to move. The tiger came to him. He felt the soft slide of the tiger's fur against his skin. He buried his face into the tiger's neck and just *held onto* that massive body.

Mate, that voice that was and wasn't Bane's said in his mind.

Mate, Nick responded back with equal measure.

Love you, the tiger told him.

Love you, too, Nick got out and increased the strength of his grip on the tiger. *Not letting you go. Never letting you go.*

He swore he *felt* the tiger smile. *Together forever. Mates. That is what we are.*

CHAPTER SIXTEEN - CHOOSING LOVE

Bane watched Nick from behind his glass and steel desk. They were in his downtown Winter Haven office waiting for Charles. Nick stood at the windows. Bane's office was on the top floor of the tallest tower so the view was fantastic. The city stretched out towards the ocean. The sky was that perfect blue. The buildings gleamed. The water sparkled in the distance. Whether Nick was actually *seeing* any of that though was unclear. He'd been in his head since the drive into the city that morning.

"My father, undoubtedly, *covets* your office," Nick said without turning around. He sounded amused, but Bane saw the tension in the young man's spine.

"This will be the first time he's been in here," Bane remarked lightly. He paused and then asked a question he had asked several times since Nick had requested to be at this meeting, "Are you *sure* you want to be here, Nick?"

"I'm sure. I have to say something to my father," Nick paused then explained further, "Well, really I have to *finish* something that started that night we made the deal to begin with. It feels right to do it now."

Bane knew that the night of the deal, Nick had planned to break from his family. Charles had told the young man in no uncertain terms that if Nick went forward with his plans to become a photographer that Nick would be out of the family. No more money for school. No more living in the family home. No more family at all. Nick chose his art over his family. But considering Nick's art *was* his soul, there was no real choice. But the deal had changed everything.

The young man turned around to give Bane a faint smile. That smile was far from the easy, broad ones that had graced Nick's face since they had gotten back together. But Nick seemed determined to stay and speak his mind to Charles.

Nick had chosen to wear one of the Fioretti suits instead of his usual shorts and a t-shirt though Bane had assured him that his casual clothes would be more than fine. He *preferred* Nick in those worn, soft, well-loved clothes. They were Nick's "happy" clothes when he was photographing beautiful things or simply laying in Bane's arms. But Nick looked lovely, too, in the pale butter yellow pants and suit coat with a dark brown belt, and, a purple and white checked oxford shirt. A purple patterned handkerchief stuck out of the right suit coat pocket.

"Don't worry about a scene," Nick added with a blythe, yet somehow *painful* wave of his hand. "Dad will be so thrilled to get the company back he won't really *care* what I have to say."

Bane winced internally at this. Even though Nick was pretending he didn't mind if his father cared or not about him, he clearly *did*. The spirit was mostly asleep but it stirred uneasily as it, too, sensed Nick's wounds.

"I do not care if Charles makes a scene. I'm concerned only with you. So ... what do you intend to say?" Bane finally asked outright.

Yesterday, they had made love, become *one*, and spent that whole day and night in bed. They had not spoken of Nick's family at all. They had focused purely on *each other* and what their plans were together. The spirit, even now, was dreaming of what they had done, replaying every glorious part, and stretching his paws as he did so. When Nick had asked again to accompany him to the meeting this morning, Bane had assumed that Nick wanted to make sure that he'd follow through with giving back the business. But Nick assured him over and over again that wasn't true yet he'd been vague as to why he wanted to be there. It was clear that he wasn't there to celebrate with Charles.

Nick rubbed his hands together now. He was clearly anxious and grim-faced, but determined as well. "I have to be *done* with them, Bane."

"*Done?* With --"

"My family."

Bane stared at him, not understanding the words he was hearing. "I don't --"

"It's not that I don't love them and maybe they love me deep down." Nick's hands rose and fell like restless birds. His expression became even more grim. "But they're ... *toxic* to me."

"I know you've always felt like the odd one out with them," Bane said non-committally. He knew that to be true but his own relationship with his parents had been so fraught that he no longer trusted himself as a guide for Nick's.

Nick began to pace in a tight line. "They don't really care, Bane! Dad and my brothers only showed up at the art show because *you* were there. They were only polite and acted semi-interested because they wanted to pretend to be a *normal* family in front of *you*. But if it had been just me? Forget it! They wouldn't have showed. So what I'm doing here is just putting a stake through the heart of something that's already *dead*."

While he agreed with Nick on one level, he'd honestly felt that Charles had been interested in Nick's photography when he'd actually taken the time to look at it. It had seemed to him that Charles was *proud* of his son. His appearance at Nick's show might have started with the intention of getting in good with Bane, but in the end, it had evolved into Charles simply wanting to show off his son.

Nick stopped pacing and wrenched his hands through his hair. "I'm so *sick* of acting like how they've treated me is *normal* or *right*. It isn't! I'm worth so much more than that!"

"You are. Of course, you are," Bane assured him and began to rise from his desk.

But before he could there was a discreet buzz from his office line. His secretary, Landon, murmured in his crisp way that Mr. Charles Fairfax was here to see him for his 9 a.m. appointment and should he send Mr. Fairfax in? Bane looked at Nick for the answer. Nick gave a jerky nod of his head.

"Please send Charles in, Landon," Bane said and pressed the off button for the speaker.

Nick was holding himself very still as if he'd shatter if he moved. Bane ached for him, but he sensed that he could do *nothing* to ease Nick's pain. Urging Nick not to have it out with his father was the wrong move. There were things that needed to be said. There were consequences to actions. Charles had earned Nick's anger and his dismissal from his life. He couldn't argue that Nick *had* to keep toxic people in his life. It was one thing if they were to *change*, but people so rarely did.

I changed. Maybe so can they. But they have to want to. Maybe if Nick makes the same bargain with them he did with me: change or he'll leave then they'll come around.

But Bane feared for Nick's heart if his father didn't even *care* to try and make that bargain. His hands curled into fists on top of his desk. He forced them to relax. There was no way to bully Charles into loving Nick the way he should.

Charles bounded into the room at that moment. The elder Fairfax was dressed impeccably as always in a light gray suit with an eccentric tie of pink and green. Upon seeing Nick's ensemble, he immediately gravitated over to his son and gripped Nick's shoulders. He shook Nick rather like he was a rag doll for all the encouragement Nick gave him for the touch.

"Nickie! Looking *smart* in one of Mr. Fioretti's originals! Never thought I would see you in purple checks, but they're really *you*, my boy," Charles chortled and smoothed down imaginary creases in Nick's suit coat.

"Hey, Dad," Nick's voice was muted. There was a faint, fake smile on his lips. He was hardly blinking.

Charles though didn't notice - or pretended not to - and turned

CURSED: BELOVED

around to face Bane. He gave Bane a large, toothy smile. "You're looking quite a bit better today than on Friday. It looks like a long weekend in the country did you some good. And I'm sure that Nick here gave you some tender loving care."

Bane hid his annoyance behind a bland mask. Though, if he were honest with himself, Charles was right that it was Nick who was making him feel and look so much better. The scar was a shadow of its former self. He could almost imagine it wasn't there.

"Yes, well, I have to apologize for my behavior that night. I fear that I ruined Nick's introduction to the art world by being so ... unwell." Bane grimaced at the lie. He had been such a bastard. His losing control to the beast hadn't been the real problem. His words about Nick's family had been.

"Not at all. Not at all," Charles assured him. "I smoothed things over. Let everyone know that the two of you were so grateful for the charitable work being done by Devon and all too happy to contribute to the cause. But that a flu bug had gotten you down and you didn't want to pass it along. Nickie went home with you to take care of you."

Charles beamed at them both with hands clasped in front of him, clearly proud of what he had done. And it was a *good* thing that he had accomplished. Bane rarely cared what people thought of him. But he did care what people thought of Nick. Charles had saved Nick's reputation. It made him *almost* feel bad for Charles about what was coming from Nick. He glanced at the young man quickly to see what Nick's reaction to his father's actions. Nick's expression was studiously blank. He turned his attention back to the elder Fairfax.

"Thank you, Charles, that was quick thinking on your part ... as always," Bane said.

Charles beamed some more then he got a rather impish look on his face. "I ... ah, *did* promise Devon a rather *substantial* contribution to his pet causes for a year or two from your company to ensure he *echoed* my sentiments."

Bane allowed a rather knowing smile to cross his own features. "Devon *always* turns potential scandal into a good cause."

"He does indeed! He's quite the sharp one himself! Glad he's using it for *good* and not *evil*." Charles chuckled and rubbed his hands together. "Now, what can I do for you today? I assume the opening isn't the reason you called me here."

Charles' expression was still happy and open, but there was a *keenness* to his gaze that showed his quick mind was working on all cylinders.

"No, you are quite correct. It is not."

Bane took out the contract that he'd had Sloan draw up that weekend. It was tri-folded. He handed it to Charles without explanation.

Charles took it from his hands and put on a pair of wire rimmed spectacles before opening it and reading it. His expression was *fascinating*. At first, he looked *blank*. Bane saw him read the first paragraph then his eyes went back up to the top of the paper to read it again to make sure he hadn't misread it the first time. The second time going through it, the paper fluttered slightly as his hand began to shake. Charles gripped the paper then with both hands to stop the movement. He started to mouth the words and a smile kept threatening to erupt on his face. Finally, he brought the pages down and stared at Bane then at Nick.

"Is there *other* good news you want to tell me?" Charles asked.

Nick and Bane met each other's gaze, unsure what he was asking for a moment, but then it was Nick who figured it out first. A dry, pinched smile appeared on his lips.

"No, Dad, we're *not* getting married or anything like that. Not *yet* anyways," Nick said.

Bane was surprised at the instant desire he had to cry out about them *not* getting married. He *wanted* to with all he was at that moment. They were *mated*. They were *one*. A wedding would just be the legal, outside way of showing that to the world. But they had just patched things up and Nick was about to break ties with his family. It was no time to think of *weddings* and, yet, Bane did.

"But then why are you giving me back the company before the year is out?" Charles asked Bane. But he quickly backtracked then, not wanting Bane to see the *folly* of his actions in doing this, "I mean: where's the pen?"

Charles laughed as Bane handed him one of the Montblanc pens from his desk. Charles held the pen above the document. His gaze still shifted between the two of them as if he couldn't quite believe his luck.

"You don't have to sign it now, Charles. You could take it to your own attorney for review," Bane offered.

Charles hesitated again, but he shook his head. "You're a man of your word, Bane. I've figured that out about you. I'm just *surprised*. This is quite *unexpected*."

"Yes, I imagine it is," Bane murmured, tenting his fingers in front of his face. "The man I was when you first met me - perhaps even the man I was last week - would *never* have done this. But your son has *changed* me."

"You've changed yourself, Bane," Nick got in quickly.

Bane smiled and bowed his head in acknowledgement. But he didn't think it was true. He'd always been a selfish creature. His upbringing had encouraged that in a way. It was only Nick's entrance into his life that had made him *want* to be different.

"What I meant is simply this: your son is worth more to me than any revenge against you, Charles," Bane explained as simply as he could.

Charles *still* looked suspicious though. Bane repressed a sigh. The man clearly couldn't believe in a love like his and Nick's. Bane had been the exact same way before Nick, hadn't he? But then the elder Fairfax gave a nod and smile.

"I loved my Emma like that," Charles said, his tone almost wistful. His eyes grew distant as he remembered this great love of his life. "Nickie is so much like her."

At this statement, Nick stiffened and Bane winced. *This* sentiment was a dangerous one though it was clear that Charles had no idea it was. But Bane already understood why. If Nick was so like Charles' beloved wife then why did he treat Nick like garbage?

"Dad, sign the papers and let's get this done," Nick's voice was flat and hard.

Charles frowned slightly and turned to his son in confusion.

"Nickie, what's wrong? Aren't you pleased about this? Bane has chosen *you* over business. That's a big deal!"

"Yes, it is," Nick agreed. "Bane has chosen *me* above the things that matter a lot to him. He's giving you and my brothers back what you *don't* deserve, because he loves me."

The elder Fairfax was frowning *deeply* now. He heard the "don't deserve". He noticed Nick's anger and hurt now, too. He clearly recognized that he was in a minefield, but wasn't sure how to get out of it.

Charles Fairfax was *not* a stupid man. That was what made him so dangerous and why Bane had wanted to eliminate him and his sons from the board.

"Son, I know that you don't *approve* of all your brothers and I have done, but it's *business* not *personal*. It's how capitalism works. Sometimes people get hurt, but more people *benefit* from it."

Nick's hands were clenched into fists at his sides. His face was white though there were high patches of color on his cheeks. "Even if one of those people is your *son?*"

Charles' forehead furrowed. "What are you saying, Nickie?" His gaze flickered to Bane for a moment. "Is he … are you being hurt in some way?"

Bane had to give him some *small* amount of credit. It almost looked like Charles would *do* something to save his son if Nick really was being injured. But the man had the signed copy of the contract in his hand. He only had to add his signature for it to be binding. Bane had signed it earlier.

"*You* hurt me. Over and over again," Nick's voice rasped with pain. "How can you *stand* there and *pretend* to care? How can you compare me to *Mom?*"

"That's a compliment, Nickie --"

"How could it be?" Nick snarled. "Would you have *sold* Mom off to Bane to keep your damned company?"

Charles reeled back slightly. His voice was weak as he said, "I didn't do --"

"Yes, you did! Goddammit, Dad, you *sold* me to Bane for a year!" Nick raged. The dam finally gave way and Nick let it all out, "And you didn't think he was a *good* guy! The very fact that you are *shocked* - yeah, you're *shocked* - that he's giving you back your company out of love for me tells me what you thought of him before!"

Charles swallowed. He was gray now, as gray as he had been when he'd realized that he'd lost Fairfax Industries. "But it all worked out. You love him and he loves you so it was a *good* thing that you and he - -"

"You didn't know that!" Nick shouted and his voice echoed in the room, silencing his father's weak protests. Nick ran a shaky hand across his forehead. "And you didn't *care* what happened to me when I was with him. Not really. I mean sure, you'd feel bad if I was hurt, but you still wouldn't have made any other decision. Because in the end you love your company more than you ever loved me."

"Nickie, that isn't true."

Nick stormed over to him, white-lipped, cheeks flushed, eyes blazing. He grasped his father's wrist, the wrist that held the pen and he moved it so that the tip was over the signature line of the contract.

"Sign it, Dad. Sign this goddamned contract. Get your company back and get out of my life!" Nick grated.

Charles stared into his son's gray eyes with a guilty, shamed expression. Nick hadn't been wrong about his actions in the past. What surprised Bane was how clearly the elder Fairfax realized the mistakes he'd made. It had taken Bane far more to recognize what a bastard he had been, but it looked like Charles had been feeling guilty about this for a long time.

"Nickie, I love you," Charles whispered.

Nick shook his head. "Maybe you do, Dad, but it's not worth a hell of a lot."

"That's not true!" Charles protested.

Nick released his father's wrist and took a few steps back towards the door to Bane's office. Bane's heart ached for his mate.

"Sorry, Dad, but you've had your chance to prove to me that's not true, but when it's come down to it ..." Nick just shook his head rather than ending that sentiment. "Whether you sign that contract or not, we're done. I'm done. I don't want anything else to do with you.

You can stop pretending to care for me and I can stop ... hoping you'll change. *Hope hurts.*"

Charles flinched. It appeared like he was being hit with bullets from an automatic rifle.

"Nickie," was all he got out.

Nick's back was ramrod straight. His gaze flickered to Bane. "I'm going to meet up with Jade. I know you're busy, but join us when you're through here."

Bane half rose from his seat. "I could come with you --"

Nick held up a hand. "It's okay. I need to talk to Jade by myself. I'm -- I'm fine."

His mate was *not* fine, but he needed to go off and lick his wounds in private.

"I will see you later then," Bane told him.

Nick nodded. He allowed his gaze to flicker to Charles once - the elder Fairfax looked like he had been kicked in the stomach - and then the young man looked away. Nick turned on his heel and left the office and the Fairfaxes.

CHAPTER SEVENTEEN - PRECONCEPTIONS SHATTERED

*N*ick blindly raced out of Bane's office building. He felt *numb*, but his body knew what his heart and mind would not let him acknowledge: that he was devastated. Ending things with his family was the *right* thing to do. Staying with them was *toxic*.

His father had *sold* him to save himself. His father had been ready to send him *packing* even before that because he wanted to carve his own path in the world and *not* destroy other people's lives and livelihoods. His brothers thought of him as a *joke*. No, it was the *right* thing to do to end this *farce*.

We're not a real family. Not since Mom died. It hurts more to pretend than simply to end things.

Maybe his father and brothers loved him in their way, but it was *bad* for him. He needed to take a stand for *himself*. How could he ask less of his family than his lover? He couldn't. Bane had proven himself worthy of his love. Bane had *changed*.

Nick was headed to the same restaurant that he and Jade had met up on that day of the deal. It was only a few blocks away. That day when they'd planned his escape seemed so long ago now. He wasn't the same person anymore. It wasn't a coincidence that he had asked her to have lunch with him there. It felt like he had finally done what he should have back then: finished with the Fairfaxes.

He saw Jade's striking black hair - pink tips were added now - and she was wearing a black skirt and top with a pair of her pink lace up boots. Her legs were crossed one over the other and her top foot was bobbing in the air. She was anxious. He didn't blame her. He'd phoned her yesterday and was incredibly cryptic about what was happening with him. He'd promised that he'd speak to her today.

Now it was today and he still didn't know what he was going to say about Bane.

Bane had told him the night before, "Only Omar, Omar's family and *you* know the truth about me and the spirit, Nick. If you wish to tell Jade, I will support it. I do not believe she would reveal my secret."

"But the more people who know, the more danger you're in, right?" Nick had asked.

Bane's gaze had slid away from him towards the moonlit silvered rose bushes. "Trust and love go hand in hand. Without one, you strain the other. I think if you had to keep lying to Jade that it would hurt your friendship with her in the end. So it is a risk I am willing to take to have her know the truth about me."

Nick doubted that Jade would believe him if he simply blurted out the fact that Bane was an immortal tiger shifter, that the spirit of all tigers lived within him, and that he was over a hundred years old. She'd stare at him for a long moment before bursting into laughter, thinking he was telling her a very odd joke. Or had a head injury.

Bane though had offered to shift in front of her, but only if Nick thought that she would not be adversely affected by it.

Like his mother. But that was her illness and the times more than anything else.

"Jade's a huge reader of shifter books, Bane. The idea of someone being able to shift into an animal form is *cool* and *beautiful* in her mind. She'll be stunned - awed, more likely - but she won't be afraid."

"Then I will shift for her whenever you like," Bane had responded.

Nick saw a duffel bag by her booted feet. She was ready to come back to Moon Shadow. Likely, she thought she was coming to save

CURSED: BELOVED

him from making a bad mistake. She had no idea why Bane and he were back together. She had no idea that he'd broken off with his family. When she caught sight of him, she immediately straightened up and brightened though there was still worry in her eyes.

She waved a hand. "Nick!"

He forced a smile on his face - he was happy and relieved to see her, just not all that he had to tell her - and jogged across the intersection. He gave her a hug and a peck on the cheek before sitting down. It was the *same* table from that day, too.

"It's so good to see you. I was worried," she said as she studied his face.

He nodded. "I can imagine. I haven't exactly been talkative since I told you I was breaking it off with Bane and then that I was back together with him."

She studied his face and what she saw there concerned her. "You don't look exactly *happy* though, Nick. Are things still ... *difficult* with him?"

Nick shook his head without hesitation. "No, things with Bane are perfect."

She blinked, clearly not having expected that answer. "T-that's great so why --"

"Why do I look like someone's kicked my puppy?" He gave a sad laugh. "Because I finally did what I should have done before this whole thing with Bane started."

It took Jade a moment to figure out what he was saying. Her lips parted in shock. "You -- you told your family off?"

He nodded. "More than that. I'm *done* with them, Jade. Let me explain."

The waiter came at that moment to see if they would like to order. Jade smiled up at him and said, "I think we need some cocktails."

She then expertly ordered their favorites. A Cosmo with extra lime juice muddled in for her and an Old Fashioned for him on the rocks. After the drinks were delivered, they clinked glasses.

"Now tell me everything from the beginning," she said as she leaned forward across the table, all of her attention upon him.

He told her everything, except the part about Bane being a shifter. He explained how Bane gave up his revenge, handing Fairfax International over to his father and brothers, and the final meeting with the elder Fairfax. He told her that Bane realized how wrong and selfish he'd been in trying to keep the deal going. He even revealed Bane's shamefaced admission that he'd done it, in part, because he still feared that Nick wouldn't stay with him for himself.

She listened intently, asked a few pointed questions, and when he was finished, she sat silently - her gaze distant - before she nodded in almost satisfaction. She reached across the table and took one of his hands in hers. Both of theirs were cool from the perspiration from their glasses. They'd had another round of cocktails as he'd spoken.

Nick's blood was buzzing with the alcohol, but he wasn't drunk. It was just loosening him up slightly as he was wound tight as a drum.

"You've done the right thing, but I can tell that you're hurting," she said as she squeezed his hand.

"Can't make them love me, you know?" He gave her a weary, bitter smile. That was the truth of it. There was nothing to be done on his part. "Maybe they're just incapable of it. Maybe I'm just asking for too much. But ... I can't stand this half-life with them any longer."

"You *are* lovable. You *know* that, *right?*" she assured him.

"I've just always been the *changeling*, you know? I get that I'm not like them and they don't care about the things I do. But they don't get to treat me like they have. I won't just stand there and take it any more." He balled one hand into a fist and thumped it against the table. The glasses and silverware rattled. He quickly straightened out the knives and forks. And it was at this moment that he saw his brothers coming down the street. He swore softly, "I can't even believe ... it's like Fate is testing me."

Jade turned around in her chair and caught sight of the two Fairfax brothers. Steven had seen them, too, and he tugged on Jake's arm to draw his attention. He then pointed them out and the two of them headed over to Nick and Jade's table rather like a pair of hunting hounds.

"Nick, do you know what Bane is talking to Dad about?" Jake

asked. No "hi, how are you?" no "what's up", no preamble at all. Just what's going on with Dad and Bane, because that's the only thing that Jake wanted from him.

Steven, because he was rigid and rule following, or perhaps less of an outward asshole, did say hello to Jade and gave Nick a nod of greeting. But it was clear that he, too, was anxious to know what was up. Some part of Nick recognized that the two of them had been under a lot of stress lately trying to win the company back and maybe he should give them some slack. They were living on tenterhooks. And family wasn't supposed to be about form over function. But still, Nick was *nettled*. Jade's gaze flickered between him and Jake, clearly wondering if she was going to have to break up a fist fight.

Nick thought of all the cruel things that he could say to Jake and Steven. He imagined yelling at them until he was red-faced and breathing hard. He imagined them looking ashamed for how they had treated him. But that was too far a stretch. Steven would have just gotten stiff and uncomfortable as he glanced around, hoping that no one associated him with Nick the madman. Jake would have exploded back, blaming him for everything. He could almost hear Jake shouting, "If you could just be fucking *normal*, Nick, we'd treat you like you want to be treated!"

So he said none of that. He let silence fall for a moment and then answered icily, "Bane's given Dad back the company. We're all free."

Steven blinked behind his wire rimmed glasses. "When you say he *gave* it back, do you mean -"

"Completely and utterly strings free, Steven. You, Jake and Dad get to go back to your old ways of dismantling companies with glee," Nick cut him off.

"You're kidding," Jake's voice was strangely flat. Nick had thought that he would have been thrilled even without the details. Jake wasn't a details kind of person. He believed what he wanted from the least amount of evidence.

"No. We're all *free*." Nick used "we" instead of "you" because this deal freed him most of all.

But still neither of of his brothers looked thrilled. When he chanced a quick look at Jade, her forehead was furrowed, too. She saw the lack of animation, and was just as confused about it as he was.

"What's the problem?" Nick asked sharply.

"I just don't get why Bane's letting us go," Jake said slowly.

Anger suddenly flared, bright and hot, in Nick's chest. "Because he *loves* me, Jake. You don't hold someone's family hostage if you love them. I can see why you guys might be surprised by that."

He couldn't help that last bit from coming out. And why shouldn't he tell them? Why did he always have to hold what he felt in and be *nice*?

"Bane did this for *you*?" Steven asked, studying Nick's expression.

"Don't sound so goddamned shocked," Nick growled. "Some people actually *care* about me enough that they're willing to give up something they really want to do. I know that's *alien* to the two of you, but --"

"I'm not surprised," Jake interrupted him. His eldest brother didn't sound angry or even look perturbed. "I'm ... I'm *glad*."

"You're *glad*?" It was the first time Jade had spoke. She was looking at Jake with her eyebrows raised.

Jake snorted. "I know what you think of me, Jade, that I'm just some asshole that doesn't give a damn about Nick."

Yeah, she's not the only one, Jake.

"But it's not true. Well, not *all* true. I *am* an asshole. But that's how Dad taught us to be in business. Bane ... Bane and his people are teaching us something else. Another way." Jake grimaced. It was clear that he was uncomfortable talking about his feelings, but he pressed on, "Look, the deal we made with him - at least the part involving you - was total garbage. It was *worse* than that. Dad *never* should have agreed to it. I was just too freaked about losing everything to speak up. I *should* have. I should have done something, anything, really. So yeah, I'm really fucking glad that it worked out. That Bane's a good guy and loves you. Because it means even though I messed up, it's still okay."

Nick's mouth about hung open. He shut it with an audible click. He finally got out, "I -- I have to say I'm surprised."

"We both realize we haven't said anything before," Steven said, pushing his glasses up his nose as he did when nervous. "But, truthfully, we've been worried about you ever since you got into a relationship with Bane. We hear good things about him in business, but his personal life ... well, the deal ... all of it made us wonder."

"Why didn't you say any of this to Nick?" Jade demanded to know, bristling. "Why didn't you call and check on him while he was working at Moon Shadow? Why didn't you stop by Moon Shadow? If you were so damned worried about your brother, why didn't you actually try to figure out if there was something to be worried about?"

"She has a point. A lot of points. A lot of *good* points," Nick said dryly.

"You didn't call us either!" Jake retorted, high spots of color flaming on his cheeks.

Steven touched his arm. "That's true, Nick. You never reached out to us either. But two wrongs don't make a right. The truth is ... that we were scared to know if something was wrong."

"What?" Jade snapped.

But Nick understood. "If you knew something was wrong then you'd *have* to do something. And working *with* Bane was the only way to get the company back and not get ruined. So if you put up a stink about me --"

"It would all be over. But if something really wrong was happening ... we figured you'd call." Jake ripped his hands through his hair. "It was such *bullshit*. I know! We both know! It's just that once we started working for Bane, we realized that his threats to ruin us? Well, he could do it."

"Not that he runs his companies that way," Steven clarified. "They're quite ... ethical. I actually am enjoying what we're doing for him. Building things. Taking care of people both inside and outside of the company."

"Yeah, I do, too. There's a bunch of people there that actually *mentor* you," Jake sounded wistful. "Dad doesn't accept failure, you know? But at Bane's companies you can offer up ideas that may or may not work. And that's okay. You don't always have to be balls to the wall all the time."

Nick felt a sense of sadness for his brothers. He realized at that moment that they had taken on the task of pleasing their father while he had stood back and done his own thing. He'd thought that they *liked* what they did at Fairfax International. But what if they didn't? What if they had felt as trapped as he did by their father's expectations? Their loyalty had made his disloyalty possible, even acceptable on some level, because Nick wouldn't have to worry about his father having *no one* to be with.

"Do you guys not want to go back with Dad and run Fairfax International?" Nick asked slowly. "Would you rather stay working for Bane?"

Steven and Jake looked at one another; it was a look that spoke volumes. He could tell that they didn't want to stop working for Bane, but were afraid to say it. So he decided to.

Nick clarified, "Would you like me to ask Bane about keeping you guys on?"

But both of his brothers shook their heads in unison.

"No thanks," Jake said. "You've done *enough* for us."

Steven added, "We need to stand on our own two feet. If Bane hires us, we want him to do so only because we're good additions to his companies. Not out of nepotism."

Nick nodded slowly. He was seeing his brothers in a whole new light. He was also seeing himself in a new one, too. Maybe he hadn't been the best brother or son to his family either.

"Telling Dad is going to utterly suck." Jake sighed.

"It's either now or never," Steven pointed out and Nick got a sense that the two of them had been plotting to escape for a long time and he'd had *no idea*.

"Well, get back to your lunch," Jake said. "We're supposed to pick Dad up and head out --"

"Wait, guys, I have to tell you something else," Nick quickly said. He took in a deep breath and scrubbed his face with both hands. "I -- I told Dad I was done with the family."

He wasn't sure what he expected his brothers to say or do, but it definitely wasn't for them both to nod in understanding.

"We figured the deal would be the straw that broke the camel's back. You're clearly really talented with your photography so it would be a waste for you to go into business. Plus, you've got Bane and Jade," Jake said.

"We do hope, Nick, that ... that maybe things at least between the *three* of us ... well, that is up to you," Steven said with a nod. "Just know that our doors are open. They'll always be open."

Nick's throat felt too tight for him to respond. He simply nodded. His brothers then took their leave, heading back to Bane's building to collect their father. Nick slumped back in his chair and looked at his mostly empty second drink. Jade picked the glass up and waggled it.

"Want another?" she asked.

He gave her a bleak smile. "I *need* another."

And another after that, too.

CHAPTER EIGHTEEN - EXPECTATIONS

Earlier...

WHEN THE DOOR shut behind Nick, an *uncomfortable* silence fell in the room. Both Charles and Bane stared at the door in those long silent moments. Finally, Charles turned to look at Bane. His face was white and he looked to have aged ten years. Bane shifted uncomfortably. He hadn't thought Charles *heartless*, but this wasn't the reaction he had expected either. He'd thought Charles would be *angry* at losing a *thing* that was *his*. A prime property leaving him would not be stood for.

He thought Charles would be raging at Bane about how ungrateful Nick was and that it was good riddance and Nick was useless! But this seemed like a devastated *father* and the businessman was nowhere in sight.

"Bane, I -- I need your help," Charles said almost helplessly. "I can't lose my son. But -- but I *have* lost him, haven't I?"

Bane cleared his throat. "I cannot help you, Charles. Nick has very good reasons for what he's doing. I cannot advocate to him a different course when nothing has ... *changed*."

And people don't really change, do they? But I did. Yet this is Charles Fairfax. The man likes who he is. He prides himself on it!

But Charles sat down heavily in one of the chairs across from him as if he'd lost everything. This was actually far worse than the night when Bane had revealed to him he'd lost his company. Bane drummed his fingers on the desk. He realized he'd had *another* expectation of Charles that was *not* being met. He'd thought that Charles would sign the papers and *leave* after Nick's pronouncement. Why was the man sitting there? Bane was *not* the comforting type. But Charles was beyond noticing anything or anyone, because of his devastation.

"I expected this," Charles said softly, almost more to himself then Bane. "After all, I *sold* my son to you. Did I really think he'd forgive that?"

"Considering you haven't even *asked* for his forgiveness ... *no*," Bane remarked dryly and looked meaningfully at the contract that still remained unsigned between them.

"I haven't, because I've been afraid to," Charles admitted, not noticing the look whatsoever. "I've been terrified to act as if any of this was anything, but *normal*. Because I thought that if I didn't mention it, if I pretended everything was the *same*, then maybe it would be all right. Somehow he'd forgive me and we'd ... go on."

At least, Charles thought it wasn't right. I did not even allow myself to recognize that. Not really. Not until Nick forced me to see how what I was doing and thinking was wrong.

"Why didn't you at least call Nick or come see him when he was in my house?" Bane found himself asking. This was, of course, extending a conversation he had been telling himself he didn't want to have. Yet here he was having it. "Why didn't you check to see if he was all right? I could have been doing -- doing *anything* to him and you wouldn't have known."

Charles lifted his head then and studied Bane. "Would you have done *anything* to him, Bane?"

Bane thought of what Dean had tried to do to Nick. He hoped that he was not that sort of man. That whatever else he was, he'd never would have done *that*.

He licked suddenly dry lips though and said, "Charles, I'm the man who offered to *purchase* your son. I don't think that *either* of us could have been sure what I was capable of."

Charles' dark brown eyes narrowed as he studied Bane. "You were in love with him the whole time. All of this - even your anger at me - was because you cared for *him*."

"I wasn't a good man, Charles. I'm probably not one now. But I'm trying to be. For Nick," Bane answered and his throat felt tight.

Charles gave him a wan smile. "It *is* possible to become a better man - if only for as long as your partner lives. Sometimes, I wish -- not even *sometimes*, *all* the time, really -- that I had died and Emma had lived. The boys would have been far happier. Nick would have never doubted that he was meant to be an artist. Who knows what Jake and Steven would have done! They might not have gone into business either."

Bane winced. There was no chance he would die before Nick. Would he change back to the creature he'd been after the loss of Nick? That was terrifying.

Bane glanced at his computer. Jake and Steven's mentors had sent their reports to him that morning, as they did not know that he was ending the deal. He'd read them to amuse himself on some dark level. He thought it would offer him yet more evidence that it was *best* that the Fairfax brothers were leaving his companies, too, before they could do more harm. But instead, the reports had told him that both Jake and Steven were *learning* his way of doing business.

Jake had averted a strike at a newly acquired firm by sitting down with the workers and finding out what the pain points were. Steven had reorganized another new company so that it would be in the black for the first time in years by renegotiating several key contracts. His people told him that they believed the Fairfax brothers could be a true force for *good* within his organization given more time.

But I'm throwing them back in with their father. All of this progress will be lost.

"I'm glad that Nick is sticking up for himself," Charles said suddenly. "He has such a good heart. It sometimes makes him take too much guff."

"Yes, he does, but he's changed," Bane said.

But people don't change. Yet I did. Nick did. Even if the change isn't set in cement yet. It could be if we support one another. What about Jake and Steven? Could their change in business stick, too? And Charles ...

"Nick is so like his mother," Charles repeated with a teary smile. "Emma was always so artistic. Everything from interior design to painting to pottery! My God, she was *always* taking art classes. And her work was really *good*. Never had to buy anything for the house or office. I'd put up her things."

Bane frowned. This was one of the many times that Charles had compared Nick favorably to his mother. This was the first time he was hearing about her artistic talent, but he wasn't surprised. Nick would have gotten it from somewhere.

"Charles, you loved your wife, didn't you?" Bane began.

"Absolutely! She was the love of my life," Charles' voice was soft and tender.

"Then why did you treat the one son that *most* reminded you of her so badly?" Bane knew this was a cruel question, but he felt it had to be asked. Didn't Charles *see* that he was *punishing* Nick for being just like the woman Charles claimed to love?

"You mean why did I try to discourage him from becoming an artist?" Charles asked.

Bane nodded. "Among other things. Why did you threaten to disown him because he wanted to pursue his photography?"

"You know that world. At least, *maybe* you do. It's *hard*. It's full of heartbreak. And, truthfully, very few artists make enough to even scrape by," Charles explained. "I didn't want Nick to have to experience that. It would have ground him down and then he'd have to take a job he hated anyways. Better for him to do it as a hobby and have a *secure* job from the get go."

That was solid reasoning though cruelly executed. He knew that Nick, like his own mother, had the soul of an artist. They were *compelled* to create. Doing anything else was painful to them. They would work hard for *little* simply to engage in their art. If they had the support of those around them - not even financial, but emotional - that was what kept them going.

"You've seen Nick's photography and people's reactions to it," Bane pointed out. "Do you still feel that way?"

Charles cocked his head to the side and considered this. "Nick is *very* good and I think - depending on if he can capitalize on this thing with Devon - that he could do well for himself. But tastes change. People go after the next big thing. I do not know if Nick's art will *always* be what people want. Yet ..." Charles gave him a wry smile. "If he is with *you*, it does not really matter, does it? You will support him and he can be happy."

"I do not know if Nick will fully let me do that. But it might all be a moot point. I've already gotten multiple inquiries about his availability."

Charles nodded. "As have I! The boy's started a firestorm! But, again, without your help, would this have happened for his work? People want to please you."

"His work is brilliant and stands on its own," Bane said loyally and truthfully. "You could have supported him, too, Charles. Checked out his stuff. Introduced him to people."

"Nick would never have wanted me to do that and he wouldn't have accepted it even if I had." Charles' arms raised then lowered. "I admit I should have *looked* at his art. I should have *known* he'd be good. Emma was so gifted ..."

"What would she have thought of your ultimatum to him to go into business or be kicked out of the family? My understanding from Nick is that you didn't just say you wouldn't pay for school, but that he also wouldn't be welcome in your house," Bane reminded him.

Charles looked miserable. "Oh, she would have never allowed me to do that. But it was only a *threat*. I wasn't *actually* going to kick him out! I just wanted him to realize how *serious* I was!"

Bane realized that he actually believed Charles. The man had thought to frighten his son with poverty to make him comply. "It wasn't going to work. You do realize that, don't you? Nick came to your office that night to tell you he was going to art school and moving in with Jade."

Charles appeared startled, but then a broad smile crossed his face. He nodded in approval. "Good! Good for him! That means that he's willing to actually fight for the life he wants. That's a good thing."

"Yes, it is. Believe me, he's willing to sacrifice much." Bane was thinking of how Nick had been willing to throw away a luxurious life with Bane for what he believed was right. "Nick isn't afraid of poverty, Charles. He's not afraid of losing unless it's about him losing himself."

Charles nodded slowly. "Yes, that is what matters most to Nick."

Landon buzzed him over the intercom. Bane was *almost* glad for the interruption. He pressed the button.

"Yes, Landon?"

"Sir, Jake and Steven Fairfax are here to pick up their father," Landon said crisply.

"Please send them in," he said to his secretary then switched off. He added to Charles with a nod of his head towards the contract, "They should see that you're all free."

"Free? Yes, I suppose we are," Charles answered, listless again. He was undoubtedly imagining what he was going to have to tell them about Nick leaving.

But will they care? They seem to despise Nick some of the time and, at others, not understand him at all.

The two Fairfax brothers came in together. Jake was in the lead like always, and there was something grim, yet oddly hopeful, in his eyes that made Bane wonder if he had some idea of what had happened there this morning. Steven followed after him, proper and refined, but he was already touching his glasses, a move he made when anxious about something. The young men stood awkwardly a few feet away from the desk. They did not crowd around their father as he had expected they would. In fact, they were standing quite *apart* from him.

Bane decided that he needed to say something right away so that

CURSED: BELOVED

the young men weren't worried they were being fired and going to be out on the streets. "I called your father here today to give him back Fairfax International. No strings attached."

Once more, he expected the young men to show *some* relief at this. But Jake and Steven appeared tenser. Steven took off his wire rimmed glasses and polished them vigorously with a handkerchief. Jake scrubbed his mouth, chin and neck with one hand so hard that his skin turned red.

Charles turned around in his seat to look at his sons. "There's no reason to be nervous, boys. Bane's doing exactly what he said he is." He held up the unsigned contract. "I just have to sign this and Fairfax International will be ours again."

The young men *still* did not act like they were happy at all. Jake looked over at Steven and some unspoken communication occurred between them. Jake suddenly was wiping his hands on the front of his pants. His eyes flickered over to Bane now.

"So ... is part of the deal that we *have* to leave Bane's companies now?" Jake asked.

"You no longer *have* to work for Bane. We have our company back. Your old jobs are back, too, of course," Charles said with a frown.

He clearly did not understand why Jake was asking this. But Bane did. He realized *exactly* what was happening here. Charles was about to be dealt another blow.

"What Jake is trying to ask," Steven said with his crisp precision, "is whether we are being let go by Bane. If we wished to remain at our current positions, could we?"

"Would you still want us, Bane?" Jake asked and that came across so *raw*.

Charles froze in his seat. His expression was one of blankness. Bane felt a twist of pain for him. Charles hadn't just lost *one* son that morning, he'd lost them *all*. Bane *could* tell Steven and Jake that they were done at his companies and had to leave. He could send them back to their father, which might be the kind thing to do for Charles. But it wouldn't be the right thing to do for the young men. Bane thought of the near glowing things their mentors had to say about them. How they *could be*, given time, really powerful forces for good.

He tented his fingers together in front of him. "If you *wish* to remain, you may. But you would be retained only with good reviews just like any other employee of mine. You *wouldn't* get preferential treatment."

Jake's eyes lit up. He was grinning. "We wouldn't have it any other way! We don't need special consideration, do we, Steven?"

Steven shook his head, a faint smile on his lips, too. "There would be no satisfaction if we haven't earned our places."

"Boys," Charles' voice was full of uncertain laughter as if his two eldest sons were pulling a not-too-funny joke on him. "I'm not sure you're *understanding* things here. We're *free* of the deal. All of us. We have the company and all of us are free to go back to the way things *were*."

Those words seemed to land with an almost audible *thunk*. The smiles on both young men's faces seemed to shrivel up like flowers in the Sahara. Again, they looked at one another and it was Jake who spoke again first.

"Dad ..." Jake swallowed and his voice became unusually gentle, "Steven and I are really learning a lot. I mean ... we've learned a ton from *you* and that's been great! Totally great." But Jake's tone seemed to indicate that it had been anything but great. "We just have this chance to learn from some of the best -- *other best* -- people and up our A game."

"You've always taught us to continue to learn and evolve." Steven set his glasses upon his face and pushed them up his nose with one finger. "Working for Bane is exposing us to a lot of new ideas."

"Really cool ideas," Jake's enthusiasm broke through before he quickly tamped it down again.

"You didn't want to work for him before. You were furious with Nick that he was endangering us getting the company back by dating Bane," Charles reminded him.

Jake lowered his head. "Yeah, I know, I acted like a jerk. But it was only because I thought the choice wasn't working for Bane or working for you. It was out on the streets or working for you."

Silence fell *again*. Bane tried not to look at any of the people in the room. He especially did not want to look at Charles. He felt as if he had stolen the man's sons away. He knew that wasn't true. Charles had made choices that had lead to this moment. The spirit was awake now and urged him to look at everyone. It especially wanted to see if Charles was all right. This was their mate's father. The spirit was worried for him.

Charles was utterly still. So still that Bane worried he wasn't breathing. But then, in a burst of motion, Charles pushed himself up from his chair. He was *smiling*. The smile was broad and looked happy. But it wasn't. His eyes were *dead*. He extended a hand towards Bane. Bane rose up from the desk and took it though he really despised shaking hands. But the spirit was even *more* concerned than before. They shook and Charles' handshake was as strong as ever.

"I must say, Bane, though I can never say I *like* losing, there's no shame in having lost to you," Charles said. His expression crumpled for one second before he forced the professional mask back in place. "Do take care of my sons, won't you? They're ... good boys. They deserve the best."

"Dad, we're not leaving *you*," Jake began, but Charles only flashed him a smile.

Steven added, "Father, really, we just want to learn more to bring back --"

"Steven, Jake, don't make promises just to *please* me. You should be doing what's right to please yourselves," Charles told them gently. "I'm proud of you."

"Dad, we've come to take you home --"

Charles waved Jake off. "Don't worry. I can find my own way. You boys should get back to your offices. You've got work to do."

Then with a nod, Charles left the office.

"Did we do the right thing?" Jake asked both Steven and Bane. He appeared shaken and Bane saw what he had not allowed himself to see about Jake before: this was a boy who wanted to please his father above all things.

"It was time, Jake. We couldn't go back to how things were. We hated how things were, especially now that we've seen how things *can be*," Steven replied quietly.

"I guess. I just ... I just hope he's okay," Jake said.

Bane did, too. It was only then that he noticed that Charles had left the contract granting him Fairfax International behind. It was still *unsigned*.

CHAPTER NINETEEN - CHOSEN

Nick stretched out his legs and put his book down in his lap He was lying on the porch's couch reading - or really *pretending* to read - for a few hours. He'd cocooned himself here since Bane had picked Jade and him up and driven them back to Moon Shadow. Jade was with Omar by the grill. They were talking and laughing quietly together. It was going to be a night of yogurt-marinated lamb skewers with a cool cucumber and mint salad along with fresh pitas glistening with butter and garlic. Bane had gone inside to get them icy cold glasses of white wine.

They were all back together again. The household felt complete. The roses glowed in the early evening sunlight. Their colors deepened in the golden-orange light. Their scent sweetly perfumed the air as faint breezes circulated it onto the porch. It looked to be shaping up to another wonderful evening.

Yet Nick was not happy.

He couldn't forget what his brothers had said to him. He couldn't erase his father's devastated expression as he'd told him off and abandoned him in Bane's office. He worried now that he had been too harsh, too cruel. What his father and brothers had done over the years *wasn't* right, but did that mean he had to respond in kind? And

Jake and Steven had valid points that he hadn't reached out to them either after the deal was made.

While his part of the deal had been doing menial labor for Bane, theirs was tough too. He hadn't called them and told them what Bane expected of them or given them any insider information to make their jobs any easier. He'd thought only of himself and acted like it was his *family's* mess, but not his. Serving Bane would *soothe* his conscience so that he could then abandon them all and go on his way. To put it simply, he was dissatisfied with his own behavior. He worried that his reasons for taking the deal were very one-sided.

He heard the tinkle of ice cubes in the ice bucket and the chime of glassware as Bane approached the back door. Bane was *talking* though, too.

"So he's in his study, Jake?" Bane asked.

Nick straightened up. Bane was talking to *Jake?* Bane had told him that his brothers had asked to stay on with his companies and he'd agreed, but Nick hadn't considered that Jake or Steven would *call* Bane or that Bane would sound like a *person* rather than a gruff boss with his brothers. He realized how stupid that was as soon as he identified his slight feeling of jealousy. He should be *glad* that Jake felt comfortable enough to call Bane.

There had been a pause and then Bane said, "Well, do tell me if ... well, tell me how he's doing, won't you? If you and Steven need to take some time off from work to be with him ..." There was another pause as Jake must have replied. Bane's tone was gentle and almost fatherly as he said, "You and Steven are *excellent* workers, but it's important to me that you don't sacrifice your personal lives for work. There must be a *balance* and this is a ... *difficult* time. Do whatever you need to do and don't worry about anything else."

Another pause and then Bane's said, "Take care, Jake. I'll talk to you soon."

Bane came out of the house then, shouldering the door open. His hands were full with an ice bucket, a bottle of Pinot Grigio and four glasses. Nick jumped up to help him. He took the bucket and wine bottle out of Bane's hands, setting them down on the table while Bane arranged the glasses. Bane then pulled of the bluetooth headpiece and stuck it in his pocket.

Nick found his mouth suddenly dry as dust as he asked, "Was that Jake? My brother Jake, right?"

Bane nodded as he cut through the foil at the wine's top and started to pull the cork out. "Yes, I asked him to give me a call to see how Charles was doing."

Nick swallowed. "It's been a hard day for Dad. First, me leaving and now Steven and Jake telling him they want to work with you. That means he's ... *alone.*"

Nick could imagine his father right at that moment, sitting in the study with its dark wood paneling and shelves of books, with a bottle of whisky and one of those heavy cut-crystal glasses in front of him. His father's tie would be tugged down and his suit coat would be tossed negligently over the arm of the sofa. His father would look rumpled and red-eyed. That's how he had been after their mother's death.

But I'm not dead! Neither are Steven or Jake, but we might as well be if we're not in Fairfax International. Maybe I'm wrong. Maybe Dad's perfectly fine. Happy that he's rid of us.

Bane's head lifted and those intense Siberian blue eyes were upon him. "Nick, what's happening to your father right now is *not* your fault."

So it was bad. He was right that there was the whisky and undone tie.

Nick sagged down onto the couch. "How can it not be? I'm the one who told him to shove off. Losing Steven and Jake though probably was more of a loss, but still ... I started the ball rolling."

Bane offered him a glass of wine. Already, the chilled liquid had formed condensation on the outside of the glass. Nick's fingers drew absent-minded designs in it. Bane sank down on the couch beside him, sliding an arm around his shoulders. Nick leaned against the much bigger body.

"This breakdown of your relationship didn't happen in a day, a month, a year or even a decade," Bane said quietly. "It built up over time to the point where you had to say: stop. You were right to say it. He was proud that you had stood up for yourself not just to him, but to me as well."

Nick nodded his head miserably. Bane had related all that had taken place after Nick had left the office. Bane had been reluctant to do so at first, not wanting to cause him further pain, but Nick had needed to hear every word. It still surprised him how many of them were *positive* about him. They were things he'd wished his father had told him himself.

Bane continued, "I do not wish to say that we reap what we sow for I fear I do not deserve even a fraction of what I have. But your father demanded certain things of all of you and you gave him what he wanted for a long time. Now though, the three of you need to make your own way in the world. Hopefully, he will come to see that as a good thing rather than a loss for himself."

Nick nodded again though he said, "You do know it's *Dad* we're talking about here? He doesn't really see benefits for others as benefiting himself."

Bane paused and there was a thoughtful expression on his face as he finally said, "Maybe he can *change*. I did. You did. Even your brothers have."

"Yeah, maybe." Nick took a large swallow of wine. He had a feeling he would be needing a lot of alcohol for the foreseeable future.

"Speaking of your brothers, I thought that it might be nice to have them over for dinner at some point," Bane suggested tentatively. "But only if you were agreeable to this."

Nick's eyebrows rose. "I -- I guess it would be okay. Yeah, of course it would."

Bane smiled. "As different as they are from you, I can see parts of you in them, too."

Nick tried to picture his brothers here. Jake would be leaning against the porch railing with a beer in one hand. Steven would have a gin and tonic with lime and be seated primly on one of the chairs. He'd be looking out with approval on the garden. Jake would think the house was "pretty all right". They'd love Omar's cooking. Everyone did. Maybe such a night would be a *good* thing.

"How *is* Dad exactly?" Nick asked.

"He is in his study. Thinking. They've knocked and gone in several times. He seems ... all right. They'll keep me informed," Bane told him.

Another nod from Nick. He was beginning to feel a bit like a bobble-head doll with all this nodding. He finished his wine. Bane refilled his glass. Casting a quick glance towards Omar and Jade, to make sure that they weren't listening in, he cast his voice low, "I didn't tell Jade about ... about *you* and the *spirit*."

Bane's gaze flickered over to her. "I supposed not, since she wasn't asking me a million questions about the spirit or asking me if you were mentally ill."

Nick snorted. "Yeah, totally."

Bane's hand ran up and down his spine. "You *do* want her to know, do you not?"

Nick looked up swiftly. "I *do*, but this is *your* secret. And if you don't want her to know then I'll make that work."

Bane's gaze flickered over to Jade. He smiled after observing her and Omar teasing each other about who got to turn the lamb skewers next. "I want her to know. She is part of our chosen family."

Nick couldn't help the smile that crossed his face. He was so glad that Bane felt that way. "I think so, too."

"We'll show her another day," Bane suggested as he urged Nick to lean back into his arms. "Today has had enough drama."

Nick totally agreed as he snuggled against the far larger body. Bane's scent wrapped around him as he rested his head against that broad shoulder. This was the place *he* belonged. And so long as he had his chosen family around him, everything else would work out. Somehow.

***

The meal was spectacular as always and there was literally nothing left of the lamb, pita or salad.

Jade patted her rounded belly. "I have a food baby in here! That meal was *so good*, Omar!"

The Indian man dabbed his lips with the napkin. "I have to agree. I am quite satiated."

"Just when I think you can't make another dish that's better than the last one, you make me a liar," Nick joked.

"Superb meal, Omar," Bane praised.

Omar beamed. "Nothing makes me so happy as seeing a well-fed group of friends."

The Indian man immediately though was rising up and picking up their plates. Nick jumped to his feet - a little more slowly than normal, as he, too, felt like he had a "food baby" - to assist.

"Do not worry yourselves! I need to clean up in order to burn off some of this lamb," Omar told them.

But the group insisted on at least taking the plates and dishes inside for him. Omar then shooed them out of his domain. Jade yawned meaningfully and said she was going to turn in early. Nick and Bane bid her goodnight and headed back out on the porch. Nick was about to sit down on the sofa when Bane tugged him up again.

"The spirit needs a run. What do you say? Up for a night romp?" Bane grinned as he used the word "romp" considering that had terrified him before.

"Absolutely!" Nick enthused.

"I have a different place I want to shift. Not the clearing this time, but by the wheat fields," Bane said.

"Wherever you want," Nick agreed.

The two of them set off, hand in hand, into the night. The moonlight was *brilliant*. The night insects whirred all around them as they walked through the long grass until they were about five hundred feet from Moon Shadow. Bane brought him in for a soft kiss. The big man's hands cupped Nick's face so tenderly that it almost *hurt* with the intensity of caring behind it. Nick was loathe to let him go when they finally broke apart. But finally they parted and he helped Bane undress, revealing every inch of that magnificent physique.

Once he was completely bare, Bane stepped away from him.

Nick's heart thudded heavily in his chest. The big man stared at him for long moments. The moon shone down brightly on his naked chest. Bane's head tilted back and his eyes closed.

Wisps of mist appeared almost immediately unlike before. They floated between the stalks of grain and flowed over the grass towards Bane. Nick's lips parted. The shift was beautiful to watch.

Nick held his breath as the mist reached Bane's feet. Bane's eyelids remained closed, his face remained tilted up towards the moon. The mist swirled up over Bane's ankles then calves then knees and thighs. It wrapped around the big man like a silken cloak. It was up over his pectorals and then his neck. All Nick could see then was Bane's beautiful face. He trembled as the mist flowed over the top of Bane's head, covering him completely.

Nick waited.

And waited.

The tower of mist glittered and then ... it collapsed. Nick scanned the area. The fallen mist obscured his view. Where were Bane and the spirit? For one frightening moment, Nick worried that both had simply turned into the mist and disappeared altogether. He waved a hand in the air, trying to see. Suddenly, a figure lunged for him from out of the mist. Nick fell back with an oomph of surprise. Then the tiger was on top of him, licking his face eagerly and nosing his chest.

"Hey! There you are!" Nick wrapped his arms around the tiger's furry neck. He buried his face in the soft, silky fur. "I missed you! Did you miss me?"

The tiger tossed its head and snorted, which was clearly a yes. Nick really didn't need anything other than to look into those eyes to know he was adored. He could *feel* Bane and the spirit behind them.

He rested his forehead against the tiger's and said solemnly, "I love you. I love you both."

The tiger licked him tenderly and he scratched behind the great beast's ears. He could have sworn he heard a rumbly purr from the big cat even though tigers were incapable of purring. Just for fun, he kissed the black, wet nose. There was no fear about being close to the tiger's very sharp teeth. He was completely safe.

Nick urged the tiger to let him up. "Come on, fur face, we need to go play. Whatever you want to do, we'll do. Tonight is your night."

The tiger let him up and then danced a few feet away, tail up and eyes wide. Nick couldn't help but laugh at the eager movements. He thought Bane was exaggerating when he had described the tiger doing that in his chest, but it was an accurate description of the tiger's cross-footed movements. Those bright blue eyes gazed into his and the tail whipped back and forth.

"Where do you want to go?" Nick asked.

The tiger glanced towards the waving waves of grain. It was clear that it wanted them to run through the field together. Nick took off towards the golden plants. The tiger immediately ran alongside him. The sleek muscles in the tiger's body covered by white fur with black stripes were a miracle to watch. Such a perfect being. The tiger looked up at him and there was such *joy* in the look.

Bane, you did this. You've done something beautiful, miraculous. You're not cursed any longer.

Nick threw his arms into the air and let out a whoop of pleasure as they raced through the field, both of them carving twin trails through the crop. They ran figure eights around one another. The tiger playfully nipped at his heels. Nick couldn't help but laugh when the tiger managed to lick the back of one of his calves. For his part, Nick took great pleasure in catching the tip of the tiger's tail. They zoomed around until Nick had to stop. There was a stitch in his side and he was breathing hard.

They both slowed down to a walk then stopped. He leaned forward, hands on his thighs, and took in long, deep breaths even as his heart rapidly beat in his chest. The tiger nosed his face and licked his cheek. Nick laughed and petted the huge head.

"You're still ready and raring to go, aren't you? Just give me a minute and we can run again." He scratched behind the two white ears. The tiger half closed its eyes in pleasure as Nick continued to pet it. Finally, when his breathing evened out and his heart rate was back to normal, he stood up and patted the tiger one last time before saying, "All right, let's go!"

They raced off again, dashing through the grain and heading towards the line of trees. They slowed again as the trees closed around them. Nick let out a wheeze.

"I'm going to have to get in better shape to keep up with you," Nick confessed as he wiped the sweat off of his forehead with the sleeve of his T-shirt.

The tiger let out a kitty sneeze that sounded a lot like laughter. It gave Nick an amused look. Nick swatted the tiger's right haunch with affection. The tail playfully whapped against Nick's butt.

"So you want to swat me out of a tree again? Is that why we're here?" Nick asked as they went deeper into the woods.

The trunks were like dark sentinels, but they weren't frightening even though only a few stray beams of moonlight came down through the thick canopy. Nick was careful to follow the tiger's footsteps as it unerringly avoided the roots and rocks that jutted up from the ground. The air was redolent with the smell of green, growing things. Nick filled his lungs with it.

"I wonder do you like the night or day better? Are tigers nocturnal? And which season do you like best?" Nick asked the questions in quick succession. "Imagine when winter comes and we're romping in the snow!"

The tiger's tail whipped eagerly. Clearly, it wanted to romp in the snow, too. Then Nick thought of being with Bane in the snow in his human form. He imagined urging the older man to go sledding or skiing. He thought of them walking arm in arm in Winter Haven's high street as fat flakes of snow drifted down around them. There would be kissing under mistletoe. Their mouths would taste of hot chocolate and whisky.

Yet there was so much to look forward to before then. There was still a ton of summer left. Plenty of BBQs and warm nights sipping margaritas, talking of everything and nothing, and then kissing until their mouths ached, as the moon rose in the sky.

Life is good. I know that things are difficult with my family right now, but I believe they will work out. He watched as the tiger went to one of the largest trees near them. *Bane and the spirit deserve happiness. I want to give it to them.*

The tiger looked up at the tree eagerly and then glanced with the same eagerness at Nick.

"What's up? What do you want here?" Nick walked over to the large tree.

The tiger crouched down. Its butt waggled and with a burst of power that stunned Nick, the big cat leaped over ten feet into the air. Its front paws wrapped around the tree's trunk while its back claws extended and dug into the bark. There was a scraping sound and huge chunks of bark flew off. The tiger then climbed to the first bough and looked down at Nick expectantly again. Its blue eyes gleamed with night shine.

"You want me to get up *there* with you?" He heard the snort confirming that he was to get his butt up there. "All right. Hold on. I'll see what I can do. But you better be able to get down. We can't very well call the fire department for you. You're too heavy to carry even by burly firemen."

Nick was able to use a few branches as handholds and hoisted himself up onto the bough where the tiger was sprawled out. The tiger's paws hung over the edges with the thick branch resting underneath its bulk. It was then that Nick realized that there was a hole in the canopy directly ahead of them that allowed them to see the field. The wheat field was silvered by the large moon. The stars studded the deep black sky.

"Wow, it's beautiful," Nick breathed. "Don't you think?"

The tiger looked over its shoulder towards him and its tail wagged. Nick could almost feel it saying, "See? Wasn't the climb worth it? Even if climbing up here made you sound like an old man?"

"Totally worth it," Nick agreed.

He rested his head on the tiger's furry back, relishing the thump of its heart. So alive. So strong. So miraculous.

He wasn't sure how long they remained like that. It could have been hours. The tiger's tail slowly wagged with contentment. The steady thump of the tiger's heart was like a lullaby. Nick's eyes half closed and he started to slip towards sleep. The moment was only broken when he heard the tiger's stomach rumble. Nick sat up and laughed. He petted the tiger's back, running his fingers through the thick, soft fur.

"Hungry again? A few lamb skewers isn't enough for you, is it? How about we head back to Moon Shadow to get you some tiger-sized portions? I'm betting Omar has a great big haunch of beef for you. Like a *huge* haunch." He had extended his hands wide to demonstrate the size of this haunch. The tiger's eyes grew wide, too, and its tail whapped harder. Nick laughed. "Don't worry though. After you eat, poop then snooze, we'll head out again to play. We have the whole night together. And tomorrow and the day after that and the day after that."

The tiger's eyelids opened and closed slowly, telling Nick that he was loved and adored by the spirit as much as Bane.

"I love you, too," Nick repeated and kissed the tiger's back.

Nick threw one leg over the branch and lowered himself down. He held onto the branch, unfurling his body fully, and then dropped the last few feet to the ground. He let out a faint oomph when he landed. The tiger lightly landed beside him and nosed Nick affectionately.

"Do you want to run back?" Nick really hoped that it didn't. He was still a little breathless from their earlier romping.

The tiger snorted and shook its massive head. They passed out of the forest and wandered back into the waving fields of grain. They walked side by side. The graceful, silent tread of the tiger made Nick a bit jealous. His feet *crunched* with every step.

He could see Moon Shadow's roof a bit over a mile and half away. If they walked through the field, it would take longer to get there than if they used one of the roads for the tractors. One of those roads was about twenty feet away. Nick debated whether it would be safe for them to be out in the open like that. But there was no one around. It was night. Who would see them? It would be fine.

"Come on, let's take the road. It'll be quicker. I can *hear* your belly grumbling from here," Nick said with a laugh.

The tiger surged forward. They both veered towards the road.

Nick had a momentary qualm as they stepped out from screen of the wheat and into the open. They really were alone though. After five minutes of walking, unmolested, his shoulders relaxed. The wind picked up behind them. The tiger roamed about ten feet ahead. Nick picked up his step as well. He couldn't wait to get back to Moon Shadow.

At that moment, a black shape rose up from the wheat on their left. There was a hoarse cry of triumph as a blurry-sounding voice shouted, "I knew it! I knew it! A *tiger*! A *bloody* tiger! That's what's been eating all of my sheep!"

Nick blanched as he realized the black shape was really a man and that man was seeing the tiger clear as day. The voice tugged at his memory, too. He had heard it before. When? How?

And then he knew.

It was his first day at Moon Shadow. There had been an irate farmer at the door accusing Bane of having exotic predators that were killing his sheep. He threatened that he would shoot whatever it was, but Nick had forgotten all about him and his threats. And clearly, Bane and the spirit had, too. Maybe neither of them had taken the threat seriously. All of this went through Nick's mind in half a moment.

Then the farmer was lifting up a stick. A stick that *glinted* in the moonlight. He shouted, "Now I'll have something to mount on my damned wall! Proof that Mr. Holier-Than-Thou Bane Dunsaney killed my animals!"

The stick was actually a *shotgun*. Nick froze. He heard the tiger growl. The shotgun was aimed at the tiger's head. The tiger prepared to pounce. But Nick *knew* that the tiger would be shot well before it reached the farmer.

"NO! DON'T SHOOT HIM!" Nick screamed.

He stepped between the tiger and the farmer.

The air was ripped apart by an explosion.

And all the world went black.

CHAPTER TWENTY - LIVING AND DYING

Bane smelled blood. He smelled it over the smoky scent of cordite from the shotgun, over the stench of alcohol and body odor emanating from the farmer, and over the dry, whispery scent of the wheat that surrounded them.

It wasn't just blood, it was *Nick's* blood. The young man's individual scent mixed with the raw, coppery stink. It was a unique smell that he would never forget. Nick's blood in his nose. Nick's blood causing his whiskers to quiver, not with desire - thank God, *no* - but with agony even before he knew anything else.

He smelled Nick's blood half a second after the shotgun boomed. The reverberations of that two-barreled blast cracked through the night. The sound echoed again and again. His sensitive ears were stunned with it. His human understanding was also stunned by it. He hoped - though he smelled the blood, Nick's blood - that the young man was fine.

Must be fine.

Surely, just a few stray pieces of buckshot had hit Nick.

Maybe a few on his side.

Maybe one or two had hit his arm.

The shot must have gone wide.

It must have.

That's what his stunned human mind told him.

But the spirit knew better. The spirit knew that sound intimately. The spirit knew that sound meant *death*. After all, had not Bane shot the spirit long ago and had not the death of the spirit's physical body followed soon after?

Bane tried not to listen to this reasoning. But his disbelief almost immediately began to peel away in layers within even less time than it had taken for the blood smell to fill his nostrils after the shotgun blast.

Because Nick fell.

One moment, Nick was standing tall between Bane and the farmer - *Brennan, the bastard's name is Brennan*. And the next, Nick was *crumpled* on the ground.

Bane felt as if the whole scene was a badly done cartoon. Surely there should be more frames between *up* then *down* in reality. But there hadn't been. So this couldn't be real. If it wasn't realistic enough for a cartoon then it certainly couldn't be happening in real life.

Nick didn't scream or yell. He simply *gasped*. One gasp and that was it. A puff of dust had risen around his body when he had landed. And then stillness.

"Oh, God, no!" Mr. Brennan yelled. His pudgy face with its oversized nose, veined from too much drinking, looked stricken under the wash of silver moonlight. "I didn't mean -- my God -- the boy! I didn't -- I didn't mean -- I meant to shoot the *tiger*! Not the boy! *The tiger!*"

Bane roared. It was a sound that would have chilled even his stout heart as a hunter. Brennan's sputtering pathetic denials froze in his throat. At that moment, Bane's humanity disappeared and he just wanted to bite and tear and *hurt*. He roared again. Brennan screamed, high and shrill. His rheumy eyes were wide in terror. He tried to raise the shotgun back up, but Bane leaped towards him and swiped it out of his hands with ease. It fell into the waving wheat and was lost from view. Brennan continued to scream.

The farmer was backing away from him now. His arms were

flailing wildly in front of him as if those puny meat-sticks could do anything against a tiger. Bane's teeth were inches long and sharp as blades. His claws could slice all the flesh from that corpulent body in seconds. The drunk farmer tripped and fell down. The wheat was crushed by his bulk as he let out a terror-soaked yip. Brennan flailed and more wheat stalks bent. The farmer was like a turtle on his back.

Bane stalked over to him and placed a paw on the direct center of Brennan's chest. The farmer wailed, but his frantic struggling stopped as if he thought being *very* still might save him. Bane leaned down and looked into the farmer's bloodshot eyes. His Siberian blue ones did not blink.

"You -- you're not -- not a *tiger*. You're not *just* a tiger! What are you?" Brennan breathed.

How odd that this man - this incredibly unimaginative man - should know the truth so easily! But this was a fleeting thought.

"I didn't mean it," the farmer babbled. His voice was low. A rushing of water over rocks. "I didn't mean to hurt the boy!"

Bane growled and the farmer blanched. Talk of Nick by this creature was unacceptable! Bane leaned down further. His mouth was a mere inch from the farmer's throat. His jaws opened. Cool night air dried the saliva on his fangs.

"We need to get him to a hospital!" the farmer cried.

The smell of Nick's blood was blown to him on the wind. The scent was stronger now and that made Bane ... *pause.*

Hospital? It was the spirit who spoke. *Hospital? We must take Nick there!*

"I can get your -- your *friend* to the hospital! There's still hope! He could be okay! With a doctor's help, he could be all right! But if you kill me I can't do that! Your friend will die!" the farmer wailed.

Hospital ... Nick ... bleeding ... so much blood ... dying, dying, dying ... what am I doing?

The mist came.

What had been so hard to do that first time, to shift and let his humanity come or go, was effortless now. Ironically, it was the spirit that made the shift possible. The spirit forced them back into a human form. Bane was still too enraged, too in shock, too much *everything* to have control of himself. The spirit though reached for the human form that had never been its before but now was and instead of a tiger on top of Mr. Brennan, it was a naked Bane. But his mouth was still open. He was still growling. He still wanted to rip out the farmer's throat.

Nick ... hospital, the spirit insisted. The irony that the spirit was more in control than he was would be lost on Bane until much later.

We have no phone. No way of contacting anyone. It will take too long for me to run to Omar and then get him out here. We need a way to get Nick to the hospital now. Bane's adroit mind kicked in seeing the problems logically, coldly and clearly.

When the mist cleared and Mr. Brennan saw who it was pinning him to the ground, his mouth opened and shut repeatedly. He actually looked on the verge of having a heart attack. He blinked. Bane drew back and his gaze again met the farmer's.

Bane's voice was raspy and the words felt alien on his tongue as he said, "Your *truck*, where is it?"

He knew that Mr. Brennan would not have walked all the way here from his farm. He would have driven and he wouldn't have gone far from the comfy cab and his stash of alcohol to hunt tigers. The farmer pointed a shaking hand past him. Bane remembered a small dirt road in that direction.

"Mr. Brennan," Bane breathed even as every cell inside of him wanted to get to Nick. "You will tell *no one* of what you saw tonight. You will *never* speak of what happened here. You will *sell* me your farm. You will *leave* this area and *never* return. You will leave *tonight* after you take us to the hospital. Do you understand?"

The farmer nodded and dug his keys out of his pocket. He offered them to Bane. "Take them. Take the truck, too. It's yours. I don't need it."

"I will *know* if you betray your promise," Bane threatened as he took the keys.

Bane didn't wait to see Brennan nod mutely again. He knew the farmer would keep his word. Bane would *ensure* that the farmer got enough money that he could drink himself into an *oblivion* somewhere far away. Bane immediately forgot about him as he went back to Nick. He vaguely heard the farmer running away as fast as his stubby legs would take him.

The smell of blood, Nick's blood, was terribly strong even to his human nostrils. He was out of the wheat and back on the road. Nick was still lying there. Face down. He had not moved.

No ...

Bane felt numb. If Nick was dead ... No! NO! He would not think it. It could not be!

Mate, the spirit mewled.

Bane went down on his knees. The ground was dry and dusty beneath him. His hands hovered above Nick's unmoving shoulders.

Nick is alive. He must be alive.

Bane reached down and turned Nick over, tenderly, *gently*, not wanting to cause more damage. The entire front of Nick's t-shirt was sticky with blood. The buckshot had hit his stomach and right side.

Nick's eyes were closed. His lips were parted. His skin looked gray.

Bane shuddered. Rage and pain so great rose up into him that he wasn't able to breathe.

Nick ... hospital, the spirit moaned even as it wanted to nose and lick the hurt.

But Bane was frozen until he saw the shuddering rise and fall of Nick's chest. Then he was *galvanized.* He gathered Nick into his arms.

He thought he heard a moan from the young man and murmured, "I'm sorry, I'm sorry! I have to lift you, my love. The ambulance will take too long to get here. I need to get you to the hospital."

Bane ran with Nick tucked against him in the direction of the farmer's truck. He tried not to jar the young man in his arms, but there was only so much that he could do. Nick's moans though meant he was still alive and that was something.

He found the old pickup sitting underneath the branches of a large tree. He wrenched open the passenger side door and gently laid Nick on the seat. He hurried over to the driver's seat and slid inside.

His hands were sticky with drying blood as he fumbled to get the car keys inside the ignition. Finally, the key slid home and the truck's powerful engine growled to life. He slammed the gear shift into drive and jammed a foot on the gas. The truck jerked and started plowing forward straight into the field of wheat. Bane cranked the wheel hard to the right and did a u-turn. One of the head lamps was out, but the moon was high and bright, illuminating the road in front of them. Bane barrelled down the narrow, rutted path not even slowing when the path emptied out onto the two lane highway. The back end of the truck fishtailed behind him as he took the turn to the left at full speed.

He headed towards Winter Haven Memorial as it was the nearest hospital. As he raced down the road, he turned to look at Nick's still unconscious form. He reached and touched the young man's wan cheek, sliding his fingers down to his pulse point. Nick's heartbeat was still there though it was thready and uneven. Terror pounded through Bane until he thought he might vomit.

If Nick dies ... He finally said the word. It was conjured out of his agony. *I will destroy myself.*

The spirit did not respond. It was watching Nick through his eyes. The spirit's grief was the same as his. This loss would be just too much.

The ride into the city seemed both eternal and short. Bane couldn't remember most of it. All he could recall was the scent of Nick's blood and the faint beating of the young man's heart. There were moments when Nick's heart didn't seem to beat at all and Bane had nearly screamed with anguish. But then the soft beating returned. He lived on a razor's edge of that thin hope.

He pulled right in front of the ER doors and came to a screeching halt. He was screaming about Nick being shot before he even got out of the cab. Nurses and doctors swarmed the truck. One of them was an African-American woman in her mid-forties. Her hair was salt and pepper, cut short and she had thick-rimmed dark glasses on. She grasped his arm as he opened the door to the passenger side and Nick.

He whirled around to shake her off, but one look into her steady brown eyes stopped him.

"They have him," she said. Her name tag said: Thandie Anderson, RN. "Are you injured?"

Her hands went over his chest, which was streaked with Nick's blood.

"The blood's not mine," he said, pushing her hands away. "It's Nick's."

She looked uncertain that he really was all right, but she said, "Tell me what happened."

"Shot. Someone shot him. My Nick," Bane's voice was tremulous. He was shaking so hard that his teeth were chattering together. He kept looking over his shoulder at the truck where half a dozen health care professionals were lifting Nick's limp form from the passenger compartment.

Nurse Anderson touched his arm again to focus him on her. "He's in the best hands. What did they shoot him with?"

"Shot --shotgun," he said.

"What is Nick's full name?" she asked.

They had Nick on a gurney now and were wheeling him inside. "Nicholas Fairfax."

"And your name?"

"Bane," he said. "Bane Dunsaney."

"Come let's get you inside and cleaned up," she said. "And maybe some clothes?"

The last she said more as a question. He looked down and realized he was nude. He had forgotten.

"But Nick --"

"They are going to take him into surgery. You can't do anything more," she told him. "We need to take care of you now."

"I don't need anything."

"Let's see, shall we?" Though she was half his size, she led him into the hospital as if he were a child.

Bane hardly noticed the people staring at his nudity in the waiting room. They paused in their own pain to gape at his. He was numb. His eyes were fixed on the gurney that Nick was on. Nick was surrounded by nurses and doctors. A set of double doors automatically opened for them. All too soon Nick was through them and they closed behind him, shutting off Bane's view.

Nurse Anderson led him into a curtained area where she insisted on checking him for wounds. She sponged off the blood while he sat on the edge of a bed without moving. He was frozen again. His mind wasn't working. The spirit was hiding its face in its paws. Both of them were deep in grief. That grief though wouldn't crest unless and until they knew that there was no hope for Nick.

He lost so much blood ...

He was unconscious ...

Did I hurt him more by moving him?

Should I have run to get Omar? OMAR!

"I need a phone!" Bane suddenly cried and nearly leaped from the bed, but Nurse Anderson kept him in place.

"There's one right here, but why don't we wait until --"

"No! NOW! Please," he softened his voice.

She reluctantly gave him a phone. It was a land line. He dialed Omar's number. The nurse stood there for a moment, but when he gave her a meaningful look she walked away, closing the curtain around him to give him some privacy. The phone was answered almost immediately even though it was near 2 am.

"Hello?" the Indian man's voice was blurry with sleep.

"Omar!"

"Bane? What's wrong?" Immediately, Omar sounded crisp and fully awake.

"I'm at Winter Haven Memorial with Nick," he said. He closed his eyes tightly. He couldn't believe he was saying this. He couldn't believe that this perfect night had become a complete and utter nightmare.

"What happened?" He knew that Omar was likely thinking that Bane in his tiger form had harmed Nick.

Bane almost laughed. It would have been hysterical laughter and if he had started he would not have been able to stop. "Nick was shot by Brennan. That damned farmer whose sheep I ... well, who lost those sheep." His hand tightened on the phone until the plastic creaked.

"No! How could he?!"

"Brennan's been dealt with or will be. We're at the hospital," he repeated. "They took Nick away on a gurney. He lost so much blood, Omar."

"Are you injured?"

"No, I'm *fine*. Nick jumped in front of *me*," his voice was threaded with agony.

"Of course, he did," Omar said and Bane could almost hear the nod.

"Nick's in surgery now, I think. They've told me *nothing*," Bane's voice rose with panic, but he swallowed it down.

"Jade and I will be there immediately," Omar answered and Bane heard a rustling. He imagined that Omar was pulling on clothes.

"Nick's father and brothers have to be called, too," Bane said and his stomach clenched. He'd been worried about Charles' mental state already that day. He'd really feared the man might harm himself from the loss of all three sons. And now *this*. But as long as there was life there was *hope*. Yet there might not be *life* any longer.

And it is MY fault that Nick has been injured! I put him in danger! Bane cried.

My fault. Sheep, the spirit lamented.

No, no, not your fault. Never. You were doing what was natural for you. I kept you -- you restrained. If I hadn't --

Nick must live, the spirit said.

Yes, he must. No matter what.

"I will inform them, Bane. Do not worry yourself. All will be taken care of," Omar assured him, his voice brisk and efficient. He was in his working mode which would allow him to function even in the face of this.

"Thank you, Omar. I -- I don't know what I would do without you ..." Bane's voice drifted off.

"No need for thanks. Jade and I will be there shortly," Omar said. There was a click and the Indian man was gone.

At that moment, Nurse Anderson opened the curtain and came in. She was carrying a set of large blue scrubs. She handed them to him along with a pair of slippers.

"Thank you," Bane said. "Any word yet?"

"He's in surgery with Dr. Vostok. She's the best," she assured him. She put a clipboard on the bed. It was paperwork for Nick's admission. "I know this is the last thing you wish to do, but --"

"It's fine." Bane was grateful for something to occupy his mind as he waited for news.

"Nick is your partner?" she asked, her voice and face expressing sympathy.

Partner? That sounded so dry and unfeeling. Nick was his *mate*. But he knew what she meant.

"Yes," he said. He started donning the scrubs as she turned and left him. Once dressed, he picked up the clipboard and began to fill out the forms, shocked at how much he did not know about Nick's medical history.

I will change that. I will ensure that ... All of his promises were based on Nick surviving. The spirit moaned softly.

Nurse Anderson came back to take the clipboard. She had no news. All he could do was sit and wait and *pray*.

Like the car ride Bane didn't know how long he was like that. He only stirred when Omar's gentle voice said his name and the Indian man stroked his shoulder. He immediately rose and drew Omar into a hug. The Indian man hugged him fiercely back. He saw Jade over Omar's shoulder. Her eyes were already red with tears and her hands were gripped in front of her chest. He reached for her and they linked hands even as he didn't let Omar go.

"My fault. My fault. My fault," Bane realized he was repeating over and over again.

Omar stroked his back. "No, no, it is not, Bane. It is the man who shot Nick's fault. That terrible Mr. Brennan. Not yours."

"But, I --"

"No. Enough now," Omar said firmly. "Mr. Fairfax and his sons are in the waiting room already. If you are well enough we should go join them so that this bed is open for other injured people."

"Yes, yes, of course." It would be Omar who would think of this while he let his misery blind him to other's suffering yet again.

Omar and Jade both took one of his hands and led him out of the curtained space and towards the waiting room.

"Have they said *anything* about Nick's condition?" Jade asked, her voice threaded with tears.

He shook his head. "I do not think that is a -- a good sign."

"Do not read anything into that," Omar cautioned them. "They are working hard to save him. They might not have time to say much."

"I brought you clothes," Omar said and Bane realized he was carrying a bag in his other hand, "but I see that you are already dressed."

"The scrubs are fine." Bane's lips felt numb as he spoke.

"Understandable. You are still ... I see that there is blood ..." Omar swallowed.

"It's Nick's. The nurse tried to clean me up, but there is ... so much," Bane responded dully. His skin itched as the blood dried. But he wouldn't touch it. He didn't want to touch it and remember.

They went down a hall and turned into a waiting room. Charles Fairfax was more than rumpled. His hair stood on end and his shirt was soiled. He was pacing. Jake was sitting on one of the uncomfortable plastic chairs. His legs were spread wide. His elbows rested on his knees and he was rubbing his face. Steven was staring at his own reflection in the window. All three of them stiffened when Bane entered. They thought he was the doctor.

Charles spun around to face him then. His face looked gray and pasty. He came to Bane and grasped his hands. This time Bane did not retreat from his touch.

"What happened?" he gasped.

"We were out -- out on my property," Bane said and stopped. He swallowed as all the saliva had left his mouth and lies left his head.

"It was a romantic evening," Omar prompted after the silence stretched out too long. "They were walking in the fields."

"Someone shot Nick," Bane said, omitting Brennan's name.

"Who?" Jake snarled. He was on his feet, his face was flushed with anger. His hands were clenched into fists. He looked ready to go after whoever it was.

"I -- I don't know. There have been animals killed recently on nearby farms. Whoever it was must have thought that we were the cause of it. They must have mistaken us for predators," his voice was soft at the end. "Nick jumped in front of me. He protected me."

Charles' dark brown eyes were bloodshot and immediately filled with tears. His lips trembled. He suddenly spun away from Bane, his shoulders shaking. "That's -- that's my Nick."

"Has the doctor said anything?" Steven pushed up his glasses nervously.

"Not yet," Bane said. "Nick's in surgery. Dr. Vostok is his doctor."

"I have heard of her," Steven said. "She had a write up in the paper. She's quite impressive."

"So Nick's in the best hands?" Charles asked.

Steven nodded.

Charles seemed to become aware of Jade at that moment. He embraced her. "It's so good that you're here, my dear. I know that Nick would want you nearby."

"Of course," she sniffled into his collar. "If there's *anything* I can do, please let me know."

He patted her shoulder gently. "All we can do now is ... wait."

"Let us all sit down," Omar suggested.

Jade and Omar helped Bane into a chair. His legs just didn't want to work. They were there for *hours*. The only thing that happened was when the police came to take Bane's statement. He made his answers vague enough that they wouldn't ever find Brennan and direct enough that they didn't think he was lying. Other than that, he hardly spoke. Omar brought them the terribly bitter coffee from the hospital's cafeteria. No one drank it.

Finally, when dawn was touching the horizon, a Russian woman, her skin as pale as milk, came in. She wore a face mask that had been pulled down around her neck. Her eyes were bright despite the hour. But she was not smiling. Everyone stared at her with such hope. There was little returning hope in her gaze.

"Doctor?" Charles' unctuous voice rose up.

"Nick survived the surgery," Dr. Vostok said and there was an audible sigh in the room. "But ..." Everyone's breath froze. "But he lost a considerable amount of blood and there was severe damage from the buckshot. He has not regained consciousness yet and his vitals are weak. But he is young and clearly has a strong desire to live. The next 24 hours will be crucial though."

Bane hardly absorbed the words. He knew from the tone what the doctor would not say. Nick was only holding on by sheer will alone.

"Can we see him?" Bane asked. Those were the first words he'd said since the police came hours ago.

"Yes, briefly. I warn you though that he is hooked up to many machines and ... well, he looks as seriously ill as he is. But I think it would be good for him to hear your voices," Dr. Vostok said.

"He's conscious?" Jake asked, his expression hopeful.

"No," Dr. Vostok qualified. "But I believe he will be able to hear you on some level."

They were taken by Nurse Anderson to the Intensive Care Unit to Nick's room. Bane allowed the family to go in while he, Omar and Jade stood in the hallway, looking in through the doorway. Nick was surrounded by machines. There were beeps and whines and hisses. He was on a ventilator that was breathing for him. His skin was gray. His eyes were closed. There was a tube going down his throat. The scent of old blood and antiseptic burned Bane's nostrils.

The three Fairfaxes were all around him. Jake was near his feet and he touched Nick's blanketed legs. Steven stood awkwardly at Nick's side and brushed his fingers over the top of one of Nick's hands. Charles leaned down and kissed Nick's forehead. Bane's lips opened and a cry wanted to escape him, but he bit it back.

"Come in," Charles urged them. "He'd want you three most of all."

Jade and Omar went to Nick. She held the young man's hand while Omar petted one of his legs. Bane stumbled to Nick's side by Charles.

"He'll want to hear from you, Bane," Charles said.

Bane lifted a trembling hand to Nick's forehead. It was the only part of his face he could reach. "Nick, please come back to us. We want you back so badly. We love you. *Please.*"

"Nickie, I know I'm the *last* person that you care about being here, but, son, I *love* you. I know that I'm a selfish bastard, but I've *always* loved you." Charles began to break down. He shook with his sobs.

"Dad, Nick knows you love him!" Jake cried.

"He does," Steven seconded.

"And he loves you," Jade said softly.

"M-my s-son. My beautiful boy! It's not right he should be this way! Take me! Why isn't it *me?*" Charles asked.

Bane put a hand on his back to comfort him. He felt Charles' agony through the heaving of his body. He kept his other hand on Nick's forehead. The young man felt cold and clammy. He had been so alive earlier that evening. So alive ... and now this ...

Nick is dying, isn't he? Bane asked the spirit. If anyone would know when a soul was about to leave a body it was the tiger spirit.

The spirit lifted its head and looked at Nick. It made a low whine and its head fell back down on its paws. That was all the confirmation that Bane needed.

Is there anything we can do? Bane asked. *If only Nick had the quick healing that I do because of your presence within me! He wouldn't be in danger! He would live!*

The spirit did not move.

Could you ... could you go into Nick? Like you came into me? Bane asked, an idea rising inside of him that he could not - would not - ignore.

This time, the spirit lifted its head. *You would die if I did this.*

But Nick would live, wouldn't he? Bane asked, his voice trembling.

Yes. The spirit regarded him quietly.

He would love you. He would treasure you. You would be freer with him than with me. And Nick would live, Bane said.

You would die, the spirit repeated.

But Nick would live, Bane repeated back. *Without Nick ... I do not want to go on. He is my heart. My heart will stop beating if his ceases to in any case. This way ... this way ... it is best.*

Bane suddenly smelled roses. He turned his head to look out the doorway of Nick's room. Except, for a moment, he didn't see the hospital hallway, but the rose garden behind Moon Shadow. And walking between those bushes was the priestess. Her gaze met his and he *knew* that she was making him an offer. His life for Nick's.

I accept.

Bane turned back to look at Nick. He did not know if he would be allowed to watch Nick in the afterlife so this might be the last time he saw the young man who was his heart.

I will love you forever, Nick. Remember that.

Bane leaned down and kissed Nick's forehead. His gaze took in Omar, Jade, Steven, Jake and Charles. He felt a wave of affection for each one of them. He knew that his death would be a special agony for Omar. But the Indian man would understand in time. All of these people would take care of Nick for him. He was leaving his beloved in the *best* of hands.

Perhaps it was magic, but none of them noticed as he slowly backed away from the hospital bed. When he reached the door, he mouthed, *I love you, Nick.*

And then he turned and left the room to go back to Moon Shadow one last time.

CHAPTER TWENTY-ONE - DYING

Nick woke up to the smell of roses. Though his eyes were still closed he knew the sun was shining. He could see the red-gold glow through his eyelids. He smiled. He was in the garden at Moon Shadow.

He must have fallen asleep out here. Maybe he and Bane had spread out a blanket and brought out a basket of food to have a picnic under the noon day sun. He imagined that there was an ice bucket with a bottle of white wine chilling in it. Beads of condensation would run down the golden sides of the glass bottle. He licked his suddenly dry lips. He was parched. The warmth of the sun must have sent him to sleep, which was a travesty. Though he loved to sleep, he always wanted to be awake now when Bane was there.

Bane ...

Something was wrong. Why wasn't his head pillowed on Bane's chest? Or at least, why weren't Bane's arms around him? The older man always touched him when they were near one another. Maybe Bane had stepped away to take a business call or maybe he went back to the house to get them something more to drink.

Nick's mouth *really* was dry so that last possibility was *delightful*, though unlikely. By the time either he or Bane thought they wanted something and were about to get it, Omar would appear with the desired object already in hand. Nick didn't believe that Omar would let them go so long without a cold drink on a fine, hot day like today. He frowned.

What day was it exactly? Monday? Tuesday? Wednesday? Could it be the weekend already? Why couldn't he remember what day it was? That was odd.

But it was more than that. He couldn't quite remember how he had gotten out here either. He didn't remember planning this picnic with Bane. He didn't remember coming out here, let alone falling asleep. He hadn't yet opened his eyes to confirm that he was indeed in Moon Shadow's garden. Some part of him was oddly afraid to. But that was silly! He must still be half asleep and that was why he couldn't remember anything. Anything at all.

He swallowed, but it was like swallowing sand. He was incredibly dehydrated. Maybe he had been out in the sun too long though it felt delightful against his skin, warm and strengthening.

Open your eyes. You've got to open your eyes, he told himself.

Nick finally did open his eyes and sat up before he could fully see. He blinked as the sudden change from dark to light dazzled him. He let out a sigh of relief when his vision cleared. He *was* in Moon Shadow's garden just as he had thought. He was lying on a checked blanket. There was a wicker basket bursting with food to his right.

Luscious dark purple grapes spilled over the side. A crusty loaf of French bread wrapped partially in wax paper struck out of the basket. There was a pile of Honey Crisp apples, their skins glossy and inviting, just waiting to be bitten into. He could see sausage, the spicy kind that was dried and had a pepper crust, just waiting to be sliced. His mouth watered as he saw that there was a cheese board already set out with melting brie and sharp cheddar. But what he really wanted was in the sleek ice bucket. There were two perspiring bottles resting inside of it. One was water and the other wine. He knew the wine would just make him thirstier.

He grabbed the glass water bottle and cracked the top. It was Perrier and let out a satisfying hissing sound as the gas was released.

He immediately drank half of it down. But his thirst wasn't even touched. The water was strangely unsatisfying.

He brought the bottle down and stared at it. He actually held it up to the sunlight to see if there was in fact water in it, which was ridiculous because he could hear it sloshing around, had felt it flowing over his tongue and down his throat, but his thirst was as strong as ever. He drank the rest of it almost desperately, but it did no good.

Other than the strangeness of the water, the day was gorgeous. The sun was high in the sky. The blooms on the rose bushes were huge and bobbed languidly in the subtle breeze, giving off their alluring scent. Moon Shadow looked bright and inviting. The porch with its comfy rattan furniture beckoned for him to come, sprawl out and drink margaritas. All in all it was a beautiful, perfect day except it was missing something or rather *someone*. Maybe that's why the water didn't satisfy, because a certain person, well, really *two* people as the tiger spirit was a huge part of Bane, too, were missing.

"Bane?" Nick called.

He set the empty bottle of unsatisfying water down on the blanket and got to his feet. The world spun for a moment and his legs trembled beneath him as if they were going to give way.

Am I getting sick? What's wrong with me?

The need for the older man hit him harder then. Sick and weak, he truly wanted and needed his lover. "Bane?"

He saw no one in the garden. But even if Bane was in the house his "super hearing" would have brought him out already. Yet maybe Bane was so absorbed he hadn't heard Nick. He had to get inside and find the big man himself. Omar was sure to be around as well. All he had to do was walk to the house and everything would be okay.

Nick took a few tottering steps forward and had to pause. His legs felt like they had leaden weights attached to them and he had this stitch in his right side. It was the worst cramp he had ever had and it was mixed with this stabbing sensation. He touched his side and immediately snatched his hand away. The pain had *tripled* the moment his fingertips had brushed along it. He thought his side felt *wet* as well, but when he brought his hand up to his face there was no trace of moisture on it.

A flicker of a memory intruded on him. More like a nightmare. It had been night. Wheat was waving all around him. Not roses like there were here. There was the bitter smell of alcohol and sweat instead of the sweetness of flowers. A man appeared out of nowhere and he had a stick in his hands. Not a *stick*. A *gun*. He was going to hurt Bane and the spirit. Nick had jumped in front of the them. Then there was a loud sound. And ... and ... *nothing*.

Did I get shot?

He looked down at his chest. His white t-shirt was pristine. He pulled it up and his side was perfectly fine. But he didn't dare touch himself.

This is insane! If I was shot, I wouldn't be here. I would be in the hospital ...

For a moment, he thought he heard beeping, like the sound a heart monitor makes, but then the breeze blew and the beeping faded away. A few rose petals showered the ground ahead of him. The peaceful sound of crickets chirruping returned. Nick wiped cold sweat from his forehead.

I'm fine. Everything's fine. Or it will be fine as soon as I get to Bane. I need him. I need him so badly.

Nick took a few more steps. His leg muscles *quivered*. He made it past the first two rose bushes before he sank down to his knees. His side was *killing* him. It hurt to even breathe. And he was so thirsty. So terribly thirsty.

"BANE!" he shouted, but his voice didn't seem to carry. There wasn't even an echo. Just a *hollow* sound.

He looked up at the house. It was so close but so far. It almost looked like a mirage. The sort of thing a dying man in the desert would imagine to keep himself going.

I'm not dying! I just need to get to the house and everything will be all right.

Bane was inside. Bane would take care of him. Bane would get him to a doctor. Bane would make everything good again.

I'll crawl if I have to.

Taking in a deep breath, or rather *trying* to as his lungs wouldn't seem to inflate fully especially the one on his right side, Nick tried to stand up. He got halfway up before his trembling limbs forced him back down again. He had to be still for several minutes before the shaking stopped and the pain reduced to a low stabbing sensation.

This is insane. What's wrong with me?

He really was going to have to crawl. He let out a hysterical giggle, but that hurt, too.

Got to crawl. Got to get into the house. Get help there. Bane's there.

Nick's legs felt numb and would hardly work though his arms still did. He grabbed tufts of grass and used them as handholds to drag himself over the path of the rose garden. Stones cut into his skin. Sweat drenched his body yet he felt *cold* not hot. The sun beat down on him, but there was no warmth from it anymore. It was just glaringly bright like a giant light bulb in an interrogation room.

"Bane ... Bane ... Bane," he whispered his lover's name like a prayer. He gasped and laughed brokenly as his hand found the bottom step of the porch. He had *almost* made it into the house.

He dragged himself up the steps. He was beyond pain and exhaustion, but somehow he had made it. He pulled himself onto the wooden boards of the porch and just laid there for a moment.

"Bane? B-Bane?" His voice was as dry as dust, it was a ghost of itself.

The screen door was in sight. The storm door was open. All that separated him from Bane and safety was a few feet. He dragged himself forward. With a shaking hand, he reached for the screen door and his fingers dragged down the metal latticework. He thought he saw movement inside the house. In the dimness of the hallway beyond, a figure moved. Nick's heart leaped up into his throat.

"B-Bane!" Nick cried and hot tears were spilling down his face. Finally, finally!

The figure - just a black shadow at first - drifted towards him. Why wasn't Bane moving faster? Why was he just leaving Nick lying there on the ground? Didn't he see that Nick was hurt? Sick beyond sick?

Dying?

The figure was still just a dark shadow even though it was only a foot from the door.

"Hello? Jade?" Nick rasped out even though he knew that it wasn't his best friend.

The woman kneeled down on the opposite side of the screen door from him and suddenly he could see her face.

"Mom?!" he gasped.

She smiled. She was just like he remembered her. Except instead of being sick, she was well. More than well. Vibrantly beautiful and *alive*. The gray caste that he had grown so used to seeing that he had assumed was her natural color was utterly gone. Her complexion was peaches and cream. Her blue eyes that had been dull and lifeless when he'd seen her last now sparkled like jewels. Her lips once gray were now as pink as roses. She was wearing a simple white summer dress that skimmed her voluptuous frame.

"Mom?" His voice cracked.

"It's me, Nick," she said and pressed a hand against the screen against his hand. He could feel the warmth of her through the metal. His chest seized with a mixture of grief and joy. His memories of her had been so tainted by the suffering of her last years. Now to see her like *this* was a blessing.

But how can I be seeing her? How is this possible?

"Mom, you can't be here," Nick said, and his throat felt tight as if it wanted to close up and not let the words out. But even though he had a superstitious fear that if he said she was dead she would suddenly become a rotting corpse, he said, "You're -- you're --"

"Dead? Yes. I actually prefer the term *'moved on'*. That's a better way of putting it, because *dead* seems terribly *final*, but that's not what death brings," she said with a fond smile.

"Am I hallucinating?" he asked her.

"No, you are halfway between life and death, Nick. In a place where the spirit and physical *almost* touch. Actually ..." Her brows drew together and the press of her hand was greater against the screen between them. "Actually you're closer to *death* than *life*. This *screen* is all that separates you from death."

Nick gasped and then he said with mounting horror, "I -- I -- I was *shot*."

He remembered it all then. He'd jumped in front of Bane when the irate, drunken farmer raised the shotgun. The man had fired. The blast had split the air. The pain in his side was from where he had been hit. He slipped his left hand beneath his shirt and drew it out. It was slick with crimson. Blood. His blood.

"I'm scared, Mom," Nick said and his voice broke.

She was nodding and her expression was all tenderness. "I know, but you shouldn't be. Death is not the end. It's the *beginning* of another journey."

"Can't you come out here with me? Why do you have to stay away?" he asked.

The thought of having her arms around him after so many years caused an ache to bloom in his chest. He could barely remember the feeling of her hugs, of the softness of her blonde hair caressing his cheek, or the subtle scent of her perfume. He wanted to feel those things now.

Attar of roses. Of course, she would wear the fragrance that Bane loves.

She hesitated and he knew that his mother wouldn't *hesitate* to come to him unless there was a good reason. Her words confirmed the reason. "I *could* do that, Nick, but it would mean ..."

"Mean what?" He truly *hurt*. And he was so *tired*.

"That you would surely die," she said. "And I don't think you want that."

"I don't want to die!" he cried, but he felt crushed by the fact that he was going to bleed alone out here.

Alone. Where is Bane?

"He left your bedside at the hospital," she said, evidently reading his thoughts.

"Where did he go?"

She hesitated again and he saw her bite her lower lip.

"Mom, what is it?" She was holding something back.

"He went to meet the Earth Mother in the rose garden," she said.

"He's here?!" Nick tried to heft himself up from the floor, but he couldn't. Blood pooled sickeningly beneath him.

"We aren't at Moon Shadow, Nick. This place," she paused, and for a moment her eyes swam with tears. "This place represents *Heaven* to you."

Nick blinked. *Heaven? Like where you go when you die? Like the best place possible? Yes, it is, but only ...*

"It's not Heaven without Bane, Mom," he said.

She nodded. Her expression cleared then. It was as if he said something that made complete sense to her and cleared up any confusion she might have. "I thought so."

"What is he doing in the garden, Mom? And what's happening here? Am I going to die? Is that a done deal?" he asked as the thirst plucked at him. He knew where the thirst came from. It was from blood loss.

She sighed and her hand rested heavier on the screen. A trickle of fear went through Nick as he knew that the *screen* was just a metaphor for death. If the screen broke then ... He thrust the thought away.

"Nick, there is a chance you *won't* die, a chance you will *never* die," she said and stared at him evenly.

"Never die?" His eyes widened.

"Like Bane. Actually, *exactly* like Bane, because ... he will give you guardianship of the tiger spirit," she said.

"He can't do that! The spirit is the only thing keeping him alive! He'll *die* if they're parted!" Nick's voice rose up.

She hunkered closer to the screen so that he could see her intense expression. "He knows that, but he's making this choice to give up his life to save yours."

"NO!" Nick nearly got to his feet then. Blood flowed down his front and he collapsed once more.

"It's all right, baby. Be calm. Save your strength," she tried to soothe him, but it did no good.

"I'll die now and then when he dies, I'll be here waiting for him," Nick said firmly.

His mother's blue eyes regarded him so soberly, so sadly, so lovingly that he had to look away from her. She didn't have to say what she was thinking. He felt her pity quite clearly.

"If the tiger spirit stays inside of him, he *won't* ever die," Nick whispered. "He will never come here. I will never see him or the spirit again."

"The tiger spirit separates you. For it is eternal and needs a host. That host benefits from its immortality. But it means that the host can never move on," she confirmed.

"So we're separated forever? Either he sends the spirit to me and I live forever and he dies or I die and he lives forever …" Nick stared ahead despairingly. His mind was curiously blank or rather it really wasn't blank. He was angry. So angry that it blotted out all thought. "This isn't right!"

"It is the curse he carries, Nick," she said.

"NO!" he shouted again with as much force as he had about Bane dying.

"You think he is not cursed?" She tilted her head to the side. She looked honestly interested.

"The spirit is *not* a curse. The spirit is a *blessing*. And that just makes *this* even more wrong!" he cried out and coughed violently. A red stain appeared on the floor. He was coughing up blood. His condition was deteriorating. He was dying.

"You feel cheated of a full life? Yes, I can understand that --"

"No!" He cried once more, cutting her off. Through coughs and hacks of blood, he got out, "B-Bane! He didn't -- didn't believe in -- in l-love! He opened himself to me! He's changed! He d-deserves … happiness!"

"You want to live *for him*?" His mother's expression was very interesting, but he was too distraught to interpret it.

"Yes!" Nick swallowed. "I'm not so arrogant to think I'm the only one he *could* love. I'm not worthy of the love he gives me."

"Oh, my son." She shook her head with a fond smile.

"But what I do know for certain is that he *won't* let himself love anyone else," Nick said. He knew that his loss would not only send Bane back to the state he had been in before Nick had chipped through his defenses, but likely send him over an even deeper and darker edge. Bane would love nobody and nothing after his death.

The spirit would be devastated. All the progress they had made would be lost. "I'm not important for myself, but for *them*. I can't die now, Mom."

"I understand, Nick. But I want to make sure that *you* do," she said.

"What do you mean?" he asked her.

"There's a third option," she said.

"What's the third option? Does it mean that Bane and I can be together?" he asked. There was a bitter, coppery taste on his tongue and in the back of his throat. There was blood *in* his mouth.

"Yes, but you need to understand the full consequences of this third option, Nick."

He swallowed that metallic taste and he knew at that moment how close he was to death. If death was a physical thing, it would be sitting on his shoulder and drawing a chilly finger down his spine.

"Tell me the consequences."

"There is a way for both you and Bane to remain together, but it means that *you* will never *move on*," she said quietly and her gaze held a heavy weight.

Nick looked at her back for long moments. "You mean ... I'll never see *you* again?"

"Or anyone else after they die. You will never continue your journey," she confirmed. "You will walk Bane's path with him as an immortal guardian."

There was no question about what option he would choose. His life -- his very soul -- belonged to Bane. And to the tiger spirit. He could not leave them. Not even for his mother, his father or his brothers. Not even for Jade.

"I love you," he said after long moments.

"You've decided," she said with a slightly sad smile, but it was also filled with contentment, too.

"I --"

"There was never any question, was there? And no, I'm *not* disappointed. I'm so happy for you, Nick," she said with quiet intensity. "You've found your *one*. And your *destiny*. That's so *rare*."

"I love you," he told her again as his throat closed up.

"I know. This choice doesn't *diminish* how much you love others, it just shows how much you love Bane," she said and then stood.

Nick wanted to stand up with her, but he couldn't. His body was completely numb. He was so cold. So thirsty. So tired. His time really was nearly up.

"What happens now, Mom? How do I choose this third option?" Nick asked.

"You already have." She smiled at him so tenderly that his eyes blurred with tears. "I will love you forever, Nick. I shall watch you and Bane in this immortal life you have chosen. Goodbye, my son."

Nick was going to beg her not to leave him, but his voice failed him. He couldn't move either. He could hardly even feel his body. His time was almost up.

CHAPTER TWENTY-TWO - GARDEN OF SPIRITS

"Bane, what do you mean you want to change your *will?*" Though it wasn't yet dawn, Sloan's voice was as alert as if he was in her downtown office at midday.

The sky was still a velvety black, though that would change soon. Bane could almost feel the sun rising behind the windshield of the farmer's truck. He pictured Sloan in her sleek apartment in downtown Winter Haven, sitting up in bed, reaching for her laptop. He wondered if someone lay beside her or if she was alone.

"I need you to simply leave everything to Nick and I need you to have it done tonight. Now, actually," Bane told her firmly as he glided around another curve of the Winter Haven highway back to Moon Shadow.

"*Now?* What -- why? Bane, what's happened?" she demanded to know. She was scared for him, he realized. Not angry that he had woken her up in the middle of the night, but more wondering *why* he had.

He gritted his teeth as a wave of panic went through him. Time was slipping by. Nick's life was leeching away. But he responded calmly, his voice clipped, "Nick was shot tonight."

"What?!" Sloan sounded horrified.

"He's going to make it," Bane told her. He would ensure that by giving up his own life. "He's out of surgery at Winter Haven's hospital,"

"Thank God," she murmured. "But why are *you* changing your will after *Nick* was shot?"

Because I want to leave Nick my estate. He will need my financial resources to live eternally.

But, of course, he did not tell her that. He told her something far more mundane, "Tonight taught me that ... that *things* can change in an instant. I want this done in case ... in case something happens to me."

"Bane, *nothing* is going to happen to you. I know that Nick was ... was shot, but the likelihood of anything happening to you is infinitesimal. Especially not *tonight*. We can meet in the morning --"

"Sloan, please draw up the document and email it to me. I'll sign it electronically," he said. "There won't be any witnesses, but this will have to do."

"Bane, that likely won't be binding! Your former heir will contest this will in the unlikely event that you pass any time soon," she argued. Some lawyers would have humored him, not brought up any possible problems, just did the work and billed for it, but Sloan was intent he understood the law and the consequences of his actions.

His "former heir" was *himself*. So there would be no one contesting his will. One had to live and die and live again in order to hide that one lived forever.

But not anymore.

"He won't contest it. He'll never appear. He's ... gone and the possibility of him is gone. I have no living heirs. There will be no problems, Sloan," he paused then added, "Please do this for me."

Her voice was gentle as she replied, "Of course, Bane. I'm typing it up right now. Once I'm done and you're satisfied, I'll head to the hospital to be with you and Nick."

He didn't correct her that she would not find him there. That would just alarm her more and she didn't deserve that. The road before him blurred as tears filled his eyes. "Thank you. You've been ... such a good friend to me. A far better friend than I deserve."

"Nonsense! You are a good man, Bane. I've always thought that."

He swallowed the lump that had formed in his throat. "Thank you again. For everything."

"I'm almost done with the document. Expect it in the next few minutes," she told him. "I'll see you soon, Bane."

No, you won't. I wish it were otherwise. But I have to save Nick.

He knew that when she found out about his death she would remember this conversation and wish she had done something. But there was nothing she could do. Bane wished he had appreciated Sloan more when he could still enjoy the privilege of her company.

He had learned so much since Nick had come into his life. He'd wasted a whole *century* feeling sorry for himself when he could have been appreciating the people around him, loving life itself.

But life is nothing without Nick.

The spirit, who had been quiet, yet very present, with Bane in order to comfort him, spoke now, *Hurry, Bane. There is little time.*

The rest of the ride back to Moon Shadow was done almost in a fugue. Bane was lost to everything, but his memories of Nick, which spooled through his mind like movies. He swore at times that he could smell Nick's clean scent, taste him on his tongue, and feel the brush of his hands over his skin.

The spirit was curled tightly in his chest, loving him, mourning with him.

You'll be happy with Nick, Bane said, trying to make the beast less sad.

I belong with you, the spirit said softly.

I've been a terrible guardian, Bane said even as his heart twisted at the tiger spirit's words. *Nick will worship you every day. He'll probably let you be in control more than he is. And Omar will take care of you both.*

I am doing this for him, but more for you, the spirit answered. Its big blue eyes were filled with sorrow. *We should have had more time.*

Without Nick our time together would be terrible for both of us, Bane said. He tried to convince himself of this.

We belong together, the spirit objected. *The three of us.*

Bane's hands tightened on the wheel. *I know.*

But there was no other choice. No way for that to happen. Nick was dying.

His phone had been buzzing constantly since he left the hospital. He knew it was either Jade or Omar trying to find him. They had no idea what he was going to do, but they knew he was beyond devastated and they likely *feared* he was in trouble. He ignored the phone and kept driving. Hearing either of their voices would be too much. And they might try to stop him.

Bane pulled into Moon Shadow's drive. The house was dark, extinguished of light and life. Bane tried to remember how it had been with Nick not ten hours before. There had been candles on the back porch, drinks glistening with condensation on the low table, and their mouths bruised from too many kisses.

After turning off the car, he checked his phone. Sloan had sent him the document. It was a simple one page affair. She instructed him to send a reply that this was his last will and testament. Of course, she warned him again that this might not be binding in case someone contested the will. But he wasn't worried. He followed her instructions. Then he got out of the truck and shut the door behind him with a solid thunk.

He didn't walk through the house. He couldn't. He thought of the house as a place where only the living should be. He didn't want to impregnate the interior with his grief at the loss of what could have been. Plus, he knew that the priestess was waiting for him in the rose garden.

He followed the winding path that circled the house and then joined the gravel maze of paths through the rose garden. The moon was sinking towards the horizon, but it still cast a silvery glaze over everything. Under other circumstances, Bane would have thought it unbelievably beautiful.

We're here now. Where is she? Bane asked. He could feel the clock ticking on Nick's life. He wasn't eager to die, but he absolutely couldn't wait with Nick's life on the line.

There. The Earth Mother is there, the spirit said and directed his gaze towards a circular grassy area where the wizened priestess stood.

Earth Mother? Bane questioned.

That is who and what she is.

The Earth Mother's back was to them. She was gazing out upon the fields beyond the garden. Bane walked towards her. His legs felt weak and he was a little afraid of what was to come, but he was determined to go through with it anyways. He'd had more than his fair share of life. Over one hundred years of it. That he'd wasted many of those years steeped in misery, was his own fault, not fate's, not the spirit's, and certainly not the Earth Mother's. He had *cursed* himself. No one else had. But Nick deserved an eternity of good things and Bane hoped this sacrifice could give it to him.

He stopped in the middle of the circular patch of grass just a few feet from her back. The grass was mown short and smelled incredibly verdant. He took in a deep breath of its fresh scent and the alluring perfume of roses. That he should die among the beloved roses that Nick had worked so hard to bring to life was fitting.

The Earth Mother turned to face him. Her wizened, nut-brown face was somber. "I did not know if I would ever see you in this place."

Her head bobbed a little like the blooms all around them. For a moment, he could believe her to be just a huge rose.

"I don't understand. I've been here hundreds of times," he said, his tone uncertain.

"Tonight this garden is *mine*, Bane. It is *not* the one you know. It is the Garden of the Spirits. It is where only the *worthy* guardians come."

Bane looked around him. While it had seemed like his garden before he realized now it was *not*. The roses, the stones, and even the grass seemed terribly sharp and clear as if he were seeing the essence of a rose or a rock or a blade of grass. The fireflies' light was blue instead of yellow. They reminded him of souls floating around them. The moon, too, had a bluish cast.

"The Garden of Spirits?" he murmured. "If only *worthy* guardians are allowed, considering how selfish I've been all my life, you were right to doubt I'd ever make it here."

"You've come far and that is a good thing."

"Now I need to go a little farther. I need to save Nick. The spirit can do that if it goes into Nick's body," Bane explained, though he was certain she already knew this. "How do I accomplish this?"

"Are you certain you wish to?" Her expression was neutral, neither encouraging him or discouraging him. "You will die if you do this."

"I know and I am prepared for that. I will give my life for Nick's." Bane knew now that he was living for *two* so it was not just himself that he had to be thinking of with this action, so he added, "The spirit will be in good hands - no, *better* hands - with Nick than with me. He has a guardian's soul. Far superior to mine. And the spirit loves him."

The spirit was glumly resting its chin on its paws. Its blue eyes were luminous with what looked like tears.

"You are willing to sacrifice yourself for another then, Lord Bane Dunsaney?" she asked formally.

With no hesitation, he answered, "Yes, I am."

Her gaze once more went to the fields as if looking for something or someone. She then turned towards the back porch and regarded that area closely, too. She remained looking away from him so long that he became uneasy.

"Forgive me, but Nick's time is short and --"

"It has been decided. Both are prepared," she said and focused on him again.

"*Both?*" Bane looked around, but saw no one, but himself and the Earth Mother. The field and porch were empty, but *she* clearly saw something or someone there. "Do you mean the spirit and I?"

She did not answer. Instead, she stepped up to him and raised one hand - *the* hand that had burned his skin and laid the mark upon him - so that it mirrored the scar on his face. He went very still. He knew the power of that hand.

"What happens now?" Bane asked, a whisper more than anything else, as he feared her touch more than anything.

"Close your eyes and do not open them until I tell you," she instructed.

Bane shut his eyes. The darkness fell around him. He waited for the touch of that hand once more. He wasn't sure what he expected to happen. Would he even know when the spirit separated from him? Would he immediately die? Or would his body just slowly age and turn to dust? Sweat broke out on his upper lip at that thought.

Please let it be quick whatever it is. If for Nick's sake and not mine.

The hand - cold as frost this time - was pressed against his face. Bane let out a gasp, not just because it was icy cold, but because it felt like his soul was *being* pulled out of his body through that touch. He actually went down onto one knee, groaning. It was then that he felt a faint vibrating *thread* connecting him to this other part of his soul that seemed to be located outside of himself.

"Open your eyes," the Earth Mother commanded. She had taken the hand away.

Bane was trembling and sweating like he had a fever even though his face felt frozen. Opening his eyes was an *effort*, but he forced his eyelids to part. He blinked a few times as his vision was blurry. Finally, he could see again and before him was a tiger. A tiger that had *his* blue eyes. It was the spirit. But it appeared clothed in a *physical* form. Bane let out a soft gasp.

"You're -- you're *beautiful*," he whispered.

The spirit's tail wagged once. But there was no joy in its eyes.

"I haven't seen you like this since I ... since I *killed* your mortal form." Bane reached out and touched the tiger's soft jowls. The spirit tilted its head into Bane's hand and purred. "You're showing you're not a real tiger, spirit. Tigers cannot purr."

I can do many things tigers cannot do. Including mourn. The spirit's eyes slowly opened. It turned its head towards the priestess. *I do not wish to leave Bane, Earth Mother. I do not wish Nick to die. There must be another way.*

The Earth Mother laid a hand on top of the tiger's head, but said nothing. Instead, she turned to Bane once more and asked, "Do you see the threads that connects the two of you?"

Bane did indeed see a silvery bunch of threads that connected his heart to the tiger's. He nodded. She reached into a bag that was on her belt and drew out a stone knife. It was as black as the spaces between the stars.

"If I cut *all* those strands ... you will die and the spirit will need another form," she explained.

"So the spirit will be able to go to Nick and enter his body?" Bane asked, wanting to be sure he understood how this would work.

"Yes." One word, so simple and so complex. "If that is what you want."

"I want to save Nick. I ... I *love* him." Bane swallowed deeply then petted the tiger gently. "Thank you for everything you've given me. I can't ask you to forgive me for –"

There is nothing to forgive, Bane, the spirit interrupted him tenderly and licked his fingers.

"I will miss you ... so very much. Please tell Nick ..." Bane's throat seized up and he found he couldn't complete that sentence. "You will know what to say. You know everything I feel."

I know, it answered.

Bane and the spirit gazed into one another's eyes as they waited for the Earth Mother to cut the thread that bound them and send Bane to the afterlife and the spirit to Nick. She raised the knife. Bane closed his eyes. He couldn't bare to see the connection to the spirit cut.

Bane thought, *I love you and Nick both, spirit.*

He felt one of the threads cut. He cried out in pain and fell fully onto the ground. He could feel the edges of the thread fluttering, yearning for the spirit, reaching out in vain towards it. He felt that thread unspooling, seeking, seeking, seeking a new connection. Then another thread was cut. And another. More unspooling. He could not move. It felt like his life was stretching out with those threads.

Darkness was everywhere.

CURSED: BELOVED

And then ... then those cut threads *found* something to connect to.

Someone to connect to.

Bane's eyelids flew open as he felt strength - such strength as he had never known - flowing back into him from this new connection. He saw the spirit was lying down on the grass, but it, too, was starting to rise, energy refilling. Its gaze was focused on the wheatfields where the Earth Mother had been gazing earlier. He turned his head to look, too.

Through the grass came *another* white Bengal tiger. It parted the long stalks with unearthly grace and padded towards them. The threads that had formerly just been tying Bane and his spirit together were now attached to *this* tiger as well. The three of them were connected.

Not just three! His spirit exclaimed and jumped to its feet. *Look!*

A glowing window had appeared in the garden just a few feet away and through it Bane could see Nick's hospital room. He nearly leaped towards the figure on the bed that was practically shrouded by tubes and wires. But the Earth Mother put up a hand that stopped him. Bane's heart clenched.

Nick. Nick. Nick.

Jade, Omar, Charles, Jake and Steven were still in Nick's room. Jade was stroking Nick's forehead and speaking to him softly words of love and encouragement. Charles was sitting on the edge of the bed, holding Nick's hands as if in prayer. Steven was by the window looking pinched and pale. Jake was in the hospital chair, resting his head in his hands. Omar stood at the base of the bed, openly weeping.

The threads ... some of them are connected to Nick! Bane realized.

"Yes, where once there was only enough power to have one spirit, now there is the power to have *two*," the Earth Mother intoned, having evidently read his mind.

Bane's head turned towards her. The second tiger spirit - this one had gray-eyes - head butted her playfully, but didn't managed to budge her an inch. She chuckled and scratched it behind the ears.

"You are young and full of mischief," she said to the gray-eyed tiger with affection.

The gray-eyed tiger gave her hand a lick and then turned to Bane and his tiger spirit. The two tigers regarded one another uncertainly for long moments before they touched noses. It seemed then in no time at all they were rubbing lengthwise against one another, their tails winding together. Bane felt the spirits' great joy in being together. They loved one another already.

"How? How are there now *two*?" he asked the priestess.

"Love has a way of making things *change* and *grow*. This is because of *you*, Bane. You opened your heart. You gave all of yourself and *this* is the result." She rested one hand on his tiger spirit's head and one on the gray-eyed tiger's head.

"This spirit ..." Bane extended a shaking hand towards the gray-eyed tiger who immediately pushed its head beneath Bane's hand to be petted. He let out a shaky laugh and obliged. "This spirit ... will be Nick's?"

"Yes, can you not feel their connection already?" She flashed a broad smile.

She was *right*. Bane could *feel* Nick in this tiger. He hugged it fiercely and breathed into its fur, "Thank you. Thank you for coming." He looked up at the priestess, "Thank you for saving Nick."

"You have shown me that my children can be safe with humans. Safe and cherished," she answered.

"Nick has done that. Not me. Without him, I would have remained unworthy, Earth Mother," Bane admitted.

"He healed your heart so you could be the man you always should have been," the Earth Mother said and Bane felt a surprising burn of tears rise up in him.

The Earth Mother regarded the gray-eyed tiger. "It is time for you to go to Nick."

Bane released the gray-eyed spirit. Without hesitation, the beautiful creature went to the window that led to Nick's hospital room and stepped through it. The new spirit went directly to Nick's bedside and immediately put its paws up on the bed. It sniffed Nick's slowly rising and falling chest. Bane held his breath.

Would this work? Would Nick be saved?

The gray-eyed tiger spirit looked up at Nick's face and within half a moment, it licked Nick's chin. Charles drew in a sharp breath as Nick's gray eyes suddenly opened and zeroed in on the tiger spirit.

Charles couldn't see the spirit. But Nick could. Even though there was a tube running down his throat, Bane could tell that Nick was smiling. The tiger let out a happy huff and then the gray-eyed tiger became a white mist that settled onto Nick's form.

It worked!

The monitors went crazy. Nick began to shake like he was having a seizure. Jake and Steven ran for the door screaming for Dr. Vostok. But before the doctor could get there, Nick's eyelids flew open again and he was pulling out the tube from his throat.

"No, Nick, no! You need that to breathe!" Jade cried trying to stop Nick.

"He's having a seizure!" Charles added as he tried to assist her.

But Nick already had the tube out. He tossed it to the side and he was taking in deep phlegmy breaths. He gripped Jade and his father's hands as he slowly got his breath back. Omar came up behind him and was gently patting his back. All of them looked like they were afraid to move otherwise, because if they did, this miracle of Nick being awake and alert would end.

The monitors settled down, showing what to Bane's layman's eyes, were the vitals of a normal, healthy person. Dr. Vostok and Nurse Anderson rushed in then. When they saw Nick sitting up in bed, breathing on his own, and rubbing at the tape marks on his face, both let out surprised laughs. Dr. Vostok immediately covered her mouth with her hand. Nick lifted his head. His gray eyes were bright, inquisitive and clear. They were the same as the tiger spirit's.

"Hey," Nick said, his voice sounding hoarse from pulling out the tube. "Don't worry, guys. I'm all right."

Bane let out a bark of laughter even as tears flowed down his cheeks. The window to the hospital room closed. Bane, his spirit and the Earth Mother were alone once more. He turned towards her.

"Thank you!" he said again, and he would say it a million times more and that would not be enough.

She smiled, showing white teeth. "It is I who should be thanking you. Because of you, the world is a much brighter place."

Bane looked down at his tiger spirit. There was such love in those matching blue eyes. "Do you choose me, spirit? Knowing my weaknesses as you do? Would you still have me? For I choose you. With all I am. It is *not* a curse, but a *blessing* to be with you."

The spirit gave him a look that appeared to be a smile then it turned into mist. That mist flowed into him. Bane let out a sigh of relief. He was *complete* again. He felt the spirit in his chest. It was circling to find a perfect spot to curl up and rest. Nick was safe. It had a new tiger companion. It was to be with Bane forever. All was finally as it should be.

The Earth Mother chuckled, drawing his attention. "And to think, you did not believe in love and you did not believe in change, but you are the epitome of those things, Bane!"

"I was a fool and very *slow* to figure things out," he admitted.

"Fast? Slow? These terms have no real meaning. You have done it and that is all that matters in the end."

"Priestess ... I mean, *Earth Mother*," Bane began again as he felt his tiger spirit mentally correct him. Their bond was so strong now and he relished it. "Who are you ... *really*?"

She seemed limned with light. "The Earth Mother."

And it was *then* that he truly saw her. Her skin was the bark of trees and rich dark soil of the earth. Her eyes were flashing precious stones. Her hair was made of vines and branches. Her teeth were ivory. Her clothes were flowers.

"Now I know why Omar seems a little saintly. He is not altogether human either, is he?" Bane asked.

"You are all my beloved children in some ways, large or small," her voice sounded like leaves rustling. "But, I have to admit, that *Omar* is one of my favorites."

And then she was gone.

He was no longer in the Garden of Spirits, but simply the garden at *Moon Shadow*. He had never been so happy, or felt so blessed. He had not thought to leave this garden alive. He had thought never to see Nick again. But he had been wrong on both counts. Now, he and Nick, along with their tiger spirits, would be together forever.

"Let's start that forever now, shall we?" he asked his spirit.

The spirit's tail thumped in agreement.

CHAPTER TWENTY-THREE - HAPPILY EVER AFTER

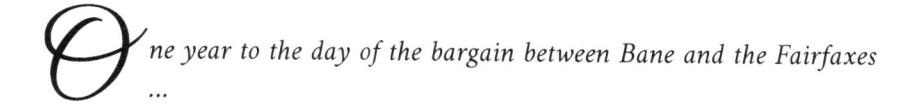

One year to the day of the bargain between Bane and the Fairfaxes ...

NICK DRIFTED through the central hallway of Moon Shadow. He drew in a deep breath and smelled green things. Summer was here. Already the sun had taken on that buttery, golden color that characterized the warmer months. It heated the dark wood of Moon Shadow's rooms, burnishing it until the copper tones came out.

Nick had now seen the beautiful mansion in the light of every season, but he had to admit that he loved summer probably most of all. The gray-eyed tiger spirit curled happily in his chest. It, too, adored summer and was looking forward to sunning its coat in the garden.

Nick passed by the kitchen doorway and saw Omar with a perspiring pitcher of his famous margaritas in one hand and a tray of glasses whose rims were limned with a mixture of salt and sugar in the other. Ice cubes clinked against the pitcher's glass sides. Slices of lime floated like playful sea creatures.

The moment that Omar caught sight of him, the Indian man's eyes lit up. "Ah, Nick! Where have you been? Everyone has been looking all over for you!" Then he lowered his voice into a whisper, "And you *must* save Bane. Your father has cornered him again about some charity event. You know that Bane can only take so much of Charles even when your father has good intentions!"

Nick laughed. "Both of them have gotten much better with each other. Bane has even stopped grimacing when Dad talks too long. For his part, Dad only shakes Bane's hand once per meeting, doesn't thump him on the back too often and limits his talking to ... well, until Bane walks away. He's not chasing after him anymore, which is a plus."

"Things have changed all around!"

"One thing that *hasn't* changed is you trying to do everything by yourself." Nick reached towards the tray of glasses. "Here, let me take that tray from you."

"Only if it gets you outside!" Omar said, laughing. But he handed Nick the pitcher as it was *lighter* item to carry. Nick shook his head at the Indian man's insistence on protecting him from any heavy lifting. Even though he was completely healed from the gunshot, Omar simply could not be convinced that Nick wasn't just a *little* fragile.

The Indian man asked suddenly, "Where were you earlier by the way?"

"I was standing at the gate actually," Nick answered.

Omar's eyebrows rose up. "At the gate? Why?"

"I was remembering when I first saw Moon Shadow," Nick explained with a smile.

"Good memories, I hope." There was a twinkle in Omar's eyes.

"Oh, yes, but more ... *amazement* at how much has changed," Nick explained. "The spirit enjoyed hearing all about it."

He had stood outside the gate, his hands on the bars, and looked in at Moon Shadow, comparing the now neat gravel drive with bubbling, crystal fountain to the haunted ruin he had first seen. Beyond the working fountain, the formerly empty drive was filled with several cars and Jade's brand new purple Vespa. While the foliage was still rampant, flowers beginning to bloom in profusion everywhere, the gardeners had finally tamed the beautiful wildness. Now it only *appeared* wild, but was really quite controlled.

The garage that had been so dark and musty when Nick had parked his motorcycle in it last year was clean and well ventilated. It didn't contain Nick's old motorcycle any longer though. Bane had gotten him *two* new motorcycles. One a very speedy Valkyrie Ryujin and the other a sleek Harley-Davidson Fat Boy Lo. There would be no chance of Nick getting stranded on a Winter Haven highway again, though Nick was sure that either his spirit or Bane's would rescue him anyways.

But the biggest changes weren't to Moon Shadow at all. They were in Bane and Nick themselves. When Nick had first arrived here, his only goals were to pay off any duty to his family and then flee them.

Bane was a person to be *endured* and to avoid any grabby-hands the rich man might want to employ against him. Nick laughed out loud as he had compared now to then. He not only hadn't fled his family, he was more deeply wrapped up with them now more than ever. And, if this second bargain was enacted, he would *never* get away from them.

Will Bane honor his promise? The gray-eyed tiger spirit asked.

You know he always does.

Yes, he does. The gray-eyed tiger spirit felt that was one of the very good things about Bane.

Besides, Jake and Steven have earned it. They're his proteges after all.

Jake and Steven's cars were in the driveway as were their father's Mercedes, Sloan's Jaguar and Devon's Tesla. They were all here for a party, to celebrate -- and *end* -- the year long *first* bargain. After nursing Nick - or more like driving him crazy - through his convalescence after he had left the hospital, his father had pleaded to be allowed to continue to work for Bane for the full year, so long as it meant he had plenty of free time for all three of his sons. He refused to take back Fairfax International until that time. Bane had agreed.

And his father - well, Charles like Scrooge of old - had been *better* than his word.

His father had become a *star* executive in Bane's companies. He adopted every single one of the traits that Bane admired in his people from a tireless work ethic - he'd had that before - to generosity. Whereas in the past, his father had been all about the bottomline to get money for himself, now it was how could he make the company better for its workers.

Also, his father had become an ardent philanthropist. Charles and Devon now worked hand in glove together. Though Nick had never thought he could like Devon, he had changed his mind. While they were not exactly *friends*, there was no longer any animosity between them. He was sure that his father was blathering to Bane about their next big event. It was to benefit victims of gun violence. It also would feature Nick's photography.

That was another reason not to hate Devon any longer. The art show that Devon had first featured him at had translated into a viral interest in his work. Nick's photographs were so desired that he couldn't take enough pictures to satisfy his very hungry buyers. Nick though still insisted on going to school, improving his art, and learning all he could.

With all the requests for photographs coming in, Nick was ever so grateful that Jade had sublet her apartment and was living full-time at Moon Shadow. She helped him with his shoots and he helped her with her Ebay business. Bane had insisted that she use the mansion as much as she wanted to sell her vintage clothing and he had encouraged her to start a fashion line of her own. She was in the midst of planning out her first season.

With all of their new businesses, they had needed a lawyer and only Sloan Wu would do. She was present at the party, too. Nick and Jade had grown to love her and call her more *friend* than advisor. But she was there not only in her personal capacity, but in her professional one that night as well. She was to unveil the documents that would cement the *second deal* that Bane wanted to make. This one would hopefully produce a far different reaction than the first.

The gray-eyed tiger kneaded his chest to make itself known. As if Nick could or *would* ever forget about the spirit!

I haven't forgotten about you! You, of course, are the biggest of big changes in me, Nick had assured the spirit with a delighted laugh.

The spirit had done the un-tigerish thing of purring in response. It had learned that pleasant sound from Bane's tiger spirit who was its "god" in all things. To Bane's chagrin, his spirit had taken to teaching all of its "naughtiness" to Nick's, like going after the sheep that Bane now owned.

Nick had just laughed as Bane tried to reason with either spirit and failed. Finally, after realizing that it was no use, and not ever, ever wanting another situation like what had happened with the farmer to happen again, Bane had gone on a buying spree so that he owned almost as much land as Alric Koenig did. Moon Shadow was a single mansion in an island of forest and fields now. But it would ensure their privacy and safety even when the spirits made mischief.

For his part, Nick was still amazed by the tiger spirit inside of him. When he had woken in the hospital, feeling that warm, furry weight on his chest and the raspy lick of that tongue on his chin, he had known what destiny felt like. He was only later to learn what had happened in the Garden of Spirits from his spirit and from Bane himself. Bane had told him, to his horror, about the billionaire's plan to give up the tiger spirit to Nick and to die so that Nick should live forever without him. In the months that had followed the shooting, Nick had the occasional, heated arguments with Bane about how he was never to do anything so foolish again. After all, did Bane really think he wanted to live an eternity without him?

But while these arguments were truly moot as they both had tiger spirits dwelling inside of them now, Nick wanted the big man to understand, without a doubt, that life was only so good because they were in it *together*. And now that the Earth Mother had granted him a tiger spirit to guard, that meant he and Bane would be in it together *forever*.

The utter joy and *rightness* of that first moment of his and the gray-eyed tiger's souls coexisting had only grown with every moment of every day since then. Nick knew he would always feel this way as the endless years followed.

Nick was brought back to himself when a burst of Jade's laughter carried through the screen door that led to the porch. Everyone was outside, eating Omar's homemade chips, salsa and guacamole. Later, there would be enchiladas oozing with chicken and cheese as well as delicate pork and sweet corn tamales in a tangy green sauce.

To Nick, this food and these tastes were the essence of summer and happiness. This was the same meal, after all, that had been served that first night he had started on his plan to save Bane from a life of loneliness. It was a fitting way to start the next chapter of their life together.

"Come, they are waiting!" Omar hurried out of the kitchen and down the hall.

Nick followed after him. Just as Omar shouldered open the porch door, he called out, "Who wants a drink?"

Immediately, there was a chorus of "ayes" from all corners. Nick poured the tart liquid into the salt and sugar-rimmed glasses that Omar held. The Indian man began to hand them out.

Jade was perched on the porch's railing between Jake and Steven. She was dressed in a purple, low cut dress and Roman sandals that went up nearly to her knees. Jake and Steven were still dressed in their suits from work. Their only concession to the fact that it was a party and summer was to have taken off their suit coats, tugged off their ties - nearly matching red ones - and to have undone the few top buttons of their shirts.

"All I'm saying, Jade, is that we can increase your profitability by 15% if you merely use the spreadsheet I prepared for you," Steven told her, all seriousness as always.

"Spreadsheets give me hives, Steven," Jade responded, hiding her smile behind the lip of the margarita glass that Omar had just presented to her.

Steven pushed his wire-rimmed glasses up on his nose and said, with a long suffering sigh, "I don't believe anyone can be *allergic* to spreadsheets, but if you are so against them then maybe *I* can fill it out for you."

Really having to hide a smile now, perhaps even a smile of success,

Jade said soberly, "If you really think the spreadsheet is necessary and don't mind doing it, then that might be the *best* solution. But I know how busy you are."

"I don't mind," Steven said.

"For Steven, spreadsheets are *fun*," Jake said, not hiding his smile or laugh.

Steven straightened up and said, "Some of us enjoy *order*, Jake. You seem to appreciate my skills when I use them for *your* projects."

Jake playfully clasped Steven's shoulder. "I *do* appreciate it. No one is better than you at keeping chaos from overtaking everything. Seriously, Steven, you're great."

This was said without any rancor, but with genuine warm feeling and regard. This was another change. Ever since Bane had taken his older brothers directly under his wing, Jake had become a kinder, gentler person and his success as a boss had increased. Steven, too, had developed a much warmer touch and was actively mentoring other people in the company.

"Well, I'm *glad* you feel that way," Steven said, no longer nettled and smiling genuinely.

"Of course! I couldn't do it without you," Jake answered.

Nick pressed a drink into both his brother's hands. "Drink more. Talk about spreadsheets less."

"Wiser words have never been spoken." Jade leaned over and kissed him on the cheek.

She smelled of attar of roses. That smell reminded him of his mother and made his smile brighter. He had come to believe that he hadn't just dreamed of his mother, but that his experience in the place between life and death was as real as this moment was.

Jade grasped his arm and turned him to look, not at the garden, but at the large flat screen television that had been brought out onto the porch. A slideshow of Nick's photographs scrolled. They showed his final series of the transformation of Moon Shadow over the years from dark ruin to bright, brilliant home. Sloan was standing in front of it, watching the transformation with a small smile on her lips.

"I think Sloan needs a drink," Jade commented.

"I think you're right."

Nick went over to her and handed her a margarita. She smiled and said in that warm throaty voice, "I believe that these are your best photographs yet, Nick."

"I agree." Devon appeared at his elbow. He took the pitcher from Nick and topped off his own glass. "In fact, I agree with that statement so much that I happened to show them to Margie Greenfield."

Nick's head snapped towards him. Margie Greenfield was *the* gallery owner in Winter Haven. To have her be interested in an artist's work was to shoot their careers into the stratosphere.

"You did?" Nick asked, his mouth suddenly quite dry.

Devon nodded. His handsome face was bathed in sunlight and a small smile was on his lips. "I *did*. She'd like to talk to you about doing an opening at her gallery next month."

Nick blinked and stared and blinked some more. "Thank you, Devon. You didn't have to do that. You've already helped me enough."

"I didn't *have* to. I *wanted* to. Because I *do* believe in your art, Nick. I can see the beauty that you bring to the world." Devon's gaze slipped to Bane for a moment.

Bane and his father were talking quietly about something in the corner of the porch. Bane didn't look *too* trapped even as Charles touched his arm and tilted his head back to let out one of his bellowing laughs. But Bane did look *beautiful*. More so than he ever had before.

"There's lots of beauty out there," Nick replied evenly.

Devon had already gone through several lovers over the past year, but Nick felt that he might never fully get over Bane. And Nick couldn't blame him. There really was only *one* Bane.

"Yes, I suppose you're right." Devon gave him a smile that did not quite reach his eyes.

Nick, feeling the lightness of the pitcher, took this as an opportunity to escape. He called out to the Indian man, "We're running out of margaritas, Omar."

"There better be enough for one more glass," Bane laughed.

Nick was grinning at that beloved voice and the spirit within him immediately sat up, whiskers quivering, at the closeness of Bane and his spiritual partner. Nick made his way over to them and was *just* able to top off Bane and his father's glasses before the pitcher was completely empty.

"I've been talking Bane's ear off," his father admitted shamelessly and chuckled. "He's only *squirmed* a few times. But I think now that we *both* need a drink."

Omar immediately whisked away the empty pitcher, urging Nick to sit down on the couch and for Bane to join him, while saying, "I will mix some more up. You stay there. I can handle this."

Nick curled against Bane's side. The big man immediately wrapped an arm around him and shared his margarita with Nick. Nick drank from the same spot that Bane had. He then rested his head against Bane's shoulder. He felt the soft brush of the big man's lips against his forehead. His father continued to prattle on, but neither Bane nor Nick was really listening. The tiger spirits inside of them were purring uproariously at being near one another and that was the only sound they heard. It was innately soothing.

Nick glanced up at Bane then. He looked so beautiful. He was wearing gray pants, a white button down shirt flared open at the collar and a green vest that was the color of new shoots. His long dark hair was tied back with a matching green ribbon. His face ... oh, his face, was that mixture of beauty and strength that was so very masculine and appealing. The plush lips. The high cheekbones. The firm, powerful jaw. The straight, noble nose. The striking Siberian blue eyes. It was missing only one thing: the scar.

The scar had disappeared the night that the gray-eyed tiger had come into their lives. Strangely, no one else except Omar, Bane and Nick seemed to remember it at all. Nick was certain that if his father had remembered it he would have asked Bane what plastic surgeon he had used, because the doctor had done a bang up job! Though Bane was notoriously camera shy, Nick had managed to get a few photos of him before the scar had disappeared yet in those pictures the scar didn't show up either. The scar had simply ceased to be. It was magic. Pure and simple. Nick smiled and curled tighter against Bane. Bane rewarded him with another kiss on his head.

At that moment, Omar came back out with a refreshed pitcher of margaritas and two glasses already filled up, one for Nick and one for himself. Nick reluctantly switched to drinking out of his own glass instead of Bane's. Bane really did need his own drink after listening to his father for so long with such patience.

Sloan turned to look at Bane then. Her raised eyebrow brilliantly asked if it was time to reveal the surprise. Bane gave a nod. They were all there. Drinks in hand. Plenty of chips eaten. It was time to get to "business". Bane cleared his throat and everyone quieted down and drew nearer to hear. Nick sat up. He wanted to see everyone's reactions.

"First, thank you all for coming," Bane said.

"Who wouldn't come for Omar's food and drinks?" Jade giggled.

Bane nodded and smiled. "Indeed, Omar has *long* been the reason that anyone has spent any time in my presence whatsoever. He's had this strange belief though that I was worth getting to know. I can honestly say that until this past year, that has *not* been the case."

"Oh, Bane! So not true!" Omar said with a broad smile.

"You're still a saint, Omar," Nick said. "For many reasons."

Omar blushed and ducked his head. "I am just a very lucky man."

After the laughter had quieted down, Bane continued, "A year ago today I made a bargain with the Fairfaxes." He lowered his head and there was a faint, sad smile on his face as he added, "One that I feel nothing but shame for now. I can't even imagine how I ever thought it was *acceptable* let alone a *good* bargain. I don't know how I could have felt justified in asking what I did."

"We drew first blood, Bane," Jake said. "We were fools to have gone after one of your companies."

"Indeed. I think of how shoddy my research was and I shudder," Steven said.

Jade patted his shoulder. "Bane holds things close to his chest."

"Bane outwitted us, outmaneuvered us, and all in all won against us," Charles said with a shrug. "The bargain was a life ring, but we would never have gotten that ring without Nick. I don't know if I can ever tell you, Nick, how *grateful* I am that you were willing to -- to do *all that* for us."

"I think I ended up getting a pretty good deal out of it," Nick assured his father as he laced the fingers of his left hand with Bane's right one.

"All that" was not defined and Nick wondered what his father had really thought he would be doing for Bane when they had first made that bargain. But it didn't matter now. He knew his father loved him. Charles' utter tenderness and devotion after he had been shot had shown him that. His miraculous recovery had not stopped his father from visiting him every day for six months and actually making those visits about *him*. Charles only talked business with Bane every other visit. Nick knew that it was a win.

And it hadn't just been his father that had suddenly come into his life with a vengeance. Over the past year, his brothers - together and separately - had insisted on him coming out with them or at least hanging out once a week. At first, he had dreaded the get togethers, sure that Jake and Steven would quickly bore of him as the shock of his near death faded away. But that's not what had happened.

Instead, *they* had won *him* over and his dread had turned to mild like which had turned into expectation and enjoyment of being with them. Now he couldn't imagine not spending one of the weekend nights with them. He swore sometimes that he felt their mother smiling down on the three of them. Well, actually the *four* of them since Jade was often with them, too. And from the way that Steven's hand just slid around her waist, Nick wondered if something more than a friendship was starting there.

"When you first met me, Nick, you must have thought something very different than you do now," Bane murmured with a shy glance.

Nick kissed him. "But I was wrong back then."

"I don't know about that," Bane said. "You made me a better man. I would not be who I am today without you. And I can't tell you how grateful I am for that, especially since you've proven me so terribly *wrong* about so many things."

They looked into each other's eyes and the purring resumed. Bane though quickly shook himself as he realized that everyone was looking at them. Charles had an unctuous smile on his face. Jade was smiling, too, though hers was sweet. Jake and Steven just looked bemused. Sloan was beaming. She was a real romantic, Nick had discovered. Even Devon looked touched by it all. Omar, of course, was crying and clasping his hands in front of him.

Clearing his throat once more, Bane continued, "But the point of this party is not to dwell on who we were then, but who we are *now* and who we will be *going forward*. And I can say without any compunctions, that my life is so much better with *all* of you in it. Even you, Charles."

Everyone laughed and Charles playfully rolled his eyes before falling into belly-shaking laughter himself.

"You're not the only one who feels that way," Jake said almost shyly when the laughter had died down. His brashness and arrogance that had come from a lack of confidence, according to Bane, and it was mostly gone now. Under Bane's tutelage, Jake was coming out as a leader. He was even in charge of their father on some projects. Nick had been shocked to watch Jake keep their father on the right course again and again without losing his temper.

"I second that," Steven echoed. He, too, had bloomed under Bane's tutelage. Though he would always be a "numbers" guy, where the weight of those numbers lay was far more important to him now.

"The bargain was if the Fairfaxes served me in *various* capacities for a year, they might earn their company back." Bane flashed a smile. "And the year is now up. The Fairfaxes have more than succeeded. In fact, they have done so well that I am loathe to lose them." The whole group went silent. Bane swallowed. Nick flashed him a comforting smile. "But a bargain is a bargain and you have met your end of it and then some. So ... Fairfax International is once more under full and complete ownership of Charles Fairfax."

Sloan came over with a leather folder in which there were papers selling all stock in Fairfax Industries back to Charles. She handed the folder to Charles and Nick's two older brothers looked over their father's shoulder. Jake and Steven looked pleased for their father. But Charles, though he had a look of satisfaction on his face and ran his fingers over the documents as if they were precious, did not appear as happy as he should have been.

"Thank you for this," Charles said, his voice thick with emotion, after long moments of silence. "You gave us back what we lost."

"He did more than that," Jake said softly.

Charles actually nodded. "More than that. The truth is ..." He was smiling, but there were tears in his eyes as he looked directly at Bane and Nick. "The truth is that I haven't had this much *fun* in years! Working with you has been a pleasure, Bane. An *honor* actually and I'm not sure ... I'm not sure I want to go back to working on my own. Obviously, my boys have made their choices to stay with you."

Both Steven and Jake nodded rather forcefully in agreement with their father. Nick's heart rose. His father didn't want to stop working for Bane. This is what he and the billionaire had hoped.

"I'm so glad that you feel that way," Bane said. He turned to Nick and squeezed his hand. "Nick and I spoke about just this possibility -- or perhaps, we spoke of our *hopes* -- and we've come up with a *new* bargain. One we both hope that you will take us up on."

Bane nodded at Sloan. The lawyer produced three more leather folders with other papers inside. She placed one folder in each of his family members' hands. Looking pleased yet flummoxed, Charles opened his first and let out a soft sound that was almost like a gasp. Steven adjusted his glasses and drew the papers closer to his face as if he could not believe what he was reading. Jake let out a laugh and pressed the papers against his chest. He grinned. Nick bit his lower lip. He was smiling so hard it hurt. Would they understand what Bane was offering? Jake did, but what about the others?

Charles finally raised his head to look at Bane and Nick. "D & F Industries? Dunsaney *and* Fairfax? Together? You mean that --"

"You won't be doing things *alone* ever again ... if that is what you want, Charles," Bane said and he rubbed Nick's back.

"Is it what *you* want? I mean ... Nick can be persuasive, but I want to make sure that you won't regret this," Charles said with such genuine goodwill that Nick was rather flummoxed for a moment. His father was risking turning down an opportunity like this because he feared it might not be in the other person's best interests? Wonders would never cease.

"Dad, I assure you that I couldn't make Bane do this, not if he really didn't want to," Nick assured him.

"This is something that Nick and I truly want to do," Bane confirmed.

"Well!" Charles laughed and slapped the papers. "Well!" he said again with a huge grin. "Well! Well! What do you say, Steven, Jake?"

"I say absolutely!" Jake beamed.

"There is absolutely no downside," Steven said and smiled.

Charles let out a raucous laugh and reached over to pump Bane's hand. "It looks like you have yourself a second bargain, Bane!"

There was an eruption of cheers and everyone was laughing, clapping and hugging. Bane even tolerated a hug from Charles. He did give genuine hugs to Jake and Steven. Jade wrapped her arms around Nick and hugged him tightly.

"How did you guys keep this a secret? I had no idea!" she cried and kissed him on the cheek again and again.

"It was hard, but if Dad, Jake or Steven wanted to go back to just Fairfax Industries, we didn't want to force them into this," Nick said.

"Force them? I may not be much of a business person, but even I know that being partners with Bane is elevating them into the business heavens, isn't it?" she asked.

"It is, but they've earned it. They've done so much good this year," he said.

"I know it! And they seem very good at doing good, don't they? People really can change," Jade said and kissed him again before moving over to Jake and Steven to congratulate the two of them.

Nick slung an arm around Omar's shoulders. The Indian man was being adorable as tears ran unabashedly down his face.

"Oh, Nick, such happiness! I have wished for so long to witness such great happiness for Bane," he got out. "I *believed* it could happen. I *hoped* it could happen. I just *feared* it would not be in my lifetime."

"I don't think I ever expected to be this happy myself," Nick said. "And I'm so glad that you helped me to see the real Bane, not to mention that you were just awesome to me in all ways."

"You are easy to be awesome to," Omar assured him as he wiped the tears from his eyes. "Ah, I have cried such tears of happiness today. I fear it will bring rain!"

But the sky was utterly clear and as it turned from day to dusk to night, the stars shone like jewels without a cloud in sight to obscure them. There was much food and laughter. There were enough toasts to make it seem like New Year's Eve. Finally, Sloan and Devon went home, the Fairfaxes clambered into their cars to hit the clubs along with Jade, and Omar cleaned up and went to bed, leaving Nick and Bane alone.

They sat on the porch's couch together. The candles were nearly guttering out as they had been burning for hours. The moonlight silvered the rose bushes and grass beyond. The scent of flowers filled the air.

"Will we ever tell them about the spirits?" Nick asked, referring to his family. Jade already knew. The first day they'd told her, she had them shifting between their forms endlessly and clapping with delight each time. She'd asked more than a million questions in between cuddling with both tigers.

"We shall need to eventually. They will notice that we never age," he remarked and Nick nodded. After a moment's quiet, Bane added, "I know that you love Moon Shadow in the summer, as do I. But perhaps in Autumn..."

Nick was practically laying on top of Bane then and he had to crane his neck up to see Bane's face. "Where do you want to go in Autumn?"

There was another hesitation and then Bane said, "India."

Nick's breath caught. The gray-eyed tiger's ears perked up. "India? I thought that you couldn't go back."

"Because I thought I was *cursed*," Bane said quietly. "But I was wrong."

"Yes," Nick answered simply.

"I've been thinking that the spirits would enjoy seeing the valley. For my spirit, it would be going home. For yours and for you, too, it would be experiencing it for the first time. And I know that Omar would *love* to show off his most excellent family to us."

"Omar would definitely love to do that and I'd love to meet his family," Nick said with warmth.

"So you'll go to India with me?"

"Yes, of course. I'd go *anywhere* with you, Bane."

Bane looked down at Nick, his Siberian blue eyes filled with love and adoration. "With you by my side, Nick, I feel that the world is new again and full of every good thing."

Nick rewarded him with a kiss.

"Do you want to go *romp*?" Nick asked. Excitement thrummed inside of him and his tiger spirit.

"I could be persuaded." A slow sensual smile flowed across Bane's face.

Nick stood up and tugged Bane to his feet as well. The two of them walked, hand in hand, into the garden. When they reached the very center of it, they tenderly stripped off each other's clothes. Looking into one another's eyes, they smiled as the mist surrounded them both. When it cleared, they were in their tiger forms. They rubbed their bodies against one another before racing off into the wheatfields under the light of the full moon.

THE END

SIGN UP FOR FREE STORY!

*D*ownload this sexy alternate retelling of how Nick and Bane meet.

In this 20,000 word story, Nick is an aspiring photographer looking for a patron, and Bane is a reclusive, lonely billionaire. Both meet at an exclusive club, Smoke, only to find that their relationship is much more than a one-night affair. It seems almost fated!

Cursed: Smoke is a fun extra that does not have anything to do with the main Cursed timeline. Use coupon code SMOKE to get it free:

https://shop.raythereign.com/shop/cursed-smoke-short-story/

Made in the USA
Middletown, DE
02 October 2017